SCATTERED ASHES

Jack Rollins

Jack Rollins Fiction

Scattered Ashes

by Jack Rollins

The stories, all names, characters, and incidents portrayed in this production are fictitious. No identification with actual persons (living or deceased), places, buildings, and products is intended or should be inferred.

Published by Jack Rollins Fiction,

Tyne & Wear, England

MMXXIII

jack@jackrollinsfiction.com

jackrollinsfiction.com

2nd Edition Paperback ISBN: 978-0-9930620-8-7

Cover design by Jack Rollins

CONTENTS

For Mick,

for everything.

1

About 'Conquistador'

Conquistador was created just in time for inclusion in an anthology about revenge. And I do love a good revenge story, so it happened that when the call-up came through to produce a piece for that book, Conquistador was almost ready to ride out.

Another writer had let the publisher down, so I was a last-minute addition to the line-up. And as it goes, when I sent them this story, the editing team were thrilled. Tonally, this was exactly what they wanted.

Some of the nuts and bolts of Conquistador come as a result of my work in the care industry, oddly enough. At least, it might seem odd by the time you've read it. Working in domiciliary care (in case you don't know, it's where carers attend the person needing assistance in their own home, rather than in a care home) in Northumberland, I spent many hours driving around beautiful stretches of countryside in all weathers. I was made welcome in all sorts of homes, from a small, draughty shepherd's cottage, to large, lavish estates.

I distinctly remember attending a lady living in an old horse farm with picturesque views out across the landscape in every direction, all visible from huge picture windows across each facing of the house. A beautiful spot, but very isolated. A patch of land outside a tiny village, which itself was in the middle of nowhere. The sort of place where a hard winter could cut a person off from civilisation and only after the snow thawed, would you know if they survived or not. This old woman lived in that place, all alone, surrounded by antiques and silverware, in a home so large, she would have no idea if a burglar was helping himself to her belongings in the other end of the house. She might have no cause to visit the other end of the house in a month, so could find it stripped bare, with no idea of who did it, or when. I worried about her quite a bit, but she had carers and help with grounds-keeping and some family fairly close-by.

There was another client who was not that much older than me at the time. I was in my early thirties and she a little under forty. The company saw fit to send young carers to her, as she had the apparent youthfulness of someone in their early twenties and had requested carers of that age group. Inevitably, she positioned herself as a friend to her carers and used social media to approach them outside of work hours and find out bits and pieces about their private lives. No matter how much the management - of which I was a member at the time - warned staff against giving away personal information and connecting on social media, one young, impressionable carer after another fell into talking about social lives and relationships. Her inability to leave her house unsupported left her desperate to be involved in their lives.

My seniors even allowed male carers to attend her on calls where no personal hygiene care was required. She made it known to her female carers which of the guys on the team she would like to fuck. I warned the company. I warned the care staff not to engage in dirty jokes with her, but she was relentless with innuendos during visits and it was only a matter of time before one of the lads on the team said too much. And that was it. He was out of a job. It was entirely his fault. He chose to make an inappropriate joke even after he was trained and briefed, but he fell into the trap of thinking they were friends.

This woman's care requirements were linked to chronic pain. Doctors believed that the pain was entirely in her head, and they continuously tried to reduce her dependency on oral morphine by gradually reducing the dosage, hoping to remove it entirely eventually. She was clever though, and craftily reduced her consumption so that she could stockpile it in case the day ever came that she found herself without the prescription.

You'll see where some of these things fit in, but the core of the story came from something a care manager told me years ago, in my very first care job, about a man whose disability prevented him from going out and engaging in romantic relationships. His social worker helped him learn how to spot adverts for prostitutes and escorts in the 'lonely hearts' section of the local newspaper.

How does this soup of stuff from my care career shape itself into a story? Only one way to find out...

2

CONQUISTADOR

Luke's prized silver Ford Focus ST-3 crunched over the gravel-covered track, and Luke prayed all the while that the skipping stones would not scratch his paintwork as they tapped and dinged under the chassis. Passing several farmhouses and cottages on the rugged track, he took his aviator sunglasses off and placed them in the hollow within the console, in front of the gear stick. Then he scanned the gates and walls, looking for Arion House.

Black gates topped with two ebony horse heads stood tall and solemn at the end of the track like two huge chess pieces. Between the bars of the gates and stretching beyond the openings and behind the brick wall surrounding the property, a two-storey house of elegant, angular timber and clean-cut stone awaited.

He pressed the control to lower the car window, reached out and pushed the call button on the small keypad on the black post in front of the gates.

After a moment, a woman's voice came through the speaker. "Yes, who is it?"

"Luke Sharp." His name had served him well on nights out while studying at university, thanks to the Dizzee Rascal song 'Fix Up, Look Sharp' - a ready-made anthem for the notorious young man about campus they said would fuck the crack of dawn if only he could get its legs apart. He inspected his immaculately sculpted nails and said, "I'm here to see a Ms. Demi Terrance."

"Just a moment."

Luke noticed a small camera eye set into the chrome panel and decided to suck his cheeks in to pronounce his cheekbones and bring out his angular jaw. He figured it was worth the little effort it cost him, you never knew who could be watching. He took in the landscape of sweeping moorland which surrounded Arion House. Such isolation was not his idea of a good time, but he could see its appeal for some, and perhaps as a holiday home or getaway for himself if the city became tiresome at any point.

"Ooh, you look as nice as you did on the website, Mr Sharp," a different woman's voice purred.

Luke turned back to the camera eye and flashed a pearly-white smile. "Ms. Terrance, am I correct?"

"You certainly are. I'm buzzing you in. Come straight in to see me."

The gates slid open in utter silence. Nothing could upset the peace of Arion House and its grounds, it seemed. Luke rolled the car forward, preserving the quiet and his paintwork. To the left stood a long stable block that he assumed opened out on the other side, into a field. Arion House loomed ahead. He parked next to a dark blue Vauxhall Astra and climbed out of his vehicle.

As he approached the front door, it was opened by a woman dressed in a knee-length grey pinstripe skirt and dark violet short-sleeve blouse cut to show off her trim figure but buttoned high enough to maintain professionalism without attracting stares down her cleavage, which Luke could tell would be a rather pleasant sight. Shoulder-length brown hair framed her smooth, tanned face. He hoped that this was who he had come to see, but suspected she was the first person to answer the intercom and likely the owner of the Astra rather than the house.

"Come on in, Mr Sharp," she said, extending a hand.

"Luke, please." He shook the offered hand and noticed a rosy tint flushing the woman's tanned cheeks. The local government ID showed that she was a social worker, and from her youthful appearance, Luke guessed she was recently graduated and appointed. A year or two of service, no more.

He flashed the smile again and locked his piercing blue eyes on hers. Always on the hunt for new clients, he occasionally found someone he liked for his real life, too.

"I'm Jo Regan, Demi's social worker."

"I see," Luke lied. A frown crossed his forehead, revealing his false concern.

"Nothing to worry about," Jo said, leading the way through the house.

A dog barked and Luke heard the animal's scampering paws long before it appeared. He prayed the thing wouldn't jump up at him and mess up his smoky light blue-grey suit. He had just collected it that morning from the dry cleaners and had no desire to see the thing covered in pet hair. The yapping persisted and Jo addressed the approaching white West Highland terrier as "Rasputin."

"Cool name."

"I know, right?" Jo enthused, bending down to scratch the dog behind the ears. "Such a big name for such a little dog."

"Oy," called a playful voice from a room just off the passageway. "He's a big, brave boy, is Rasputin. He protects his mama."

Rasputin capered off back to his mama, followed closely by Jo and Luke.

"Ahhh, here he is," the woman Luke assumed to be Ms. Terrance announced. She was sat in an armchair with what reminded Luke of an old person's Zimmer frame, but this one had wheels and a tray a couple of feet away. Ms. Terrance wore her dark brown hair in a neat bob, and whereas the social worker's blouse was fastened for privacy, Ms. Terrance liked to put on a show, with her two full rounds of flesh and deep cleavage displayed with pride.

"Ms. Terrance," Luke said, stepping forward, offering a hand.

"Demi. Call me Demi." She took his hand and gently pulled, so Luke lowered his head and she planted a kiss on his cheek. "Mmm, you smell good."

"Thank you. So do you. Is that Viktor and Rolf?" he asked.

"Good nose."

"Flowerbomb?"

"Very good nose."

"I'm wearing Spicebomb. I know my V and R."

Jo cleared her throat, taking a seat. She grasped a notepad and pen. "If you please, take a seat, Luke. This will only take a few minutes."

Luke sat down then smiled at both women, waiting for one of them to begin.

"Would you like me to set the ball rolling?" Jo asked.

"If you don't mind," Demi said.

"Well, I'm sure if Demi would like to, she may well tell you about the accident she suffered and the repercussions of that. I think it's okay for me to say that while you don't want to live in a more built-up area, you recognise that social life is a problem for you, isn't it, Demi?"

"Absolutely. I can't really meet people up here, but this is my home. I don't want to give it up just to make it easier to get out to a pub only for people to ignore me while I'm there."

Luke nodded, wondering what the hell this had to do with him.

"Since Demi's husband left her..." Jo paused, looking for the correct phrasing.

Demi smiled at her social worker. "Look, that bastard left me for someone else. One of my friends... or so-called friend, as it turned out. I had an accident... I fell off a horse, actually. And I was left with crippling pains as a result of that. Some days are better than others, and I've got some pretty powerful pain relief so I can sleep on those bad days. Jo is here because, well, since I'm registered as disabled and I need some treatment, some adaptations were needed for the house and a vehicle in the early days, at least." Demi sighed. "What Jo is beating around the bush about is that I sometimes feel like I need," she paused and shot a mischievous glance at her social worker, "a good beating about my bush."

Jo chuckled, rolling her eyes. "You have such a way with words, Demi."

"Well, he's a man-whore. He's heard worse, I'm sure."

Luke erupted into laughter. "Excuse me, Madam. I am a professional escort."

The two women laughed as well, and Demi said, "A professional shagger, more like."

"My job is providing company for people. I provide a vital service," Luke said, frowning in mock indignation.

"Essentially, as Demi has experienced periods of low mood, I have to ensure she has the capacity to remain in control of the decisions she makes regarding certain physical needs," Jo explained. "I'm satisfied that you're quite happy with your decisions so far, and I feel it's appropriate for me to withdraw from this particular aspect of your support, Demi."

"Thank you for helping me arrange this, Jo."

"No problem at all, Demi." Jo stood up with her pad and pen in hand. "If you need me for anything else, you know to give me a call." The social worker left, with little Rasputin trotting along at her heels.

"Close the door, Luke," Demi said.

Luke complied, then paused before her, letting her see his full form in his well-tailored suit. "What do you like?" he asked.

Demi blushed and giggled. "My God. You're direct."

"I want to please you. I want to make you happy."

"I don't want... *that* today."

Luke smiled. There was something girlish about the woman before him. At first appearance, she was a woman of confidence, humour and control, but it was becoming clear to him that her confidence had been crushed. Crushed by the accident. Crushed by her husband leaving her. Crushed by pain.

"I'm not really able to... to do anything today." Demi waved a hand over the little table at her side, indicating the shot-glass size medication pot with the remaining trace of some sort of medicine or suspension. The thick grey droplets clinging to the plastic pot reminded Luke of semen, but the large brown bottle on the table indicated that it was Oramorph.

"Morphine?" Luke muttered. "Demi, your pains must be terrible."

"They are. But that does the trick. For a while, at least."

"Do you feel okay right now?"

"Yes, and if my pains start up again, I'll be laid out on my couch until the carers come to make my dinner and again until they come back to help me to bed."

"I see." Luke sat at the edge of the couch.

"Stand up."

Luke jumped back to his feet like a child who had done something wrong and been caught in the act. "Sorry... I thought you just wanted to talk for a while."

Demi bit her lip and narrowed her eyes. Her gaze seemed to radiate confidence now, the vulnerability of moments before eradicated with a single thought. "Show me your cock, Luke."

Luke's smile spread slowly across his lips. He grasped the lapels of his jacket and began to peel the garment off his shoulders.

"No," Demi interrupted. "Keep it on. I just want you to show me your cock. I want to see it just as you are, like that."

Luke unzipped his fly, reached his fingertips into the opening, and pulled aside his *Aussiebum Wonderjock*, releasing his genitals from the concealed pouch that kept everything pressed into a tight, neat, impressive package. He grasped his shaft and stroked, exciting the muscle to give Demi a little more to look at.

"Don't do that," Demi said. "Just show me it. Just take it out exactly as it is."

Luke raised his eyebrows and exposed himself. His flaccid penis hung in the opening of his trousers. Without the full erection to show her, he blushed and looked around the room, unable to meet Demi's gaze.

"Don't be embarrassed. Do you know how long it's been since I saw a man's cock just sitting there normally? If I want to see a massive, throbbing hard-on, I just need to turn on my laptop, don't I?"

Luke levelled his eyes on Demi's face once more, hoping she would instruct him to do something... *anything*... soon.

"Come here."

Luke positioned himself in front of his client and she leaned forward. Her warm breath tickled the flesh of his exposed penis. Demi reached into his fly and gently stroked his shaft with her middle fingertip.

A shiver of excitement ran through Luke's spine. He felt the throb as hot blood flooded his meat. Demi leaned her face closer, brushing his shaft with her lips. Her tongue flicked out, licking his flesh, tracing the engorged blue vein as his erection swelled and rose towards her mouth. She kissed the tip, then placed a flat palm against his shaft and pressed her cheek against it. She nibbled at his skin and tilted her head, his cock running beyond the width of her lips. She applied light pressure with her teeth, never hurting him.

Demi pulled her head away and shifted back in her chair. "You can put it away now."

Luke zipped himself up.

"It's a hundred an hour, isn't it?"

"Yes."

"The money's waiting for you on the kitchen table. Was that considered an extra? I know I'm paying for your time only."

"No, my time alone is fine today."

Demi looked him up and down. "I'll be in touch with the agency again soon."

Luke returned to his car. The moorland around him was cast in a wonderful orange glow as the last vestiges of the winter phase of afternoon sunlight washed the countryside and tinted the metalwork of his vehicle. He considered the woman living all the way out here on her own. Carers checked on her four times a day, as it turned out, but that only amounted to about two hours of contact time on most days, with extra time for shopping and domestic duties on two separate days in the week. Luke wondered why

Demi hadn't just sunk a couple of bottles of Oramorph and finished herself off in a fit of sheer boredom.

He was about to step into the Ford when a sudden snort startled him. He spun on his heels, crunching the gravel beneath him, and turned to the source of the noise. A bay stallion stood at the corner of the left-side north face of the house. The animal's eyes were fixed on him, as though weighing him up and forming an opinion of him.

Even standing perfectly still, the power in the creature's musculature was plain to see. Its tightly braided chocolate brown mane and tail set against its latte-coloured body perfectly. He knew nothing of horses, but he could see that this creature was exquisite.

The stallion snorted once more and turned away, disappearing out of view around the corner.

Luke drove to the console by the gates, wound down his window and pressed the button to open them. He glanced in the mirror and could see all along the north face of the property, but the horse was gone.

***

Luke's next appointment was not until the evening: one of his regulars, a woman in her sixties whose husband had suffered a stroke and couldn't get it up anymore with all the blood pressure medication he took. She was attractive in her advanced years; he thought of her as a MILF who'd turned into a GILF. Sometimes, when servicing older clients, he had to drop a pill to guarantee a performance. With her he had no such problems, and he preferred that, preferred to find something he liked about the client, something natural that would give him the ability to perform. She was a good tipper, and all she wanted was to lay there and be fucked by someone she found attractive. Missionary, bareback, and he had to come inside her, that's what made her happy.

He trained at the gym for an hour, working his back, knowing he would need his arms and chest for the night's activity. Once his workout was done, he showered and wrapped a towel around his waist, collected his Speedos from the locker and slipped them on before entering the spa.

Resting the base of his skull on the lip of the Jacuzzi, he let his body float up to the surface of the water. The bubbles tickled his body, soothing his tired muscles. He closed his eyes, passing into a perfect state of relaxation. Focused on the bubbles surging against his flesh and the blackness behind his eyelids, he blocked out his troubles and let the moment take over.

The moment, however, was short-lived. Rough hands grasped Luke's head and pressed him beneath the water. The surface of the water erupted as his arms and legs thrashed. The downward force relented, and Luke burst from the water, gasping for air, coughing and retching. He cleared his eyes and saw before him John Kelly, clad in a fine charcoal suit and pale blue shirt. Kelly's condescending laughter echoed around the tiled spa. A couple of curious patrons peered out from the steam room and showers but ducked away when they saw the feared and most notorious member of their club.

"Sorry, pal, I thought you'd nodded off. I thought it safest to wake you," Kelly said, sneering.

"You're fucking unbelievable, John. Really you are," Luke managed to whine between gasps.

"Well, it doesn't do you good to rest for too long. Work's good for the soul, my friend. It's good for getting me the money you owe me, too."

"You said I had 'til the end of next month."

"You do, pal, but I don't think you're setting aside as much as you should be. Maybe you need to go and bang some more old women or something, eh... or maybe you'll need a good plastic surgeon to fix up Luke Sharp, when I've finished with you." Kelly said, almost singing the taunt. "Nothing quite like being debt-free, my friend, but some folk... well, the more they earn, the more they want. Isn't that true?"

Ignoring the question, Luke climbed out of the Jacuzzi and snatched up his towel, patting his body down, pleased to hide his almost naked form behind something while Kelly was present.

"Anyway, I'll leave you to it. I saw you come up here and couldn't resist. It's been so long since I last saw you, I absolutely had to come and have a little catch-up." With that, Kelly gave a patronising wave and left the spa, his message well and truly delivered.

Luke ended his spa session prematurely, his relaxation time spoiled. A flash of panic tore through his concentration: The car.

The chill air cut into his damp hair as he raced across the car park, his suit jacket crumpled over his left arm, gym bag flapping against his thigh. He paced around his cherished vehicle, braced for a dent or scratch in the paintwork to break his heart. To his relief, Kelly's spite, it seemed, did not extend as far as vandalising vehicles. Then it occurred to Luke that the reason may be that it would reduce the value of it should Kelly see the need to relieve him of it when the day of reckoning arrived.

He ran a hand over the rain-streaked roof and climbed in, throwing his jacket onto the passenger seat as he settled behind the wheel. He slammed his hands against the steering wheel in anger and frustration at Kelly catching him off-guard like that. The thing was, Kelly was right: he hadn't been setting aside enough to get the debt cleared. He hadn't been working as hard as he should. He'd been picky about taking on new clients, preferring instead to milk those he was established with. He'd taken on Demi purely because he'd known her age, mid-thirties, and if his luck was in, she'd be an attractive woman he'd happily fuck anyway, and the money would just be a bonus. His luck was in, as it turned out, and he hoped he'd hear back from her soon. It seemed likely to him that she needed companionship as well as sex. That could lead to lots of additional hours and money beyond what he made with his dick alone.

Being an escort meant Luke made his money off the books, with no tax or national insurance payments, no student loan repayments and no paper trail with which to impress upon a bank his ability to repay a loan. When he had decided to take advantage of the property boom, he'd formed a limited company with his uncle Phil, who'd put in five thousand pounds. Luke had added the same amount, borrowed from the shark. They had then used the money as deposits on two homes, one of which they had let out immediately and the other which they'd discovered had serious foundation damage not highlighted in the initial survey.

Any money they had made from the rental had been quickly swallowed in the cost of the underpinning work on the other building, along with legal costs accrued from suing the surveyor for negligence.

And that was how in three months a five-thousand-pound debt had swelled to over twenty-thousand pounds.

Three days later, Luke received his usual email offering him some work. He knew immediately that the three-hour visit was with Demi, and he was correct in his assumption. This meant three hundred pounds basic, and whatever was negotiated for any sexual contact in that time. Had he not been so desperate for money, he might have given her that for free to secure frequent business from her, but time was of the essence and he needed to take as much as he could as soon as he could.

Everywhere he'd went, whether it was the shops or the gym, Kelly or one of his lackeys had seemed to be there, hovering around, watching him. Sometimes he had caught a glimpse of a knife, a club, and once even a power drill in their hands. A sense of desperation had risen like a flood tide within him, he couldn't even masturbate, which was, in his trade, most concerning. The urgency for money might just eradicate the only means he had to make it.

Stress burned in Luke's veins, tensing his muscles, making him push the car a little harder than usual on the moor road. Even on the track approaching Arion House, he sped along, sending gravel clattering up beneath the chassis to clank on the panels and his precious paintwork. He didn't care. It's Kelly's fucking car soon, anyway.

The speed rendered the hedgerows translucent as the gaps merged into one, opening up a view into the field to his right. Keeping pace with him raced the bay horse he had seen on his previous visit. A determined eye peered through the hedge, and although the animal must have been looking ahead as it ran, Luke had the odd sensation that the horse was observing him, or had at least recognised him.

The offside wheels of the Ford Focus thumped up onto the grass verge and Luke wrenched the wheel around to force the car back onto the track. His heart thudded in his chest as adrenaline sent his body and mind into overdrive, flooding him with thoughts of what would have happened had he crashed the car.

He didn't mind putting a few scratches on the paintwork for Kelly to inherit, but it would be no good if he wrote the whole thing off. Then he'd really be in trouble. He eased off the accelerator, drawing to a complete halt at the intercom at the gates.

Demi opened the gates remotely. Within moments, Luke stood before her in the lounge. She sat with a table like those found in hospital, with a frame forming three edges of a rectangle so it could slip over her chair, with the main surface positioned over her lap. Upon the table stood an easel, a pack of charcoals open and at the ready.

"Strip," was all she said.

Luke smiled and did as he was told.

The first thing Demi did was photograph him as he lay across the sofa in a classic pose for a still-life drawing, with one hand supporting his head and the other arm draped over his midriff. "In case I don't get to finish while you're here," she informed him.

"I didn't know you were an artist," Luke said.

"I'm not a very good one, but you're such a nice thing to draw, I thought I would take advantage."

"I see."

"I used to draw my horse a lot."

"I suppose it's difficult if you don't get outside much. Plus, from what I've seen, he'd take some keeping up with."

Demi frowned and looked up from her work. "What do you mean?"

"He's bloody fast. He was racing me on my way in."

"Couldn't be my horse. Conquistador died not long after our accident."

"Oh. You're right then, it must have been another of your horses."

"I don't have any more."

"There was a horse bolting along the field out there. It must be one of your fields. Right next to the road approaching this place."

"Yes, that's my field, but I don't have any horses at all. Not since the accident."

"Bloody hell, then someone's missing a lovely bay racehorse."

Demi continued to work in silence for a long while. Eventually she said, "It's funny, you know, how you saw that bay horse. My Conquistador was a bay stallion. He was beautiful. Such an intelligent animal. He understood me more than any man could."

"Maybe you just haven't tried the right man. I think I understand what you need. Probably better than any horse could. I'd stake money on it."

"Really?" Demi grinned at him and wiggled her eyebrows. "Would you stake your fee for today on it?"

Luke groaned inside. "How do I know you'd be honest with me?"

"I'd be honest with you. If you can make me come, you'll be worth every penny. Not even my husband could make me come."

"It's a deal."

Demi slid the table away from her chair and grabbed her walking stick. "Right, then. Let's see what you're made of."

Luke excused himself and snorted a quick line of coke in the bathroom. Then he hurried to the bedroom where Demi had positioned herself in the centre of the bed. He undressed her gently but quickly. Her ex-husband had been an idiot, Luke decided. Even after a disabling accident, her body was toned and tight. Excitement coursed through him and he traced his fingers up her legs, working upwards slowly, deliberately. Demi shivered with the anticipation of one never touched sexually, or one who had gone without such contact for a long time.

Luke pulled Demi's legs apart and positioned his shoulders beneath her knees. She pushed her hips forward, squeezing his neck with her thighs, her shaven pussy only inches from his face. She giggled and so did he, finding her girlish excitement both funny and something of a turn-on. He slid his tongue along her right thigh, sending shivers of pleasure through her. As he reached the top of her thigh, he turned his head and listened as Demi took in a sharp breath, holding onto it, probably waiting for his tongue to make contact with her lips or clitoris. Instead he worked his tongue up her left thigh.

This time, he didn't make her wait. As his mouth moved closer to her opening, he found himself salivating and unable to resist a second time. He pushed his tongue inside her, making her gasp and squirm. He withdrew and brushed the tip upwards over her clit, tracing circles, altering the pressure, shifting from the tip of his tongue to the blade, then back to the tip.

Demi came within two minutes, covering his mouth and chin with hot juices.

"Now," he said, shifting his weight on the bed as Demi released the pillow, she had clutched throughout the trembling orgasm she'd enjoyed, "get on your hands and knees."

After her third orgasm, Demi doubled up on the bed. Luke slid his cock inside her again, but she moaned and wriggled away.

"Please, I'm sore. I can't do any more."

"Have I hurt you?"

"No," she whispered. "It's my pains. I should've known this would happen. Should never have done this."

"God, Demi, I'm sorry. I really am. If I'd known…"

"Don't worry about it."

For a couple of minutes, she rolled from one side to the other, onto her back, over and onto her front. Tears streamed down her cheeks.

"Please, Demi, let me get you something for the pain."

"Can you bring me my morphine and one of those little medicine cups, please?"

Demi described the location of the morphine in the kitchen and Luke hurried to collect it, still naked. He was glad she lived so remotely and had no little old lady neighbours to shock.

When he opened the cupboard where Demi's medication was stored, his eyes bulged. Six bottles of Oramorph sat in a row before her blister packs of tablet medication.

He took the already opened bottle with a medication pot up to the bedroom and placed them on the bedside cabinet. "I see you're well-supplied. Plenty of morphine in that cupboard to keep you going, eh?"

She chuckled as she shifted into an upright position and twisted to see the medication. "What, those six bottles? That's a fraction of what I've got."

"Seriously?"

"Yeah, they've been trying to get it off me for years because they're saying the pains are all imagined. They say I'm just an addict, so I've been trying to take only tiny amounts over time to build up my stockpile. You know, just in case they eventually do stop prescribing it to me."

"So how many bloody bottles of this stuff have you got?"

"On your way out, have a little look in the old tack room in the stables. Then you'll see what's been going on. It's not all from the doctors, though. One of my friends is a pharmacist. Every now and then they claim a spoiled delivery box of them, break some of my empties, and give me a few bottles on the side." She poured herself 5ml of the liquid and knocked it back.

"Very clever."

"Well, they don't do it for free, but it beats dealer rates, put it that way." Demi lay back on the pillows once more and closed her eyes. "Hopefully that'll settle things down. Not a word about that stuff to anyone, okay?"

"My lips are sealed."

"Your lips have done quite enough for one day. Well... I suppose you've earned your fee. I forgot to ask, what do you charge for the extras?"

Luke ignored the question. He had a question of his own, and the coke seemed to insist that he ask. "What happened to you, Demi?"

"What do you mean?"

"What happened to you when you fell off the horse?"

A long sigh escaped her and she shook her head. "Did you take some of this when you were downstairs?"

"That? No. God, no. I had a little line before we got started, but that's it."

"Really?"

"Really. I swear."

Demi nodded, eyeing him with distrust. "If you really have to know, I lost a baby. I didn't even know I was pregnant. My period hadn't stopped or anything, but when I fell... that was that. Conquistador... he turned around in the middle of the track and stood over me, blocking the other horses. They collided with him, and one of his hind legs was broken. He collapsed next to me, but somehow pulled himself past my head to protect me. I was on my way to hospital, screaming the ambulance down. I remember them bringing the screen around him, and that was that. He was no longer worth keeping, as far as my dad thought, and... they killed him. My beautiful Conquistador."

Demi descended into a flood of tears, pressing her palms firm against her eyeballs. It occurred to Luke that the loss of the horse meant everything. The loss of a baby she hadn't known she'd carried meant nothing.

An idea bubbled away in Luke's brain. Demi's upset faded into the background as he turned over the possibilities. He didn't like the idea, but it would get Kelly off his back. And he might get to keep the car after all.

"Help me," she whispered, pointing to the bottle.

Luke poured another 5ml measure and pressed the cup into Demi's trembling hand, guiding it to her lips. When she had swallowed the syrup and collapsed back onto the pillow, Luke waited with her as her eyes grew heavy and she slipped off into sleep.

It was then he made his move. He raced down the stairs three at a time, then inspected the loops of keys on the hooks by the front door. He found one for the stables and a key labelled Tack Room. As he lifted the key, he heard a massive metallic thump. He thought, I hope that wasn't my car. Then, his shrill car alarm sounded to confirm the worst. Luke almost tore the front door off its hinges as he flung it open and leapt out onto the gravel.

He raised a hand to his mouth and cried out in anger as soon as his eyes fell upon his vehicle. A huge dent had appeared in the centre of the bonnet. "Who the fuck did this?" he shouted. "Who's out here?" He pressed the button on his key fob to deactivate the alarm.

Luke hurried around the house, finding nothing but empty garden and fields beyond. He returned to the car and looked around to see if any clues lay nearby. He expected to find a huge chunk of broken chimneypot, but there was no sign of what had damaged his car.

"Fucking brilliant," he muttered. His anger burned hot and bright, but he managed to return his attention to his main purpose and approached the stables. He accessed the tack room easily. It held a dusty assortment of saddles, bridles and stirrups, and in one corner he saw the sort of locker one might use in a garden, to store tools or a lawn mower. A brass padlock held the locker door closed. The smallest key on the loop opened the padlock and Luke pulled back the thick plastic doors to reveal the contents.

Demi had not exaggerated. Luke guessed she had amassed about fifty half-litre bottles of Oramorph in the locker. She really was worried they would take her precious pain relief away. He wondered if her pains were even real anymore. The jigsaw pieces began to slot together. The accident. Her love for that horse and her belief that it had sacrificed itself to save her. The pains that were no doubt real and intense enough to be prescribed some heavy-duty relief. Her husband leaving her. Her ability to trim the amount of morphine she took in order to save it up in case they ever took it away from her. She was an addict, nothing more. A clever one with some level of control, but an addict, nonetheless.

In a moment, the phone was in his hand, Kelly's contact details on the screen, and the tone was in his ear as the call went through.

"John, it's Luke."

"I bloody know that already. Your name came up."

"Whatever. Listen, is Oramorph any use to you?"

John went quiet for a few moments. "Some. Why?"

"Some? How much? Is it any use to you or not?"

"As it is, it doesn't give a massive high, but I know some boys who'll plug anything up their arses and they'll have a fucking field day with the stuff. Why, like? Have you got your hands on a bottle?"

"How much would you give me for a bottle?"

"How big's the bottle, and what's the dosage?"

Luke grabbed one of the cardboard boxes from the locker and inspected it. "Says here it's five milligrams per ten millilitres and it's a five-hundred-millilitre bottle."

The phone went silent as John did the mental arithmetic. "I'll get a few quid for it, Luke, but it's going to take a lot of that shit to clear what you owe me. Why the fuck are you bothering me about this?"

"John, I'm looking at about fifty to sixty bottles of it here."

"Really? That's a bit more interesting. And would you care to tell me how you've come by that amount of this stuff?"

Luke proceeded to explain about Demi, the lonely woman on the moors, her morphine addiction and the stockpile she had built up.

"If you're doing this, Luke, you must be fucking desperate to pay me back. Now listen, you're looking at about ten grand for fifty bottles, right? I'll make more than that, but I have to split it right down to shots for these idiots to stick up their arses. That's a half of what you owe gone. We're still looking at the car and whatever else I can lay my hands on up there to clear the rest, yeah?"

"What do you mean, 'whatever else'?"

"There'll be some *ket* or something up there, I'll bet. All sorts of interesting shit I can use on horse farms."

"But don't hurt her. Just leave her alone, okay?"

"What do you give a fuck, Luke? You called here, inviting me to burgle the place right underneath her. Anyway, what if I give her for free what you charge her money for?"

"This is a joke, right, John?"

John remained silent.

"Tell me you're fucking kidding me."

"What do you take me for?"

"I know, but... don't say things like that." Luke's legs felt like jelly as he stepped outside into the orange-grey moorland dusk. "The car... it's got a right dent in the bonnet, John."

"Will it tap out?"

"Probably."

Another pause. "Well, I'll still take it."

"And what if there's no ket?"

"I'll take a gamble on that. There'll be something else I can take. She got any dogs?"

"A little terrier thing. Yappy, but not big."

"When will her next carers come?"

"They'll be here shortly for half-an-hour, then not again until nine, gone again about ten, I think."

"Lovely. Stay up on the moors. You know that ruined church?"

"Yeah."

"Park near that. I'll meet you up there and you can give me the guided tour when we see the carers drive off."

Luke did as he was told and waited by the ruined church. Its stone skeleton appeared black against the darkening sky as the last shreds of orange sunset slipped behind the Cheviot Hills in the west. He saw the carers approach. Two cars, both with their headlamps on, racing along the track with no regard for the condition of their vehicles. He knew they were probably rushed off their feet with dinnertime visits, with little time to get from one place to the next.

He made a private joke to himself that he should stop them on their way back and give them some career advice, as he could be paid ten to fifteen times what they made in an hour and all they would have to do is stop selling care and start selling themselves.

This naturally led him to thoughts of his time with Demi. Rarely was he gripped by excitement as he fucked a new client, but she had been different. He enjoyed her. She looked good, she felt good, she tasted good. Under different circumstances, she might have been good for a relationship, but once they were a client, it was difficult to see a woman as anything else.

The carers left after about twenty minutes at Demi's place. It seemed to be a short visit, but he imagined that if she was doped up, her needs would be minimal. Then he wondered who had let them in. It was a brief wonder, as he realised, they probably had the numerical code to open the gates without the need for help from the inside.

The carers headed back for town on the road snaking off to the north, and they had barely slipped out of view before the lights of another two vehicles became visible.

Luke shook his head in disgusted awe when he realised that John Kelly had brought two of his thugs and a black Ford Transit van. He climbed out of his car as Kelly did the same.

"Jesus Christ, John. You planning on emptying her house?"

"Hey, you never know what there might be in there, lad. Out here, these farmer types like an antique, you know?"

Luke told Kelly about the problem he anticipated with the gate access.

"She never gave you the code?" Kelly asked.

"If she had, I wouldn't be saying it's a problem, would I?" Luke snapped.

"Wind your fucking neck back in, you silly twat. I'm doing you a fucking favour taking this shit in lieu of payment. Speaking of which, giz a look at this bonnet." Kelly stepped up to Luke's Ford Focus, activating the torch on his iPhone. "Aye, that'll tap out no bother. You didn't fucking miss it, did you? Got a pretty good smack on you, eh?"

"Miss it? I don't know how the fuck it happened." Luke stroked the metalwork. "Anyway, what about this gate?"

Kelly pointed over his shoulder with a thumb aimed at the van and its two occupants. "They can get into anything, those two. I'll be surprised if that lock will keep them out." Kelly turned to face the men in the van and nodded to the passenger, who emerged from the vehicle rubbing his stubbly jaw as he walked around Luke to the Ford Focus. "Since the car's mine now, he's going to drive it. You can ride with me. I'll drop you off when we're done."

Luke's face creased with concern. "I thought I was only showing you the way. I don't want to be there while you knock the place off."

"Tough shit." Kelly sneered and climbed into his car. "You think I'll let you call the fucking coppers on me while I'm in the middle of the job? I don't think so. Get in."

In minutes the vehicles idled outside the gate at Arion House as one of Kelly's men worked on the console. It took less than a minute for the man to override the system and the gate swung open, allowing them access to the grounds.

Kelly pulled his estate Subaru Legacy up outside the stables, stopping at the door Luke had told him led to the tack room. Kelly opened the car boot and withdrew his crowbar. He pried open the black wooden door with a quick and heavy downward jerk. Wood splintered and the locking mechanism tore out of the old door.

"Follow me," Kelly said.

Luke stepped into the tack room with the loan shark. Behind him, Kelly's men worked to breach the house.

"Silly cow, how was plastic ever going to keep anyone out?" Kelly muttered, smashing the locker open.

"I'm sure she didn't expect anyone coming up here to rob her."

"And then she met you, eh?" Kelly snarled. He had a way of ensuring Luke could not distance himself from the crime, reminding him that he was not only an accomplice, but the mastermind behind the whole caper.

"You'd better help me get this shit out into the car as quickly as possible."

They worked fast and lifted the boxed bottles of Oramorph into the boot of the waiting Subaru. Kelly covered the packages with a thick grey blanket and slammed the boot shut. "Let's get over to the house."

One of Kelly's underlings, the grey-haired, mustachioed man who'd driven the van, stood in the front doorway. At his feet lay a pile of silver plates, Demi's laptop, a blu-ray player and her forty-inch TV. "Mark's upstairs," the man said, stepping aside as Kelly entered the house.

"He'd better not have hurt her," Luke cried.

Without warning, Kelly spun on his heels with the crowbar outstretched, striking Luke across the side of his head. A lightning flash of pain preceded a red shroud over Luke's vision. His legs wobbled and he fell against the kitchen door, which opened upon impact. He hit the slate tiled floor with a heavy thump. As his consciousness faded, he caught a glimpse of something small and white beside his head, but before he could focus on it, all was blackness.

Luke woke, cold and with the corners of objects jabbing into his arms and midriff. It took him a moment to realise that he was in the back of the van surrounded by everything Kelly and his two accomplices had stolen from Arion House. He pressed his fingers to the left side of his head. Wet, sticky blood met his touch, and excruciating pain planted in him fears for the integrity of his skull.

Sitting up, Luke heard footsteps crunching over the gravel and the voices of two men grumbling about the raw deal they'd received.

"I don't know why he gets to have all the fucking fun. I tied the bitch up."

"Always the fucking same. We get the sloppy seconds."

"Well, you can have the sloppy thirds, you old fart. I'm not stirring your fucking porridge for you."

Luke climbed to his feet and readied his fists, preparing to jump at the men as soon as they opened the doors.

"What the fuck's that?"

"Is there an animal loose or something?"

Luke couldn't hear what had caught their attention from within the van, but he noticed that their footfalls moved away from his position. He crept to the doors and pulled the handle, hoping the men were too preoccupied to hear the judder of the door when the catch disengaged.

He peered out into the darkness. Beams of torchlight cut across the gable end of Arion House as the men approached the rear of the property. Luke stepped down from the back of the van and left the door open in his wake, creeping to the cover afforded by Kelly's car, which remained parked at the stable block.

One of the men turned, flashing his torch back to the van doors. Luke kept his head down and waited for the light to pass once more before chancing another peek. He saw the two men disappear around the far corner of the house and considered calling the police. He checked his pockets for his mobile phone, but of course, they had taken that from him while he was unconscious.

Luke rushed from the cover of the car to the front door. The house lights burned bright and Luke stepped inside with hesitation, placing his steps as carefully and quietly as possible. Kelly could be anywhere and would see him once he entered the light. He needed the element of surprise, there was no way he could overpower the man in a straight fight.

As he passed the kitchen, he saw Rasputin sprawled on the floor, his tongue grey and limp and hanging from his head, which had been twisted around to face backwards. He saw a cordless telephone handset and considered using it to call the police, but the coward in him decided against it. What was he meant to say? *I wanted us to rob her nicely?* They made it nasty. He knew it wasn't a wise choice if he valued his freedom.

He instead grabbed a knife from the angled wooden block by the cooker and charged up the stairs.

"I'm almost done here, wait your turn," Kelly barked upon hearing his approach.

"You're done," Luke cried, plunging the knife deep into the loan shark's back. He felt the metal blade grind against bone.

Kelly writhed, trying to reach for the knife handle.

He slid off the bed, falling face first to the carpet, his bare backside pointing up to the ceiling.

Demi lay still and silent on the bed. Her lips glistened with what at first Luke thought was semen, but he then noticed the empty bottle of Oramorph next to her and realised he'd been fooled by her medication. The bottle hadn't been full when he'd administered it to her earlier, but there had to have been about 400ml or so. He placed his ear over her mouth and could neither feel nor hear any breaths.

He pulled the quilt to conceal all but her head, covering her bare legs and torn knickers and exposed breasts, which were bruised from rough handling. Hot tears burned down Luke's cheeks as he considered the dead woman. *I did this to you. You gave me money because you were lonely, and because I wanted more money, you're dead.*

Luke's tears were not solely for Demi. They were for himself, too. He was a murderer and an accomplice in a second murder, as well as a number of other charges that could be brought against him in this whole affair.

He checked the clock and realised the carers would return soon for the bedtime call. He might be able to flee the scene without issue, but he had no idea where his mobile phone was. He dragged Kelly clear of the bed and turned him over. The handle of the knife acted as a stand, propping Kelly up and keeping him from lying completely flat. Luke rifled through his pockets, finding Kelly's phone and wallet but nothing else.

That meant one of the two thugs outside had to have it. He rolled Kelly over once more. Pressing a foot into the small of the dead debt collector's back to stabilise himself, he applied the force required to break the vacuum within the wound and yanked the knife free of his spine.

Luke crept out to the top of the stairs, straining his ears for sounds of anyone approaching. He glanced down the staircase, then found his attention drawn to the open doors of the ransacked spare bedrooms, one of which had been used as something of a studio for Demi's sketching and painting. Sketches, charcoals and tubes of oil paint lay scattered across the carpet. Luke remembered the sketch she had made of him. Then he thought of the photograph, or photographs, she had taken of him. Not necessarily incriminating evidence, but certainly something to connect him to the place.

Of course, there was the record of the appointments she had made with him, and her social worker's knowledge of the arrangement at the outset. No matter what happened, he would have questions to answer, but he could do his best to make those questions simpler and fewer by removing any traces of himself.

Staying low, he tiptoed into the room, careful not to stand on the oils, which would split the tubes and cause him to leave a lovely set of footprints at a murder scene. He leafed through the scattered notebooks, working frantically, desperate to get out of the house, off the moor and back into town where he could at least have time to think up the next part of the plan.

As his eyes flicked over every one of Demi's lovingly rendered sketches, he saw many of various horses and ponies, but the ones that really stood out were the ones she had marked 'Conquistador XXX'. Those sketches were so lifelike, so precise, that even the knowing look in the animal's eye was captured there on paper. Luke had seen the look before. He knew those eyes. He had been in the presence of this horse more than once.

Impossible, he thought. Conquistador is dead.

In that moment, he heard a blood-curdling scream from outside. Grabbing the knife once more, Luke charged downstairs and made it to the kitchen door before he heard the scream again. He knew it was a man's scream, and for one of those men Kelly had brought with him to be screaming, they must be terrified.

His grip on the knife tightened and he pressed a hand against the open door, using it to steady his nerves, prepared to shove off from it should he suddenly need to turn tail and retreat. Luke peered around the door frame, hearing footsteps kicking up gravel nearby.

He saw one of the thugs, the one referred to as Mark earlier, sprinting towards him, light from inside the house catching the dark stain across his face, making it glisten as he raced past the windows.

Luke stepped outside and raised the knife. "Where's my phone, you thieving bastard?"

The man skidded to a halt on the gravel and changed direction, turning towards the parked van. "Fuck the phone, get out of here. She's killed Terry."

Then he heard the hoof falls, a casual trot somewhere in the darkness. The steps were solid thuds; no splash of gravel accompanied them. Luke peered out beyond the edge of the stable, to the fields where the horses would have been more comfortable than on the loose stones of the driveway. He could see nothing.

"The keys. The fucking keys," Mark cried, dropping from the driver's side of the van.

Luke ran to the back of the van and grabbed the thief by his jacket. "What's going on? You said she... *she* killed Terry. Who do you mean?"

A wet snort sounded from the gate. Gravel crunched under heavy, steady steps.

"The woman. The woman who lives here." Mark shoved Luke aside and broke into a sprint as he reached out for the open door, desperate for the relative safety of the house.

"She's dead, you fucking idiot," Luke cried.

Hooves fell like thunder. Stones whipped up and struck the side panels of the van, clanging louder and louder, closer and closer. Mark froze in the space between the van and the house, turning his head to the source of the furious commotion. He screamed.

Luke clasped a hand over his mouth as the silhouette of a horse and rider cut across the light projected from the front door. He heard soft, wet crunches as Mark's ribcage and head collapsed, his organs and vital fluids bursting out of his smashed body in lumpy, glistening spurts.

Luke took his chance and ran for the door, jumping over Mark's tattered body as he went. He slammed the door shut behind him but didn't bother to lock it, suspecting that whatever Mark or Terry had done to the lock to get in there in the first place had probably rendered it useless.

He had no idea what to do next. There were three vehicles outside and he had the keys to none. There was photographic and sketched evidence of his involvement with Demi, and four corpses on the scene. The only thing he could do was make a run for it, but there was no way he'd outrun a marauding horse.

The knife thudded on the carpet and Luke paced back and forth in the passageway with his fingers clasped behind his head. Finding no answers to his predicament in the confines of the short corridor, he burst through the lounge door like he was a narcotics officer on a drug raid. He scanned the room and saw, sat on the table where she had left it, the little easel, some charcoals and a sketchbook. He tore the book open and flicked through it, finding the nudes Demi had drawn when he'd posed for her. He ripped them out and stuffed them into his pocket.

It was then that he noticed the next picture in the book. Demi had drawn herself in a blurred, dreamy image, standing with one hand on the glass of a window, beyond which was the handsome head and knotted mane of Conquistador. The composition made it clear that the two were locked in eye contact, but the strangest thing of all was that Demi's other hand disappeared behind the thigh of her bent leg. It was unmistakable: she was masturbating in this picture, and it looked like the focus of her desire was the horse.

Luke flicked through more and more of the images, finding more sketches of this kind. He wondered if they were fantasies but considered that Demi might have been drawing memories. Conquistador lying in a bed of straw, Demi naked, sprawled across his back. Pages of rough sketches of what he imagined to be a horse's engorged phallus.

"Fucking hell," he muttered, wide-eyed. "She loves it. She loves the fucking horse."

Demi's voice came from the passageway and Luke turned to face her.

"And he loves me. He never left me. Everyone else did, but not my Conquistador."

Her naked body, supple, healthy, vital, sat tall and proud, riding bareback on the powerful stallion she had loved beyond its death. Her position was not one common to comfortable riding, as she seemed to sit forward slightly, closer to Conquistador's neck. The animal stared deep into Luke's eyes, transfixing him as it strode into the lounge, Demi ducking her head beneath the door frame.

Luke gasped, backing away around the sofa. "This is impossible. This can't be real. You are not real. I saw you.

You're dead. You're lying dead on your bed." The sketch-book slipped from his hand.

Demi's weight shifted with each movement of Conquistador's muscles, shifts which Luke could see caused one of the braided mane knots to rub against her clitoris.

"I'm dreaming this. I'm dreaming all of this, surely to God." Luke continued to back away and stumbled over a side table. He toppled, taking a reed diffuser with him. Passion fruit and coconut oil pooled on the carpet and soaked into his clothes, thick and cold, the scent, normally pleasant, now too strong, cloying. Before Luke could scramble back to his feet once more, Demi towered over him and Conquistador's muzzle hovered inches away from his face, nostrils flaring.

"Demi, I'm sorry. Please, Demi... I didn't know he was going to rape you. I didn't know he would kill you."

She said nothing, only smiled.

A shuddering sigh escaped Luke's lungs. He sobbed and wept as terror gave way to relief.

Conquistador snorted as its lips peeled back, revealing two great barriers of gum and teeth. Luke screamed as the teeth clamped down over his wide-open mouth and white-hot pain consumed him. Tooth and bone snapped and crunched as the mighty animal's powerful bite crushed the escort's jaw, tearing his tongue and lower lip off.

Coughing on the blood racing to the back of his throat, Luke thrashed out, finding his left hand in Conquistador's mouth. Over the crunching bones, he heard Demi moan with pleasure, the same groans he himself had provoked from her with his fingers and tongue earlier that after-noon.

There was no fighting the warm, cotton wool cloud of unconsciousness as the horse clamped onto his left cheek and eye socket. The darkness pulled him down. As he departed, Demi screamed at the peak of her ecstasy and he realised that even in death, he'd fulfilled the purpose of his chosen trade.

3

— · —

ABOUT 'SPORES'

I wrote *Spores* for inclusion in a charity anthology published by the lovely guys over at Sinister Horror Company. Having met some of the company's founding fathers at the first Horror Con in Rotherham, and being impressed by their setup, I was really excited to be invited to produce a story for them.

Body horror taps into something deep within me. That sense of wanting to survive, but also wanting to stay intact. Spores looks at the normal and very personal being corrupted by the unnatural. Or in this case, being corrupted by something from nature itself. This is the kind of story that sticks in the minds of people who can't help but peel a scab off their skin, or who take twisted satisfaction from those YouTube videos of zit popping, or mango worms being squeezed out of infested dog flesh. Do a quick Google search for *trypophobia* and find yourself sucked into a grotesque fascination with warping, corrupting bodies, not by decay and ruination, but by the idea that some parasitic life-form has burrowed into you, made you its home and is making changes against your will. I'm equally fascinated and repulsed by such things. I cringe, but I can't look away. It looks satisfying to poke at, to squeeze, to get the tweezers out and have a dig around. And that's where Spores has its origins.

The characters Bill and Sheila are loosely based on two people I know very well: my daughter's grandparents. My former in-laws. And the horrible part of this is, they are really lovely people, so part of me feels kind of bad about writing a grotesque story with them in mind. Since the original version of this story was published, sadly, Bill is no longer with us. Even as I type this, I'm fighting the urge to change the character names. The house and garden, are very much based on their real home and I couldn't help but have them in mind when I wrote the story, so I will leave the names as they are. I enjoyed the process of writing them into the story, because they are nice people and they just seemed like perfect casting for the story I wanted to tell. It does me good to have them in my mind every now and then, so it was done with love. But then again, we're talking about the love of a horror writer...

4

— · —

SPORES

The property development show ended, and Sheila switched off the TV, balanced the remote control on the arm of the chair and stood up, arcing her back to relieve the dull pain in her lumbar. She wished she had known how much value would have been added to the first home she and Bill had taken on when they were young. If they had rented out some of the homes they had lived in over the years, they would have been worth a fortune by now.

On the television stand, two photographs stood guard at either side of the screen – her youngest grandchildren. Their little smiling faces caught Sheila's eye as they always did when she got in and out of that chair. This action in turn always made her glance at a larger family photograph, mounted above the fireplace, taken before those little ones were born. Bill hugged her tightly on the photo, they were all dressed up on their silver wedding anniversary, with their three sons, daughter, and seventeen (as it was back then) grandchildren arranged around them.

Could have had a lot of money to split among you lot when we're gone, she thought, letting a smile of resignation flicker across her face for a moment.

She padded across the passageway and into the kitchen. She filled the kettle and stared out of the window, taking in the garden's decline into wet and muddy autumn. The *Blaze of Fire* salvia plant that was one of her favourites, clung to its last few stray scarlet leaves. This imbued her view of the garden with a hint of sadness. It felt like even the plant did not want the summer to end.

Switching on the kettle, Sheila returned to the window and looked over at the greenhouse, in the corner of the upper garden, off to the left. She looked for Bill's green flat cap bobbing in and out of view as he worked, but there was no sign of him. The only place he could be, out of sight in this way, was the paddock.

The paddock was a small field to the rear of their garden, which Bill had purchased at the same time as he bought the house, to ensure that no housing developers could snap the land up and build a house that would spoil their view, overshadow their garden in the afternoons, and generally encroach on their space. The corner of the paddock was devoted to Bill's huge compost heap and Sheila guessed that her husband was there, throwing on all the dead plants to keep the cycle of deterioration and growth going in their garden.

Sheila prepared two ham sandwiches and poured the tea, arranging lunch at the kitchen table rather than the dining room, so that Bill wouldn't make a mess of the good dining chairs with his gardening clothes. She peered out of the window, expecting to see Bill trudging up the garden path, whistling a tune she couldn't hear through the double-glazing. There was no sign of him.

It wasn't like him, Sheila thought. Since his army days, he was a real stickler for time and lunch was at 12 noon every day. Never had she needed to go and seek him out – she always joked that she could set the house clocks by Bill's appetite.

The stillness of the garden brought about a stirring in the pit of her stomach - a feeling of butterflies as her nerves seemed almost to stand on end. She opened the back door and stepped out into the garden, feeling the chilly air and the cold of the paving slabs cut through her flimsy slippers in an instant.

She glanced at the salvia just in time to catch another tiny red petal fall loose. For a second a silly notion played across Sheila's mind; she wondered if the petal had waited for her to look before it chose to let go of the stem, or had the movement simply caught the corner of her eye and drawn her full attention?

She passed the pond and noted a ripple playing across the surface, a disturbance, caused no doubt by something unseen, hidden within the murky water. A crow let his presence be known with a throaty call from the stark branches of an oak at the bottom of the paddock.

Tall leylandii formed a natural, green border between the garden proper and the field beyond, the arched opening at the centre forming a portal between order and the wild, unpredictable land beyond.

Sheila's footsteps slowed as she reached the gap, as the enormity of these final steps took prominence in her mind. A vision remained fixed in her imagination: Bill, lying face down in the grass by the compost heap. Becoming compost himself, she thought. Her hands raised to her mouth in shock at this careless, callous, unspoken joke.

She took one more step and jumped with fright as a burly figure burst through the opening, half of his face obscured with dirt, clothes streaked with wet mud. Dirty hands grasped her upper arms.

"Sheila," Bill gasped, "you almost gave me a heart-attack."

Sheila pressed her hands to her bony chest and raised her eyebrows, waiting for the shock to subside and her heartbeat to settle into its ordinary rhythm. "Heart attack?" she cried. "I thought you'd bloody-well had one already."

"Don't be daft. A specimen of health like me won't die of a heart-attack. I almost set my neck, though. I slipped and went right over."

"Why didn't you just come back in then?"

"Well... I think I may have been unconscious for a few minutes."

"We need to take you through to the hospital," Sheila suggested.

"Nonsense, I'm fine." He wrapped his arms around his wife and planted a kiss in the centre of her forehead. "I'm ready for a spot of lunch now, I must say."

Sat at the table enjoying their sandwiches, Sheila asked, "So, how did you manage to fall over?"

"I slipped on the damp grass. I found some toadstools growing, a real cluster of them. I don't know, I was just in a playful mood and couldn't resist giving them a kick. Next thing I knew, I woke up, flat on my back."

"Silly old sod," Sheila chided, chuckling.

"You know when you see something, and you just can't resist?"

"Like bubble-wrap?"

"Exactly... I'm the same with ice on the pond, I can't help myself, I have to crack the surface as I go past."

Sheila sipped her tea. "Well, they say men never really do grow up, don't they?"

"Ah, but I was a boy soldier," Bill replied, smiling, sticking his chest out with shoulders back in a jovial demonstration of pride. "I was made to grow up fast."

"Perhaps you're having your childhood now, then."

Bill scratched behind his right ear for a few seconds, then took a draught of tea.

"You still with us, Bill?" Sheila asked.

Bill shook his head for a second, as though suddenly roused from a deep daydream. "Sorry, what was that?" He rubbed his hand behind his right ear again.

Sheila frowned. "Are you sure you're all right, Bill? I think I should drive you down to A and E, get that head checked over."

Bill shoved his chair back from the table and almost leapt to his feet. "I told you I'm all right," he snapped, then stormed out of the room.

Sheila stared at the kitchen door long after Bill had vanished through it to stomp off up the stairs. His temper had shocked her – he hadn't been so short with her, so angry with her in years. Age certainly had mellowed him. She had always hoped it would stay that way.

* * *

Bill stood at the guest room window, breathing in the soothing smell of the lavender and chamomile reed diffuser positioned on the windowsill above the radiator. The pleasant scent could not take away the envy he harboured, staring out over the box hedge that separated his garden from that of his neighbours, the McKies.

Fred McKie, twenty years Bill's junior, worked his garden from morning until night every weekend. He was some sort of business law hotshot for a German manufacturing company with offices in North Tyneside. The McKies had no children and Fred threw a lot of his money into plants and beautiful wooden furniture for the garden.

Bill watched as Fred scarified the lush green lawn on the second of three terraces that formed a colourful cascade of lawn and blooms year-round.

"He works that grass too hard," Bill muttered to himself. "I've told him before. It'll all die off over the winter."

Once more, his fingertips returned to the spot behind his right ear, and he scratched again, but this time, something caught his attention, breaking the unconscious nature of the movement. He traced tiny circles with his fingertip, trying to locate the thing he had felt moments before. After a few seconds, he found it. The bump felt like a large pimple, but he knew from experience that pimples, moles, warts and wounds always felt larger than they really were when you couldn't see them. He hurried into the bathroom, listening for a moment at the top of the stairs to make sure Sheila wasn't heading in his direction. Her worry was the last thing he needed.

He flicked on the strip lamp above the main mirror and twisted his head aside, eyes strained to the right extent as he bent his ear forwards, trying to reveal the abnormality. He couldn't see it, so he grabbed his shaving mirror from the shelf and placed it on the windowsill. He had to change the mirror's angle twice before he got a view, and even then, the reflected reflection revealed only a tiny spot behind his ear. He dismissed it as a skin-tag or some other similar unwanted, benign growth related to his age.

It was when he replaced the shaving mirror that he noticed a cluster of bumps in the webbing between his right thumb and forefinger. Stretching the skin as far as he could, he probed the tiny growths with his fingernail. He tugged at his flesh and a tiny gap appeared between his skin and the lumps. These things were embedded in his skin, but not part of it – not the epidermis, at least.

He glanced about the bathroom, paused at his Gillette razor, dismissed it, then opened a drawer. He produced a pair of nail scissors, opening them so that the blades sat wide apart. Using the tip of one of the blades, he pressed down against one of the fleshy bumps. The structure gave way and he brushed it aside. He then pressed the blade tip down alongside one of the other bumps, opening that gap between his skin and the growth once more. Shifting the blade's angle, he applied pressure and lifted, popping the tiny sphere of matter out onto the rim of the wash basin.

He found the process most satisfying and began to dig again.

Sheila left Bill alone, feeling it was better to let him sulk alone upstairs than to force the issue. She settled on her favourite lounge chair with the latest Jo Nesbo thriller and determined to wait the afternoon out and see if Bill's humour improved later.

The grandfather clock in the hall chimed the arrival of three O' clock. Sheila finished the paragraph she was reading, set her bookmark in place and put the book aside. She put the kettle on and decided that a nice cup of tea and a Kit-Kat were the most effective peace offering she knew of where Bill was concerned. She carried the drink and biscuit upstairs, surprised by the stillness and quiet she found there. She wondered if Bill had fallen asleep and thoughts of delayed shock set her heart pounding, and for the second time that day, the horrific possibility of her husband lying dead flashed into her mind.

She burst into the bedroom, spilling dribbles of hot tea onto the cream carpet, and to her relief she found the bed empty and no sign of Bill there.

A cough startled her and drew her back to the bathroom. "Bill," she called. "Bill, I have a cuppa for you."

"I'll be down in a second," Bill replied.

"Is everything all right?" she asked, wondering what he was up to. She hadn't heard the bath running, and no movements had indicated his heeding the call of nature within a reasonable time-frame. She reasoned then, that something must be wrong. "Have you fallen again?"

Another cough broke the silence of the bathroom. Sheila pressed down the door handle and entered the room. Dark red splatter marks punctuated the brown cork tiles across the length and breadth of the room. The white of the washbasin was spoiled by brownish-red marks as blood broke down against drops of water.

The teacup and saucer smashed off the floor sending fragments of china skittering across the room as tea splashed and splattered across the tiles. The Kit-Kat landed at Bill's bloody foot as he stood naked before his wife, his hands, stained red, clutching the open nail scissors.

"What have you done to yourself, Bill?" Sheila cried, taking in the series of punctures her husband had apparently dug into himself. His hands and arms had borne the brunt of the self-harm, but she noted a dozen or so wounds in his chest, a half dozen across his tummy and several on his legs, more prominently around the ankles.

"I couldn't stop myself, Sheila. There are just so many of them."

"So many of what, Bill?"

"There's something growing in me. It's all over my body. I need to cut it all out."

Bill turned and Sheila could then see the horrific work he had carried out on his back, with skin roughly hacked and torn where he couldn't reach and see what he was doing effectively.

"I need to call an ambulance. Put those scissors down, would you?"

"No ambulance, Sheila. I'll be fine. I just need to clean these cuts up."

Against her better judgement Sheila agreed to help Bill clean his wounds with surgical spirit, sticking plasters and dressings. The sting of the spirit elicited sharp intakes of breath from Bill, some of which in turn triggered a deep, hacking cough.

"Bill, at least let me make an appointment for the doctor. For the cough alone, if not the rest of this mess," she suggested.

Bill pondered the idea and, knowing that it would be at least a couple of days before he would have to attend the appointment, he agreed. By then, no doubt, the cough would have cleared up and he would be able to cancel the visit.

Every now and then, Sheila inspected a scabby patch at the back of Bill's head, where his hair was sparse and the relentless march of balding had taken its toll. It was impossible for her to determine if his head had been injured in the fall he described, as the self-inflicted wounds masked anything sustained earlier.

At dinner, Sheila managed only a few forkfuls of food. Bill ate voraciously, but his swallows were punctuated by thick, rasping, wet coughs and deep, grunting inhalations through his nose, snorting back globs of snot.

"Sounds like you caught quite a cold while you were lying on the damp ground."

"Must have," Bill agreed, barely looking up from his plate.

Sheila raised her eyebrows, disgusted at the sight and sounds presented before her. Revulsion at her husband was an entirely new experience for her; she had always found him lovable, but there was something about this odd behaviour, and the frustration of not being able to help him, that made her resent him.

She carried her plate into the kitchen and scraped her barely touched dinner into the bin. As she filled the kitchen sink to wash up the dinner plates, shallow, rasping breaths sounded above the noise of the pouring water. Sheila turned to see Bill leaning against the pantry door.

"Sheila, I need to get myself to bed," Bill groaned. "Sorry, love. I don't think I can help with the dishes."

Sheila slipped an arm over his back and led him out of the room. "Bill, you look terrible. I don't care what you say, but if you're still ill tomorrow morning, I am calling a doctor out and that's the end of it."

Bill leaned against the banister, letting it take the bulk of his weight as Sheila assisted him up the stairs. His feet dragged over the carpet and every step seemed to draw a noticeable chunk of vitality from his muscles. When he reached the bed, he simply flopped onto the quilt and wriggled upwards so that his head eventually settled on the pillow.

Sheila watched her beloved husband for a moment as he descended rapidly into sleep. She felt guilty for the resentful thoughts she had engaged in at the dinner table. He was poorly, more poorly than she had ever seen him. It wasn't his fault that he was all snotty.

With the kitchen tidy, Sheila settled in her comfy chair once more and picked up her book. Just an hour, she thought, then I'll check on him.

The warm house, and the stresses of the day made Sheila's eyelids feel like lead weights. Her eyes seemed unable to focus on the words in the paperback and in minutes, sleep claimed her.

A noise somewhere between a slap and a thud shocked Sheila awake once more. The shadows of the room, beyond the pools of light offered by the twin lamps, lay deep and dark. Sheila realized that she had slept past sunset. She glanced at the clock and saw that it was a little after seven O' clock. As she stood, she noticed the Jo Nesbo by her slippered feet and realised that the book, having slipped from her hand, had served as her alarm.

She collected the paperback, slipped her bookmark back into place and set it aside. Wondering if Bill fancied some supper, she walked up the stairs at a slow pace, feeling the tingle of increased blood flow into her legs. Upon entering the bedroom, she flipped the thin, brass switch and the wall-mounted lamps cast their comforting, soft glow over the room.

Bill seemed not to have moved a muscle in all the time on the bed. He lay exactly as she left him, naked, on top of the quilt. At first, Sheila thought that some of the sticking plasters had become dislodged by the blood collected beneath them, but as she stepped closer, she realised this was not the case.

Wanting to call his name to try to wake her husband, Sheila found the words caught within her chest. She tried to clear her throat, but the air she forced seemed to have no purchase, no power to it. Both the sensation in her throat and the sight before her eyes initiated a panic within her. She crossed the room in a sort of staggering lunge and collapsed on the bed alongside her prone husband.

With shaking hands, she extended her fingertips towards his back, which had erupted in clusters of mushroom-like growths in white and red varieties. Of these growths, half of them bore heads the size of a thumbnail or smaller, and the other half had spread open to the size of a milk bottle top.

Thin, inch-long stems of orange and yellow held the red mushrooms above her husband's flesh, and white stems held the white caps in place. She touched one of the red growths first, just above Bill's right buttock. The cap had a waxy feel to it and as she enclosed it between her thumb and forefinger, with a mind to pluck it, she had the strange feeling that the mushroom had a pulse.

She stared at the clusters across Bill's back, positioning herself low, with her chin resting on the bed, she held as still as possible. It took a few seconds to really notice it, but the white and yellow gills under each of the caps certainly did seem to pulse – to breathe.

Sheila gasped and in that same instant, her finger and thumb increased pressure and she snatched the red cap up from its stem. The instant she did so, she investigated the thin black tube of the hollow stem and noticed that it was full of a dark red liquid. She knew the liquid was Bill's blood immediately, as it oozed down the outside of the stem as though she had opened a wound.

This discovery forced her to take note of the cap in her hand, which she squeezed. The plump, saucer-like growth split open under only a little pressure, and blood trickled out into her palm, running between her fingers as though she had wrung out a sponge.

She turned her attention to one of the white growths, which seemed to occur in the centre of the clusters, surrounded by a dozen or so red caps. Reaching for the white cap, she unleashed a deep, hacking barrage of coughs and heard the phlegm loosen in her chest and throat. She tried to encourage further coughs to bring the uncomfortable mass up into her mouth, but it seemed to settle in place again, restricting her breathing to a thin wheeze.

Sheila's fingers inspected the white cap. It felt completely different to the red variety. Gone was the waxy, gelatinous feel; in its place was a rigid structure, with a surface which, although it appeared to be a single colour, was in fact two different textures. Some parts of the surface felt rough, grainy, while other areas felt smooth, almost glazed.

A desperation built up within her. Curiosity bubbled at the surface of her consciousness. She considered the fact that this was her husband lying before her, no more than Bill had considered the grass when he kicked apart the mushrooms earlier that day. She pulled the white mushroom, but it didn't break away. She tugged again and noticed that Bill's flesh rose around it with each exertion, as though the mushroom was somehow anchored into place. Adjusting her grip, she twisted the white cap and observed the flesh pulling as she did so. Eventually, she was treated to a sharp snap, like a wishbone breaking, and the white cap came loose in her hand. Rubbing her fingers over the upper surface, she realised that the glossy surface reminded her of tooth enamel. Staring at Bill's back, she noticed that a porous, pinkish matter filled the broken white stem.

Rubbing her fingertips over the underside of the white cap, she discovered that the gills were flexible, but somewhat delicate, almost brittle like fine china.

Another fit of coughing forced a lump into her windpipe which triggered her gag reflex. She raced to the bathroom and hung her head over the toilet bowl. She retched and coughed until her mouth filled with solid lumps which she promptly spat into the toilet.

The toilet water immediately darkened as bloody clouds curled and dissipated before her eyes. Lumps of deep red and purple bobbed on the surface and clung to the porcelain.

Sheila clasped a hand over her mouth, then inspected her palm to see thick, dark blood smeared over the pebbled surface of her flesh. She inspected both of her palms to find that both were rough with growths the size of pin heads. She screamed and plunged her hands into the toilet, her fingers frantically breaking apart the lumps she had coughed up and vomited.

Holding the glistening fragments in the light, Sheila could see pieces of red caps, just as she had found on Bill's back, and a purple, gelatinous variety, very similar to the red caps.

Her legs felt as though they could no longer support her weight and she staggered to the bedroom once more, where she fell upon the bed, collapsing partially onto her husband, squashing, tearing and breaking the fungal eruptions as she did so. The tang of fresh warm blood met her nostrils as she clawed at the bedding and wriggled until her head was next to Bill's.

Crying his name, pushing against him, Sheila tried desperately to wake her husband. Her arms seemed to have no power in them as she raised her hands to the back of Bill's head, rocking him. "Please. Bill, wake up."

Bill's thinning hair jutted out of his head at odd angles, where growths had burst through his flesh between follicles. Red caps even sported some of his brown and grey strands as they had become entangled in the rapid fungal growth.

Sheila's body shuddered as she was overcome with tears and dread. She could feel that Bill was warm, but his lack of response left her with no alternative but to assume the worst.

Then he breathed. The breath was a shallow, liquid wheeze, but it was a breath. He twitched as consciousness began to fire inside his brain once more. He pressed his palms down on the bed and pushed, arching his back.

Sheila heard a sickening crunch from Bill's hands, which were spotted with clusters of red caps, punctuated with the white variety. Bill moaned in pain, but his voice was strained, weak. He raised his head and slowly turned to face her.

She gasped as torn stems leaked blood from his cheek and lips, and bony white caps encircled Bill's left eye, which was blinded, itself ruptured by a cluster of red caps bursting from blood vessels.

Another garbled moan escaped Bill's lips as the inability to focus properly created panic.

Adrenalin burst into Sheila's bloodstream and she sat bolt upright immediately. Bill shifted his weight, trying to turn to face his wife properly. All his upper body weight shifted to his left shoulder and he rolled his hips. Another crunch emerged and Bill's left arm collapsed. Rolling onto his back, Bill unleashed a gurgling scream. Speckles of blood sprayed into the air, peppering his face, Sheila's face, and the white and floral bedding around them.

Bill's right hand lashed at his left shoulder and he tore at the growths he found there, snapping the white caps which seemed to hold the strength and substance that his own skeleton now lacked. Red caps burst, leaking blood across the bedding. He tore at his left eye, snapping away the white caps, then pulling at the tough, spine-like stems, before plunging his fingers into the shell of red caps protruding from his eyeball.

He howled again, tearing at the growths on his lips, scratching at tiny white nodules on his teeth. At length, his fingers reached his neck, where red and purple mushrooms grew beyond his vision.

Sheila cried out, begging her husband to stop, but he either could not hear her, or would not take note. He tore away a handful of the fungi, unleashing a hot jet of bright arterial blood across the bedroom. Sheila screamed, pressing her fingers against the broken stems. Bloody bubbles, like red spittle, burped from the stems which had born purple caps, as his windpipe released air.

Sheila bucked and lurched as another fit of coughs broke loose. She took her hands away from Bill's neck instinctively, raising her hands to her face, where the fact that the swellings on her palms had grown became evident. Not only that, but she felt a strange sensation as though someone else's hands touched her face, and her hands touched someone else's face. She knew that if she looked in the mirror, that her cheeks would be stippled with spores.

Bill ceased to move, his eyes rolling back in his head as his blood pressure dipped dangerously low.

Turning towards the bedside cabinet, Sheila reached for the telephone. Her fingers felt swollen, transformed, and she cried in frustration when the telephone thudded on the bedroom carpet. Scrambling onto the floor, Sheila grasped the telephone and stabbed at the keys to reach the emergency services.

Sheila rasped and coughed into the receiver and the operator was unable to take any useful information from her.

"If you require emergency assistance, please press any of the keys," the operator instructed.

Sheila complied, squashing several keys down at once. The operator, hearing the tone, recognised that the person at the end of the line, Sheila, was in danger and that this probably wasn't an accidental or prank call.

Gurgling, liquid breaths built up in Sheila's chest and again she descended into a fit of coughing. More solid pieces broke free and burst from her lips.

The operator called out, asking questions, trying to get to the bottom of the problem, believing Sheila to be choking on perhaps a piece of food.

Unable to explain or give any indication at all what was going on, and afraid that the emergency services would not arrive and diagnose her correctly in time, an idea flashed in her mind. Sheila clawed across the floor and out onto the landing. She reached and grasped the newel post at the head of the stairs, hauling her body up off the thick olive carpet.

Her vision became grainy – she prayed it was from lack of oxygen and not a series of mushrooms preparing to erupt from her eyes. Clinging to the banister, she managed to make it to the foot of the stairs. She staggered to the front door, coughing and wheezing. Her thighs burned as the oxygen in her blood ran low, starving her straining muscles.

She tumbled on the stone paving by the pond and her forehead thumped down hard. She closed her eyes as her vision filled red and faded to black. Her ears seemed to fill with the sound of static as she battled to stay conscious. Blood cooled in the night air, dribbling down her brow and into her eyes as she rose to her feet and grabbed the wooden trellis to her right.

Her flesh seared with white-hot pinpricks of pain and she clawed at the backs of her hands, where the pain was most intense. The topography of her flesh had changed, as had the texture. She felt waxy pebbles coating her skin and her fingers curled into fists involuntarily as the growths dictated the behaviour of her tendons.

Barely able to flex her fingers, Sheila knew that her plan was running out of time as she arrived at Bill's garden shed. Her knotted hands slid over the damp brass door handle again and again as her coughing intensified. She pressed down with her elbow and the handle gave way, allowing her to access the interior. In the darkness she was unsure that she would recognize the fungicide bottle, but she squeezed her hands together, trying to break her fists open once more.

Knocking spray bottles of weed killer aside, Sheila fought against her closing fingers. She grabbed a tub of slug pellets and threw them to the floor, breaking open several of the growths on her palms, sending a fresh cascade of blood over her hands. She turned and yanked the pull-cord to turn on the single bulb and tried to ignore the sickening sight of the parasitic growths colonising the flesh on the back of her hands, and the bleeding stumps on her palms.

She scooped up a grey plastic bottle with a ridged grip at the sides and tried to grasp the black bottle cap. Her slick, bloody hands could gain no purchase on the plastic and so she looked about for anything that she could use. Her eyes fell upon a garden trowel hanging from a hook by the door.

Her hands faltered as she reached for the trowel when a fresh bout of coughing carried her off-balance and blinded her as her eyelids clasped shut and teared up. She spat a ball of matter from her mouth that was more solid than liquid, but which left the metal tang of blood on her tongue.

She wiped her eyes with her sleeve and grabbed for the trowel once more as the growths tugged at her tendons, forcing the fingers of her right hand to lock closed again. She picked up the tool with her left hand and felt her fingers tighten involuntarily around the rubber hand grip, with no little satisfaction - she finally had what she needed within her grasp.

Sheila returned to the bottle of fungicide and plunged the trowel down as close to the bottle cap as she could, two of the teeth biting into the plastic. As she pulled the trowel back, the fungicide bottle came with it, slipping off the teeth to fall to the floor, spilling the contents, with heavy glugs providing a countdown to her doom.

The siren of an approaching ambulance met her ears from a distance. She dropped to the ground and squeezed the bottle clumsily between her two knotted hands, the left of which was still locked around the handle of the trowel, ever more fungicide spilling out of the rents she had created. She opened her mouth and held the container up, feeling the chemicals splash across her face, pooling against her closed eyelids, burning inside her nostrils.

Sheila hoped the paramedics would check the shed soon, and she hoped that they could treat her for poisoning quicker than they would have removed the fungi from her compromised airway.

Fred McKie sighed deeply on his way to the kitchen. "Can't you just get into this? You've seen all those programs about having a forage and getting it into your home cooking."

His wife, Laura stared at the sizzling pan of mince, garlic and onions, then glanced at the red mushrooms she had chopped and set aside on the wooden chopping board. "They just look nothing like the button ones you get at the supermarket. I mean nothing like them."

"That's because these ones have some flavour to them. Probably, anyway." Fred raised his tablet and pointed at the picture of the red mushroom on the screen. "Look, it says here it's edible. Scarlet Hood, edible. See? There are some down here it can be confused with, but they are black when you cut into them."

"Yeah, that they know about," Laura protested.

"Oh, so you think that growing in our garden would be a brand new, never-before-seen type of mushroom. Come on."

"Well, you never know."

"Living off the land, Laura. What could be better for you than that which nature provides in your very own garden?"

The idea did appeal to Laura, she had to admit it.

Fred flipped the leather cover back over his tablet emphatically. "Look, if you don't want to use them, chuck 'em in the bin. I just thought it would be nice to use what we have around us, that's all."

"I know, and it's a nice idea, but mushrooms are just one of those things I was always nervous about. Dad said never pick them and never eat them unless they're bought from a shop. He was always on about poisonous toadstools."

"Every dad goes on about them, but not one of them knew how to describe them, I bet. They didn't have the information we have at our fingertips. Christ, they didn't eat mushrooms unless it was in a fry-up, let's be fair."

Laura chuckled and slid the contents of the chopping board into the frying pan.

5

— · —

About 'Once Tolled the Lutine Bell'

I was invited to submit a piece to the Scarlet Galleon Press anthology *Fearful Fathoms*, a collection of aquatic-themed horror tales. For this one, I summoned up another 19th century story, this time about a shipping magnate with some unscrupulous plans to get an edge in business.

Let me tell you about the title. The French-built *Lutin* was acquired by the British in 1793 and rechristened *HMS Lutine*. Six years later, heavily laden with gold, she was lost in a storm at Vlieland in the West Friesian Islands, where shifting sandbanks disrupted attempts to salvage the ship and its valuable cargo (the majority of which was never recovered). Maritime insurers Lloyd's of London acquired and preserved her salvaged bell - the *Lutine Bell* of the title, which is now used for ceremonial purposes in their London headquarters.

Lloyds mounted the bell in their underwriting room, where it was struck upon the receipt of news on lost ships whose cargo the had insured. The bell was struck twice for good news, and once for bad. In modern times, it is

67

struck to mark the passing of members of the royal family, or to commemorate such disasters as 9/11, the London Bombings, the Asian tsunami and is rung to mark the start and end of the two minutes' silence observed for Armistice Day.

It was easy to imagine nervous investors waiting for news of their cargo and fleets, praying for delivery, fearing disaster and financial ruin... or wishing it on their competitors.

Those familiar with *Doctor Blessing* might find some familiar faces in here, and when you get to know more about my Tilwick stories, you'll doubtless spot a connection there, too. Mark at Scarlet Galleon was very enthusiastic about this story. He actually approached me to develop it into a novella and offered to publish it, but I like it as it is. I don't like the idea of going back and padding a story out, after I've written it to be a self-contained capsule of a tale. Still, it was nice to have a piece of work met with such enthusiasm.

I hope you'll enjoy it, too.

6

—·—

Once Tolled The Lutine Bell

"Yer a damned cold, hard man Jack Snow," said the silver-haired Scotsman, Matthew Dent.

"Dent, now ye know as well as I do, that business is business."

"Now you sound like your father. You're becoming him through and through."

Snow cast his old mentor an angry glance, his narrow jaw clenched, and head cocked at an angle almost suggesting curiosity. His mouth betrayed his mind with the question, "Now what on earth do ye mean by that, ye old conniving bastard?"

Dent chuckled. "It means yer a throwback to the auld man after all."

"And do ye mean tae suggest that this is a bad thing, Dent?"

Dent pursed his lips and turned to gaze out of the window of the luxuriously appointed offices of Snow and Sons, at the scuffed masts and battered chimney of the aged Red Scout, noting the ragtag band of men scurrying about her, making ready for sea. "Yer father was a successful man, Jack. But he wasnae a very happy man."

"I'm not sure I care for your line of conversation, Dent."

"If ye dinna care for the men oan that ship, then I dinna expect ye tae care for the ramblings of old friends. But ramble I will. I've lived long enough tae earn the right tae ramble awhile. It always aggrieved your dear mother that she couldnae lift the spirits of old Jock Snow. I want you tae think about that, Jack. Think of how your mother was, and I want you to think to your own household, in future, a family, if ye should see fit." Dent turned to face his young master once more. "You see, what she found out the hard way was that it is impossible to lift the heart of a man, when that organ is so weighted with regret."

Snow stood and took position at the window, staring down at the doomed vessel. "You sound like a man tempted to offer his resignation."

Dent sighed and patted the younger man's bony shoulder. "I'm with you 'til I drop, lad. Not because I want to, but because I see in you my destiny."

"Which is?"

"With what I know, Jack, my resignation letter might as well be a suicide note."

Snow squeezed his mentor's fingers, with a firm pressure meant only to reassure, not to threaten. "I have seen what I have to become to make way in this world, Dent. If I stand idly by then I get to bear witness to this company, the legacy of my father and his father, waste away. The Burton Company has pecked and nibbled away at us for decades. I can't let that old bitch take it all away from me now." His fingers danced across the lip of a hat-sized, ash-filled brazier stood on a steel pedestal to the left of the window.

"This superstitious nonsense will do you no good, either, Jack," Dent sighed, noting Snow's preoccupation with the brazier. "What good it does to burn money while you say you are so in need of it, is anyone's guess."

As Snow observed the busy London and St Katherine Docks he considered the Red Scout standing convincingly fast as ominous tendrils of fog probed her starboard side. Laden with the poorest quality coal he could purchase, to then run with the shabbiest sails in his fleet. The battered steamer and the crew of drunks he had assembled to man her made for a damned pitiful sight by comparison to the vision of next berth, where the Red Stallion made ready, a sturdy crew cutting about her with rapid, precise movements.

He turned to his selection of whiskies, trying desperately to stifle the gulp he could feel swelling within his throat. He had to conceal this show of concern from Dent.

"Something on your mind, Jack?" Dent asked. Dent was wise enough to turn his gaze back to the bustling docks, rather than maintain his watch over Snow. He knew the younger man would unleash that savage tongue of his, should he realise that his gulp had not gone unnoticed.

Snow did not respond. Not with words, anyway. The heavy bottle of fine Basker's single malt thumped against the back of Dent's skull, felling the man with one blow. Dent's legs gave way and his forehead struck the glass pane before him.

A crack arced across the blood-smeared glass and Dent settled in a heap on the floor. Dark blood soon matted the grey waves of hair that met his crisp white shirt collar, and leaked from his broken nose.

Snow strode to the office doors, snatching them open. The red-faced Dutchman, Gosseling and one of his foul-smelling ship thugs stood ready. "Take this traitor aboard and make away within the hour. Nobody, nobody is to approach this man until you are ten miles out, do ye hear?"

"Aye, sir."

"And when ye reach Calcutta, ye are tae drop him there with only the clothes oan his back."

The doors closed once more and Snow opened his strongbox. He selected a wedge of twenty valuable pieces of paper - debts he was yet to collect - debts which any of his advisers would instruct him to call in immediately, or sell on to a factor to free up the cash. Instead, he strode to the brazier, stuffed the documents into the aperture and picked at the shilling-sized scab on his left palm. He scratched the raw skin beneath the scab, exciting blood from the wound. A few drops was all he needed and before long, thick dark crimson droplets splattered heavily on the notes. Snow struck a match and coaxed the flame to catch the corner of one of the bills. Within seconds, the paper curled and blackened as the confined fire devoured it.

Snow bowed his head, muttering incantations under his breath, with his eyes shut tight. Beneath, on the docks, Dent's polished shoes scraped across the wooden planks of the gangway and up onto the deck of the Red Scout.

The Red Scout lurched over the back of another crushing wave and Gosseling cursed his orders, cursed that bastard Jack Snow and cursed the treacherous Portuguese coast. He wiped briny spray from his thick eyebrows with the sleeve of his greatcoat and stalked amidships of the beleaguered steamer in his charge. Around him, the crew worked to shut and seal with tarpaulin every hatch and opening they could, fearful that this terrible gale could only get worse before their situation could improve at all.

"Dacre," he yelled, eyeing the sails as the wild wind threatened to tear them from the ship, masts and all.

"Aye, sir."

"Where is my steam? Do these men intend to power this ship under the heat of but a single candle?"

"Sir, with God as my judge, the men spend so much coal I fear we won't make it but ten more miles. It gives off no heat, sir. They would be better suited with a handful of candles, I would swear to it."

"Reef these sails, damn you," Gosseling bellowed, then his eyes caught sight of the great grey swell rising before the ship. "Brace," Gosseling roared in horror as the churning sea reared up before the Scout, tipping the bow skyward. Men staggered even more drunkenly than their usual disorderly gait as they fought against the violent lurch of the boards beneath them.

The wave broke, pouring gallons of frothy brine over the deck. The bowsprit dipped low as the Red Scout surged forth, tipping down at ever such a steep angle that for a moment the captain feared they would sail in a straight line downward, ever downward, fathom by fearful fathom, right to the bottom of the sea.

Wood groaned against the irresistible force of the sea as the beautiful Cherokee girl figurehead vanished beneath the waves and the bowsprit cracked as the Scout fought to right herself once more, scooping up another treacherous wash of rushing water to flow across the deck.

"Man overboard," came the cry.

"Dacre, take the name," Gosseling bellowed as a clutch of crewmen leaned over the port side bulwarks, throwing ropes to their doomed fellow, screaming as the furious waves smashed his head against the waterline, before pressing him into the crushing deep.

That the Red Scout had turned a few degrees was almost imperceptible, but even years of sloth and drink could not dampen Gosseling's instincts that much – least of all his survival instinct. The captain turned to face the bridge, where the pilot, a weather-beaten fellow Dutchman name Van Semple swayed and clutched the helm as though his life depended upon it. Unfortunately in doing so, he had allowed the ship to veer starboard ever so slightly, revealing more of the port side to the elements. "Van Semple, you fool. Turn this bitch three degrees to port." Gosseling had mistaken the shift for an intentional move. He feared the pilot was about to order them men to attempt a starboard tack, to work upwind without the benefit of the engines. He knew that with such powerful waves, that the ship could be forced over and capsize and that they had to sail dead ahead to cleave through the wild sea.

Van Semple responded with a booming, "Aye, Sorr." But it was too late.

Before the ship could correct its course, another almighty wave carried her aloft, not breaking until she had risen forty feet. "Jesus Christ," Gosseling bellowed, grasping the starboard bulwark and hanging on with both arms locked in place.

The damaged bowsprit finally gave way, tearing loose as the wave broke over the bow, carrying the timber rod backwards where it lodged against the forecastle, splintering planks of that structure, prevented from flying further back across the deck by the sheer tension of the rigging. The Scout lurched to port with a sudden, jerking violence that cast another three crewmen into the deep.

Gosseling gritted his teeth in anticipation of the righting moment, as Van Semple battled to carry the ship a few degrees to port. He shouted with exertion and the captain tried to haul himself along the deck, against the downward momentum of the ship as it finally tipped over the back of the wave, trying desperately to get to the pilot to assist him to return the ship to a safe course.

The rigging squealed and snapped at the front of the ship. A capstan broke loose, freeing the fore mast boom, allowing it to swing wildly in the gale. The capstan whipped across the width of the deck. Gosseling yelled a warning, but it was too late. Dacre took the full force of the bulky iron node in his chest, sending him cartwheeling across the ship to land in a bloody heap against the port bulwark.

"Davis, you're with me," Gosseling called, beckoning the most capable hand he could see and the two pushed into the shelter of the cabin, beating a course straight to the engine room where the stokers and greasers swore and damned the poor coal Snow had provided them with. One of the engineers took a long swig from a bottle of cheap gin he had picked up in London.

Gosseling snatched the bottle away and hurled it into the open jaws of the starving firebox. "Drink will do no good, lads. If we can't get some power into this bitch, we'll all be on the bottom, now I need your wits about you."

"Wits? I've wit aplenty, but unfortunately wits are as combustible as this fucking coal, Sorr."

Gosseling should have been shouting to be heard under the normal conditions of a steamer's engine room, but the engines were so underpowered and the pistons driven so slowly that the conversation was held at an almost civilised volume. The captain's ears pricked up as a sound met his ears, one as unwelcome as the lack of sound in the engine room. The sound of laughter. Hysterical, mad laughter.

Dent lay curled up in a shadowy corner to the stern of the cargo hold, tied to a metal ring fixed in the deck, usually reserved for tying crates down. It was usually an effective way of keeping the ship's goods in place, but ropes and chains groaned against their burdens as nature's frenzy tested the Red Scout to the very limits of her design.

Dent's laughter came in fits and starts and he cowered, averting his eyes, as Gosseling's bullseye lantern cast light across his face.

"You appear to find humour in the strangest of situations, my friend," Gosseling growled, steadying himself against a crate.

The hold had begun to carry water and Davis called the crew to man the pumps. This command brought about the greatest response from the men, either because they knew this meant they could all be about to drown, or because it meant they could work as far from the battered deck as possible.

"Snow has murdered us all. We are to be chalked up along with the goods and chattels lost on this ship, I am afraid."

"He would never do that, liar," Gosseling roared.

"You and all the drunken wee miscreants aboard signed a contract to take this ship to hell. Any minute now the hull will begin to fracture; he paid well to have this ship sabotaged."

"Impossible."

"Gosseling, you've lost your touch, man. You are every bit of you the rum-soaked idiot Snow took you for. Ye set sail and didnae check your ship properly. You were too busy taking your pay for dragging my arse aboard. Well, my friend, here we go, down to the fucking bottom together. Lloyds have Snow well insured for the loss, and as soon as that Lutine bell tolls, he'll be at those underwriters and a handsome wee profit will be made from our souls."

"You are a liar and a traitor, Dent."

"You hesitated, Gosseling. You hear those bilge pumps doing their work and all that clanking is like the cogs in your fucking thick head turning over. If ye dinna believe me, check these boxes. What is it supposed to be, barley, wool, whisky and soap or some such?"

Gosseling firmed his jaw, not wishing to confirm Dent's assumption, but his eyes averted the old Scotsman's gaze. He could no longer pretend. "Davis, open these crates. I want to see what our Mr Snow has arranged for us to carry."

"That's my boy," Dent encouraged. "Do as he says, Davis. And then ye'll see. Ye'll see that this is a ship bound for Hell."

As Davis pried open the first box, Dent fell back into his maniacal laughter. Worthless rags fell loose from the opening and Davis reached in deeper, drawing out a clutch of paper. "Sorr, Sorr, it's money and... I think it's paintings, and chairs."

"It's fucking what?" Dent howled, delirious in these, his final moments. "Listen to me, Gosseling. Snow is a desperate man. He has appealed to a force darker than you or I could believe possible. He has struck a bargain, sacrificing his personal wealth and it is we who are to be forfeit."

"The Devil? I need no ghost stories here, old man."

"No' the Devil, but you're close. 'Tis Mammon, the demon of greed. Now, when I heard about this, I thought old Jack had gone mad under the pressure of the Burtons making ready to take his company off him, but your old pilot up there, he's done nothing to get you out of this fucking tempest has he?"

"The storm came upon us from nowhere," Gosseling snapped.

"Then a deal indeed was struck. You and your men best be on good terms with God, is all I can say."

Gosseling ran full pace against the tilting ship, bursting out onto the deck in time to see the fore topgallant mast plummet towards him, harpooning the redundant chimney. Eyes narrowed against the lashing rain, the captain scanned his ship, assessing the despair of his wounded, bleeding crew, the shredded sails, tortured rigging and collapsing masts.

Metal and wood screamed off the port side and Gosseling dared to peer into the deep, black sea in time to bear witness to the coppered hull splitting apart, opening a vast rent into which hundreds upon hundreds of gallons of water rushed.

The captain tore at his hair, screaming defiance to God, who even in his limitless power could not save them now. Producing a dagger from his belt, Gosseling wept bitter, angry tears as the Red Scout dipped down, the sea seeming to suck away from her, impossibly shallow and at a terrifying, sharp angle. Before him grew the killing wave, the final stroke. He knew that the ship could never right before the surging tower of water claimed them.

"Snow, you bastard. You are not the only man under the sun who knows the dark old ways. I pledge my soul to vengeance. I pledge the souls of these poor doomed bastards before me. I shall have my revenge on thee." The captain yelled to any crewman who could hear him above the roaring sea and the panicked cries of those who knew they had met the end, "Hear me, men. All hands, if ye would visit vengeance upon the whoreson who sent us to die, take any lanyard, chain and scrap of rigging ye can find and lash yourself to this damned vessel."

Davis heard the maddened captain scream even against the deafening rumble of the impending swell of death and watched as the men scrambled to fasten themselves to the ship in vain hopes of surviving the cataclysmic wave approaching. He bore witness to the captain's suicide, the plunging of the dagger deep into his own heart. Gosseling turned to him, teeth grinding together in agony, chipping and snapping apart under his bite, his eyes bulging in utter insanity as he twisted the dagger, chewing through the cardiac muscle, opening the wound into a gaping, crimson maw. The captain withdrew the dagger once more drawing with it a fountain of hot blood and gristle, only to plunge the dagger in deeper, this time with such force that the tip of the blade tore through the back of his dirty greatcoat.

Davis fell to his knees as the sky before him became the sea...

Jack Snow raised the bottle of Basker's to his lips after his left sock was in place. He did so again after the right sock, his shirt, his tie, his trousers and every item of clothing he applied to his person. By the time he strode past his concerned servants and out to the waiting liveried brougham, he was a man halfway to drunkenness even as his untouched breakfast of soft-boiled eggs still steamed in the dining room.

Snow had detected the whispers of shocked conversation over the days spent tearing oil paintings from the walls, freeing them of their frames and hurling all into the mighty bonfire he had set in the ornamental garden. His loyal manservant Ackley had confronted him in horror as Snow tore down the priceless Pond collection and committed to the flames what he had not placed in crates and sent to the docks.

Chanting and dancing around the fire had instilled in his staff the belief that he had completely taken leave of his senses. They saw him burn a fortune in antiques and heirlooms, but could not understand, could never even learn that this was not the random act of a madman, but the mad strategy of a man committed to restoring glory to his family's name. Restoring the glory, and retaining it forever.

The coach bumped and bounded along the route to the Royal Exchange. Dribbles of whisky stained his once-pristine white shirt and soaked into the lapels of his black jacket. He stared out of the coach at clutches of ragged flower and match sellers, the glint of a shilling catching his eye every now and then as a transaction took place in mere seconds.

The coach slowed to a crawl, joining the crush of traders and businessmen eager to learn of their fortunes and to create new ones, at the Exchange. Snow's hands trembled at the realization he was so close to learning the fate of his dynasty's fortune.

He gazed through the coach windows at those perfectly framed portraits of trade. So straightforward, so beautiful in their simplicity. Give me tuppence and I shall give you this thing. The purity of that fundamental idea of trade was long lost to him. Thinking of the dark master he now served, he could only think that the lifeblood of that creature had flowed at one time solely on one man's happiness to trade and another man's desire to have more.

He allowed himself a wry chuckle as he thought that Mammon could have no better wife than the widow Burton. Every thought in that woman's mind would serve to keep the master alive for a thousand more years.

The coach drew to a halt and the footman opened the door. Snow decided, in something resembling pride, to leave the whisky behind and stepped out into the bustling crowds of the City. A card table showdown thrill rushed through him as he glanced once at the statue of the Duke of Wellington. That grand statue, forged from the canons of his defeated enemies, just as his own throne was to be built of the bones of the Red Scout's crew.

The crew, and Dent, of course. Dent, who would have been there with him on any normal day. Dent, whose wise counsel always seemed to stave off the fear of tangling with these savage creatures who mounted the Royal Exchange steps alongside him.

He had barely set foot in the foyer of this vast center of commerce when he broke step, only for a second. She was already waiting for him.

"My dear, dear Mr Snow," the widow Burton gushed, hobbling across the checkered floor to meet him face to face. "But I have simply been dying to see you this day." She extended a gloved hand, which Snow received, kissing the black velvet at her knuckles.

"Oh, if only that were true, Mrs Burton, I should have been sure to wait a wee while longer."

Burton was attended by two young men, both dressed alike in greatcoats, buttoned tight across broad, muscular chests and shoulders, each man sporting a top hat, their faces framed with neatly trimmed mutton-chops. They looked like twins. One of them stepped forward with his fist clenched. "My Lady, would you have me cast this man into the street?"

"Down, boy," the widow growled in a playful tone, with a flirtatious glint in her eye, which excited in Snow a faint sense of nausea. "Mr Snow here is our friend. I have travelled here with the sole purpose of conversing with him."

"Well, that is rather kind of you, Mrs Burton, but I must be moving along," Snow insisted, stepping aside with a mind to circumnavigate the group.

"It was lovely to see you, young Mr Snow. I look forward to meeting with you later as we discuss monies outstanding on the Red Stallion."

The insinuation was clear, but Snow feigned ignorance. "I believe you are mistaken, my good lady. You see, the ship you mentioned was constructed by Russell and Aspinall's, in Baltimore. It is to them that I owe the belated funds."

"Ah, but I thought that with your business so far in-debted, perhaps I should grant you a boon and so I bought the debt from them to save you having to send that money on its exhausting trip all the way to Baltimore. True, Russell and Aspinall were happy to wait and accrue interest at first, but when my American agents delivered telegrams from your other erstwhile creditors, they were only too keen to take my offer of sixty percent. Does it not make more sense for the consolidation of all of your debts? To have all your debts held, in fact, by a friend?"

"Were it only that I had a friend in our line of business, Mrs Burton."

The widow clutched at his hand once more, squeezing with a pressure totally at odds with her fragile, aged form. Closing in for the kill seemed to wipe years away from her, filling her with new vitality. "Oh but you do, Jack Snow. You do have a friend. And like all friends, I will guide you back into honour by ensuring that you repay every single penny owed on Red Stallion by the end of this day."

"It is a risky business, owning one's ships outright. A lot of capital is shed in the early days as well you might know from your dear departed husband... or, did I not read somewhere that he was a pirate and a thief? Well, who knows, eh? One mustn't believe everything one reads. I bid you good day."

The widow snatched back her hand as though avoiding a venomous snakebite. She muttered curses under her breath. That arrogant bastard had dared to cast aspersions at the memory of her beloved Henry. Even more than before, she relished the moment when she would bring about the end of Snow and Sons.

Notes and calls passed back and forth on the trading floor and Snow felt the thrill of the action. He could see the lifeblood of Empire coursing about him. He could feel the pull of Mammon's influence. Wealth and gain justified the loss of any lives. So it had always been. So it always shall. In that sense, he could almost admire the ruthlessness of the widow and the whispered tales of her long-dead husband.

Snow could not help but notice the widow watching him across the trading floor, flanked by her foreboding guards. She sipped at a delicate china teacup and whenever their eyes met, a sly malevolent energy seemed to radiate from her.

One thing was clear to him: the news she awaited was exactly the same as he. The outcomes they wished for, however, were polar opposites.

The resounding chime of the mighty Lutine Bell brought the trading floor to a standstill. The traders held their breath, waiting for the second chime which would indicate the news received was of a late ship now found to be safe. The second chime did not come. It was bad news and that news spread like a wave throughout the room, filtering its way to Snow.

The widow clapped her hands and tugged at the sleeves of her henchmen, pointing at Snow as he learnt that the Red Scout had not arrived to replenish coal reserves at Tripoli as expected. The ship had not been seen by others who had left London shortly after her.

The underwriters scrambled to make their deals, conspiring to make business to offset the anticipated loss of a mighty cargo.

Mrs Burton could not contain her amusement, but found, to her chagrin, that Snow maintained an impassive look. Through narrowed eyes, she began to wonder why the man, whose last lifeline appeared to have sunk into the briny sea, seemed not to care. She decided that her young rival was in shock. She raised her cup in salutation, mocking her fallen foe.

When he heard murmurs of Red Stallion passing around the floor ten minutes later, he braced himself for a victorious salutation of his own.

The Lutine Bell chimed once more. Snow looked around, wondering which poor bastard was about to receive bad news.

Again the announcement passed around the room and reached his ears. Red Stallion, it seemed, had not collected her coal either. Snow clamped a handkerchief over his lips to catch the acidic whisky and bile mix that scorched his throat and filled his mouth.

Mrs Burton had the reaction she wanted. Her laughter rose above the hubbub of commerce and tore into his soul.

***

Smoke billowed from the chimney of Red Stallion, as good quality Newcastle coal brought life to the vast condenser and pistons driving the screw paddle at her rear, driving her onward, ever onward. Her precious cargo, 200 tons of soap, wool, candles, books, glass and china thundered ever closer to Calcutta.

The Stallion's captain, Charles Hollingworth stood to receive a hefty payment from Jack Snow for his secrecy on this mission, carrying a cargo over-insured and supposed to be carried on the doomed Red Scout. Every ton of opium collected in Calcutta upon the sale of the aforementioned goods would travel to Lintin on the Stallion, there to trade for silver. That silver was destined for Hong Kong where 200 tons of the new tea crop would be loaded and raced back to London. Not a shilling received in London would reach the accounts of Snow and Sons, as none of the trades or cargo would be borne in the company name. All transactions and monies stood for Jack Snow personally. Jack Snow and of course, those who had assisted him in this daring bit of maritime fraud.

"Sorr. You should see this, Sorr," came the call from the poop deck. Hollingworth strode across the deck to join a gathering of men staring overboard into the deep. "Do you see it, Sorr?"

"See what, exactly? I see only the glare from the sun, you fools."

"That's not the sun, Sorr. That's fire."

Hollingworth wanted to berate the man for his folly, but the more he stared into the deep blue-green of the water, the more he realized the shimmering white-orange glow did look like fire.

As they plowed across the sea, the glow seemed to follow them, as though something deep below kept pace and tracked them.

"Keep watch on this phenomenon, men. But keep it to yourselves." The captain turned to his First Mate and ordered him to send word to the engine room: "Full steam ahead."

Hollingworth checked his pocket-watch, noting that half an hour had elapsed since the phenomenon was made known to him. He returned to the ship's aft, where a silent vigil was held. The men appeared almost hypnotised.

"What do you think it is, Sorr?"

"If I knew I'd have fucking told you by now, boy." he barked. It was then that he noticed the activity of the water. Even in the wake of the racing propeller, the sea seemed to be unusually disturbed. Not only had the orange glow of the deep kept pace with them, but it had grown larger. Larger, or closer. Squinting, Hollingworth tried to determine if the vapour he could see rising from the turbulence of the propeller was simply the mist of churned water, or steam.

"Do you see it, Sorr?"

"Be specific, man."

"Do you see how the sea boils?"

In that moment a muffled horn sounded. Hollingworth looked about the Stallion, expecting to see a distant ship, but he saw nothing. The horn sounded again, closer this time, but still no ship could be seen.

The raging orange glow exploded from the churning surface of the water, and a chimney reached towards them, spewing thick, black fumes. The ghastly, screaming horn blast that emerged with the chimney sent a chill down the captain's spine.

"'Tis the Devil," came the cry, and in that moment, all was panic and the chimney was followed by a bowsprit constructed of an array of bones. The figurehead appeared next, in the form of a screaming skull whose arms swung back and forth, seaweed clinging to each vertebrae of the spine.

The demon ship's mighty prow exploded from the sea, reaching almost to the deck of the Stallion, before reaching the tipping point, where it slammed down, shattering the waves.

It was then Hollingworth noted the name of the ship, cut deep and proud either side of the figurehead. "That's no devil ship. It's the Red Scout."

Hollingworth stood frozen in slack-jawed incredulity at the sight of the ship's crew. Bloated with seawater and gnawed upon by the denizens of the sea, the roaring crew waved cutlasses and brandished rifles, threatening his crew.

Flames grasped for the sky from the opening of the cavernous chimney as the ship, now fully revealed, bore down upon the Stallion.

Although he knew it was impossible for the gunpowder to be dry, shots roared out from the firearms of these ragtag raiders. A man Hollingworth vaguely recognised as the ship's captain Gosseling stepped to the fore of the throng, placing a tattered boot above the bony bowsprit, his chest a slick, cavernous wound and with eyes that glowed as ferociously as the chimney's flames this creature met his gaze and bellowed, "Prepare to be boarded."

The Stallion lurched as the Scout, at some point beneath the Plimsoll line, made contact with the screw propeller.

Metal screamed as the mechanism was forced to a grinding halt. The propeller tore away as ropes and hooks flew up onto the Stallion's deck. In moments, the bilious sailors of the Scout began to clamber along the tethers.

Hollingworth called his crew to arms, but too late, as he turned back to face the enemy as Gosseling's gnarled hands clasped his head. "Your weapons serve you no good, lad. Not against the dead."

***

Jack Snow watched the approaching coaches and waggons, knowing fully well what lay in store for him that afternoon. Red Stallion had gone unseen for days. The news had spread far and wide of the imminent downfall of Snow and Sons. Stockholders harassed the servants at his home and banged on the doors of the warehouse at the London and St Katherine Docks,

At his feet lay the black brazier in which he had burned so much of his money in worship of Mammon. It seemed, as the debt collectors closed in, that his prayers had gone unheard and a plan that at first seemed foolproof had disintegrated into the same ashes as the fortune of his family.

That sixty men were sent to their deaths, knowingly, by Snow, barely registered with him. That sixty more, it seemed, died in his service on the second ship, again, mattered not to him. His only thought was that all he owned was either gone, or about to be taken away. He had bet all on a single coin toss, and lost.

The staccato drumming of horse-hooves and the rumble of trundling wheels ceased and he dared to look out of his window once more. As he expected, she was there, the widow Burton, a glad spectator in attendance of the death of his business.

The insurance for the loss of Red Scout could cover the money outstanding on Red Stallion, but Burton had called in all of his outstanding debts. His gamble had been on that new tea crop returning in Stallion's hold, in his own name. He could have raised credit against that and kept the old bitch at bay for a time. Now the insurers were certain that Stallion was lost, if he were to reveal that he had knowingly over-insured Scout and under-insured Stallion, then he would not only lose his company, but he would lose his liberty for the fraud.

He had no choice, and as the collectors broke the warehouse doors in, accompanied by bailiffs and police constables whose job it was to see that the acquisition of the property of Snow and Sons was carried out in line with the law, Jack Snow knew that there was no escape. His fate was sealed.

In a trance, he signed over the warehouse, stock and chattels. He took one last swallow of whisky, fastened his coat and trod the stairs with leaden steps, down into the warehouse and out onto the cobbled dock.

"It is simply devastating to see a fellow giant of maritime trade laid low," goaded Mrs Burton from her coach.

Snow set his jaw, eyeing the wrinkled, pudgy, white face with sheer hatred. Unable to speak a word, he simply spat on the Burton livery upon the carriage door, to the disgust of those gathered.

"Your father would be ashamed," Mrs Burton snarled. "Speaking of your father, when I finally take your home from you, when all of our business is settled, there is the matter of the Snow family mausoleum. I believe it to be on the grounds of your home. You must put your mind to it now, young Jack, where those bones shall go when I have my men exhume them."

Jack stared into the swirling greenish brown Thames water, fancying that to die gulping down such a filthy liquid would be almost the perfect end to this foul ordeal.

Burton's coach made away, and before long, Snow was alone. No more a master, but a simple observer of the shipping trade, watching the ships come to port, watching them slip away into the growing twilight. His shoulders sagged as he wandered the docks, without aim, without purpose. He had no money on his person to buy even a small beer or fare for a ride to his home. It was then that he made out alarmed whistles, bell chimes and horn blasts to the East, all along the Thames.

The ever-present Thames fog shrouded the ships by the time they reached the end of the dock and so any ship arriving would be within the berths before he would see them. So it was that Snow heard the approaching vessel long before he saw it. A mournful horn blast filled his heart with dread and a steam engine surging ever closer, with thunderous pistons hammering so loud that he thought the crew of this ship must be deaf.

An orange glow swelled within the gloaming and within moments, the fog seemed to part as though cowering aside.

Snow's eyes remained fixed on what he knew to be flames and the ship's chimney came into view first, through the dissipating head of the fog. The maddening hammer of the pistons grew louder and louder with each moment and although he wanted to run, a mad curiosity compelled him to stay. He covered his ears, certain that his eardrums would explode any second.

Dockworkers and sailors stood agape, bearing witness to the spectacle as a wide-mouthed skull presented its chilling image at the head of this hellish steamer. Another blast of that horn, that chilling, dying animal howl, made Snow tremble, as suddenly the hammering ceased, the flames died down, and the hulking steamer glided into port right before him.

His eyes confirmed what his rational mind could not believe. He saw the name of the ship and fell to his knees. Hollow eyes and cavernous mouths loomed over him from the bulwarks as the gangway clattered into place only feet away from him. The spectral crew spoke no words, they merely hissed through cracked and blackened teeth.

Footsteps on the gangway made Snow's heart tighten. Only when the footsteps approached him on land did he dare to look. He opened his eyes to see Hollingworth glaring at him.

"Jack Snow, you are a disgrace and a murderer." Hollingworth announced.

"Hollingworth, I thought ye were dead."

"Well now, Jack, it appears I know a thing or two about death more than you do."

Snow recognised the voice immediately, as Gosseling's ghastly, cadaverous form lurched into view.

"I sank your Stallion and with it your fortune, Snow. But I'm no murdering bastard like you. Every man on board the Stallion is here, safe and sound. My men and I may have made for a shabby looking crew to your eyes, but we have some honour, even beyond death."

Hands caked in salt grabbed Snow's coat, pulling it down over his shoulders and bracing his upper arms. Jack cried out, gagging on the foul death-smell of his captors as they hauled him up the gangway and onto the gently rolling Red Scout.

"A friend wishes to greet you," Gosseling snarled, gripping Snow's hair, dragging him across the deck to the prow.

"Please, not Dent. Tell me it's not Dent. Don't let me see him like this."

"Like this? What, like us? No, I'm afraid your old friend was not part of the crew, so he became part of the ship. In fact it is his hatred for you that fuels the fires in that engine to such extremes as the depths of the sea could never extinguish the flames."

Bone ground against bone as the skeletal figurehead juddered into life. The skeleton's spine creaked and groaned as the skull came around and arms reached out. Finally, Snow's legs buckled as the figurehead's spine snapped away from the fused bones of the bowsprit, freeing its reach.

Gosseling's men thrust Snow forward, towards the embrace of Dent's waiting bones. Snow screamed, pleaded, promising anything, promising the world, if only they would let him live.

Dent wrapped his arms around his former ward, turning him, drawing him close as his ribcage creaked open, accepting Snow's upper torso, so that the businessman's head rested against the bones of Dent's neck. The ribs closed as Dent tightened his embrace. Snow's screams renewed when Dent's ribs closed in around him, puncturing his flesh, biting into his chest deep enough to hold him, but not deep enough to penetrate his organs.

"You said you were no murderer, and yet here you come to slay me," Snow wailed.

Gosseling chuckled as Dent crept back beneath the bowsprit with Jack Snow held fast. "Who spoke of slaying you, Snow?"

Beneath the decks, the engine room thrummed with life once more, the pistons hammering a slow, steady tattoo, rising in volume and speed with each repetition. The ship stole away from the dock, turning about to point east once more.

The crew of the Stallion gazed on in awe, as their erstwhile paymaster screamed and cursed, thrashing his head about, kicking wildly at the head of the ship now slipping away to the river proper.

"As I said, Jack, I spoke nothing of your murder," Gosseling called down to Snow from his position at the ship's prow. "But we have decided to change the route we're bound to take, now that our colleagues from the Stallion have been returned safe and sound. I must confess that on this particular journey, it does make travel more comfortable when one has no need to breathe."

And upon Gosseling's final word, the Red Scout's engine roared, the horn screamed, and the pistons hammered out their deafening beat. The ship slid deeper and deeper into the frigid, foul water of the Thames, filling Snow's nose, filling his mouth, smothering his screams. And his greed.

7

—·—

You Are Now Entering Tilwick

Get used to Tilwick, dear reader. Hopefully, I'll convince you to spend quite some time there. Tilwick is my hellish response to the town I grew up in, Alnwick. Many years ago, I worked for Alnwick District Council and before that, for Morpeth Borough Council, where I met my friend of some twenty years now, fellow horror writer David Basnett (who edited this collection).

Working for these town councils I saw cronyism and nepotism almost beyond compare. Cover-ups and scandals, backstabbing, back-biting. Sometimes I felt like I was in ancient Rome. It was all fuel for the fires of the series of novels I was working on in my twenties, centred on a young man called Matt Carsun, in the town of Tilwick. Over the years, I found it increasingly difficult to get those stories into a shape I'd be happy to release. It will come. Carsun will appear with the right story, but in the meantime, I enjoy working on other pieces set in his town.

Tilwick doesn't appear on any conventional map. Its history blurs with legends so unbelievable that people con-

97

signed it to myth. As if it could be possible that the demon of greed lives in a town in North East England. As if such a small, insignificant place could be the origin point of an enormous matrix of power and trade reaching around the globe, into every government and major corporation in the world.

In that town, the residents show their devotion to a god they believe may live on among them, the creator and protector of their home: Mammon.

The two stories that follow each have their own introductions, so I won't say too much about them. I wanted them to feel like everyday occurrences in a strange rural town. The less said, the better, right now. They say if you talk about Tilwick to people who aren't from there, you die. So I've probably said too much alrea-

8

About 'Home, Sweet Home'

Just before the birth of my second son, my then-partner and I moved into a detached house on a friendly little cul-de-sac on the outskirts of town. There we had gardens front and back for our oldest son to enjoy - he was at the age where he needed to be out digging, climbing and playing in his own garden, and we needed an extra room for his soon-to-arrive baby brother.

While moving into that house, I cleared some things from the garage and in an elevated storage area, I found some old cases and boxes. I remember having a strange feeling as I inspected the contents, trying to determine if the landlord had left useful items, or if these were just the abandoned possessions of previous occupants. The odd sensations as I rummaged came purely from the creative parts of my brain, of course: the inner horror writer telling me there could be anything in here. Murder weapons. Nazi artifacts. Bones.

It was, of course, all useless, harmless tat destined for the bin. But the idea stayed with me, of a house on a cul-de-sac with secrets known to some of the residents who looked out of their front windows and into each other's homes like living in a goldfish bowl.

I remember an evening in late January, that time of year where the days are still short and darkness falls quickly. My ex was off to bed early, exhausted at this late stage of her pregnancy. I washed up the last few dishes of the day and suddenly found myself struck with dread. The movement of my own reflection had caught my eye, making me stop in my tracks. I peered outside, paranoid now, in case it hadn't simply been my own movement that alerted me. With the kitchen lights on, the windows revealed only a reflection of me and my surroundings. The view of the dark garden was completely obscured. The black wall of conifers that cut the garden off from the road beyond was perfect for blocking silhouettes. Anybody could be stood in that garden, out in the open, yet perfectly concealed by the interplay of light and darkness. Someone could be out there, I realised. They could be watching me.

It sent a chill up my spine and I hurried out of the room. To my computer, where I wrote...

9

HOME, SWEET HOME

"I know it's not our dream house, Keith," Amanda admitted, pressing her firm body against her husband. She kissed the tip of his chin. "But we can make the place our own and I'm sure we'll be happy here."

"I know, I know. I just loved the old maisonette. I'll get used to it," Keith said, sighing in resignation. The maisonette was sold, and he was officially a resident of Tilwick's Golden Acre Park estate.

Peering over Amanda's shoulder, brushing her blond hair up behind her neck, Keith observed the collection of brown-brick detached and semi-detached homes arranged around the cul-de-sac, washed in the muted orange of sunset. Keith remained silently thankful to have taken up a detached property with a good stretch of tree and shrub-lined garden on all sides, baffling the noise to and from the neighbours. He considered that his battered Ford Focus appeared somewhat out of place among the BMWs and Land Rovers of their neighbours. The patchy lawn of the front garden, the cracked driveway, the too-small-to-park-a-car-in garage, the one-hard-cough-and-down-they-come fences, all of these things, they made Keith feel as though a huge sign reading Lowest Earners in the Neighbourhood should be erected out front.

Keith had voiced his opinion before the move and Amanda had reasoned that since the property had been uninhabited for two years, and the landlord had left the running of the place to an estate agent, nobody would be surprised that the place needed some work. Plus, she had added, our friends live here. By our friends, of course she meant her friends, who had recommended the place to her.

Handing him a glass of a fruity summer red wine, Amanda attempted to free Keith from the mental swamp he kept falling into when he thought about the house and its gardens for too long.

He took a gulp of the wine, recognising Amanda's distraction tactic and hoping that it would work. She slipped a hand to the front of his jeans and fondled him with just the right amount of pressure in the right place to state her intent without hurting him.

"Which room would you like to christen first, Mr Corgan?" she purred.

Keith almost spat his wine across the window, only just managing to swallow his drink in time. In doing so he avoided the destruction of the white vertical blinds he had installed the previous morning. He clasped a hand over his lips and let out a half-laugh, half-cough.

The white baby monitor plugged into the four-gang extension by the TV flickered to life, with two of the three green LEDs blinking, showing that only a low level of noise had been detected. Little Alex's cries usually drove the baby monitor up past the third green light and into the two red LEDs that indicated a loud noise had been detected. A second later, with the LED's still flickering slightly, a snuffling noise was heard through the small speaker. Alex let out a little moan and settled down once more.

"I wasn't expecting him to settle in his new room so well, tonight," Keith commented.

"He's very adaptable," Amanda said. She pinched Keith's bottom, adding, "You could learn from him."

Keith frowned at his wife, something was missing. "Hey, where's your wine?"

Amanda flashed him a grin and rested her head on his shoulder. "I have some news for you... Daddy."

"You're fucking kidding me?" Keith cried, returning his wife's wide grin. "Really? Well, it must be true, or you'd be drinking, nothing as sure as that," he said, answering his own question.

"You're happy then?"

"Happy? I'm over the bloody moon. How long have you known? The move, Jesus the move... Mandy, are you sure everything's alright?"

Amanda stroked Keith's upper arms. "Everything is fine. I've known for a couple of weeks, but I knew if I told you, you'd probably call off the move."

"Tricky cow."

"Well, it's done now."

"And you won't be lifting a finger 'til he's here," Keith warned.

"He? Another little chap, is it? We'll see. And besides, I'm only about six weeks pregnant. I'll be doing plenty right up until I can't move anymore. Alex needs his mummy."

"I know, I know. I just don't want you to get stressed out again. You know how it was when you were carrying Alex."

"Yes, Mr Corgan. But this is different, we're here. We've got a view, and space, and nice neighbours."

"So you say, I haven't met them yet."

"Well, that's the next bit of news. I've invited them over this weekend."

Keith rolled his eyes toward the ceiling. "Oh, brilliant."

They chatted excitedly about the baby and how Alex was going to be a brilliant big brother. Keith drained his glass and returned to the kitchen. The wine bottle rattled against the lip of the glass as his hands trembled. The thick red liquid poured across the oak veneer of the work surface, trickling over the edge to splatter and pool on the marbled linoleum floor. Keith cursed under his breath and slammed the wine bottle down before him. He pressed his flat palms onto the work surface and pushed a hissing breath through his clenched teeth.

Closing his eyes he felt the sting of tears and the lurch in his stomach as the reality of the situation – that they would never again leave Tilwick, that the second child would essentially root them to this evil old place – took hold and squeezed all hope from his heart.

Alex squealed with excitement as Keith gathered speed, pushing the toddler faster and faster on his ride-on tractor. The chunky plastic wheels clattered over the stone slabs of the lower portion of the back garden.

Amanda peeked out the kitchen window and smiled as the green tractor trundled past her view. She chuckled as Keith wrestled control of the little black steering wheel to stop Alex steering up the grass embankment leading to the overgrown grass terrace.

"Back down we go, Farmer Corgan," Keith said, guiding the vehicle back to the paved area. "I don't want to lose you in that jungle up there."

Keith had been putting off tackling the terrace, and especially putting of the collection of overgrown shrubs beyond. The truth was, he knew nothing of gardening and the maisonette, with the yard out back, had needed no more than an occasional run over with a broom.

Then again, he thought, it could be sort of a workout. The thought of working up a sweat in the garden, of running around with the new tools he had picked up at the local garden centre, suddenly appealed.

"What's this, Daddy?" Alex asked. Keith suddenly switched his attention back to his child, who was off his tractor and stood staring intently at a small item he had picked up from the ground.

"Give it here, son," Keith said, hurrying to Alex's side. He took the curved nail from Alex's hand and noticed a red smear on his son's fingers. "Did you prick yourself with this?" he asked. Keith's mind suddenly raced. What age do they get their tetanus jab? Amanda's going to fucking kill me for taking my eyes off him. I'll never hear the end of this.

Wiping Alex's hand with his own fingers, he squeezed gently, trying to promote further bleeding to discharge any dirt driven into the wound. No fresh blood came. Keith realised that the blood had already been on the nail when Alex found it. "Where was this, little man?"

"There," Alex said, pointing at a spot by his feet.

"Everything all right?" Amanda called from the back door.

"Yeah, it's fine. I just really need to give this garden a good going over." Keith tossed the nail into the bushes. A cat must have caught a loose nail in the fence or something. "Come on, Alex, let's get our hands washed and get back into the house, eh?"

Alex made off on his little vehicle, pumping with both legs at once, attempting what he really knew was an impossible escape. He squealed with delight as his father scooped him up, growling and nuzzled the back of his neck. Alex held onto the tractor for a moment before letting go when his dad's tickling became too intense and he scrunched his shoulders up and drew his hands to his face, letting the tractor clatter to the ground.

Keith fastened Alex into his booster seat and Amanda placed an orange plastic Finding Nemo plate in front of him. Alex grabbed a wedge of cucumber in one chubby fist and a cube of cheddar cheese with the other.

"Don't forget your sandwiches, Alex," Amanda called.

Alex pretended not to hear, and commenced to eat the cheese and cucumber, picking the ham out from between the slices of bread.

"He really does love that garden," Keith said, smiling as he peered out the window. "I suppose I really should become a gardener."

"Well before you do," Amanda said, her tone becoming a parody of a disapproving mother, "you can get that garage tidied up. You can't see two feet in front of you in there."

"I know, I know, it's heap-lie-on, but I needed a place to work from when I was decorating, didn't I?"

"Maybe getting rid of the mountain of empty cardboard boxes from the move would be a good start."

Keith wiggled his lower jaw from side to side. Amanda's tone had changed. She was becoming serious. Her suggestions, he realised, were in fact orders. "I'll make a start after lunch."

"I thought we were taking Alex to the park after his nap."

"I can't do it all, Mandy," Keith snapped.

Amanda's eyes immediately turned to Alex, who was still happily munching away on everything but the bread on his plate. "Really, Keith?"

"So what, Mandy? It's the real world. You can't protect him from everything. People get pissed off with each other."

A tiny voice rose from the table, "... pissed off with each other."

Amanda's eyes widened. Keith's closed. He knew he was for it now.

"Daddy said a naughty word," Keith said. "We don't say that."

Amanda hissed, "Don't draw attention to it, he'll just do it all the more."

"Well... whatever... but listen, if you want that garage cleared, I'll do it. But other things will have to wait. And besides, you two will have fun together and I'll get on much faster without the little man checking in on me every two minutes."

"You have a point," Amanda accepted. "Anyway, the sooner you hit the garage and turn your hand to the garden, the better. Want the place looking good for Saturday when the girls come over."

"Marvellous," Keith deadpanned. The girls weren't the problem, he could just leave them all chatting away in the lounge, but it wouldn't just be the girls. He'd have to have awkward, stunted conversations with their husbands and partners about Christ only knew what. Cars and work, probably. And the gym. Keith sucked in the tummy he had gained since Alex was born. Fuck it, he thought, best crack on, I need the exercise.

Keith flicked the switch and stepped into the garage as the light flickered on. With a deep sigh he took in the scene before him. At the far end of the garage, at the large rolling door, the empty cardboard boxes were stacked, but they had toppled and slid over each other into an unruly mess. Easy win, Keith thought, get them away to the waste depot.

Moments later he was at the front of the house. He clicked the button on the remote control, activating the automatic garage door. As the entrance opened, flattened boxes slid out onto the driveway and two of them had become caught in the cables on the back of the door, and rose with it, dangling down perilously. Keith playfully smacked the boxes down from the raised door and began to gather the cardboard up. It was then that he noticed the boxes in the storage space just beneath the ceiling.

He frowned, not believing that Amanda would have gone to the trouble of placing anything up there, and knowing that he himself had not. Probably a load of shit left by the last tenants, he thought, may as well get that gone while I go to the depot.

Keith dropped the back seats of his Ford and stuffed the cardboard in to get it out of the way. This opened up a little room to manoeuvre within the garage as he dragged and scraped some boxes of DVDs and CDs back across the concrete towards the door. Keith closed the garage doors in case any of the neighbours should see him messing about in there, he hadn't any inclination to engage in small-talk. He opened out a red metal step ladder and climbed it until his head was above the level of the storage space.

The space was only large enough for an adult to slide across on their tummy, not even enough room to crawl, but he found three boxes and a battered leather suitcase up there. Without care, he pulled on each item and let it crash to the floor. He didn't really give a shit what was in any of them.

When he was back on the floor, Keith tore away the parcel tape from the first box and pried open the flaps. "Hideous," he muttered, lifting out a garish orange and gold lampshade and a gold painted lamp. He inspected the plug, thinking he might play a trick on Amanda and set it up in the bedroom. He found that it had the rounded pins of electrical good of yesteryear.

He delved into the box again and found a neatly folded set of pink pillow cases.

The second box brought no treasures, either. A pink double sheet matched the pillowcases and a few green tinted copper fittings from plumbing jobs before the plastic fittings came along, were all he was offered.

Expecting more rubbish, Keith unzipped the suitcase, purely because it looked more interesting, more personal, than the cardboard boxes. Probably just some old granny's stinking fucking swimming cozzie, he thought.

He raised his eyebrows at the mysterious treasure trove within. A dozen small bundles of brown paper greeted him, just begging to be opened. He grasped the first item, a roughly oblong shape, rounded at the edges, about six inches long. Keith cursed as he grasped the item and a point jabbed the centre of his right palm, drawing forth a warm dribble of blood.

"Bastard," he hissed, unwrapping the item carefully, to find a Stanley knife. The blade looked to be dull, but the triangular tip evidently still had a bite to it. The knife handle had once been chrome, but was now tinged with an orange-brown coating of what first appeared to be rust. Keith soon began to wonder how many people had cut themselves with the blade, and how much blood accounted for the discolouration. He tried to figure out when he had last had a tetanus shot and if he was still covered.

He wiped the small puncture wound in his palm against his trouser leg, drawn back to the contents of the suitcase. He found a claw hammer, stained similarly to the blade. There was a tenon saw, complete with dull brass back and well-worn wooden handle. Keith inspected the blade and noted a fine powder between and across the saw's teeth. He lifted out an almost horse-shoe shaped item and unwrapped it.

Keith's fingers opened wide, immediately rejecting the item, letting it fall into the suitcase. He clasped his bleeding hand over his mouth and squeezed his eyes shut for a moment as though expecting the scene to have changed when he reopened them.

But no, the jawbone was still waiting for him.

The door connecting the garage to the kitchen opened and Amanda peered in. "Everything alright?"

Keith kicked the suitcase, flipping the lid over to conceal the bone. "Yeah, it's fine. Just this fucking suitcase. It's fucking stapled together and I cut my hand on it. Dropped it on my head and nearly fell off the steps."

"Mind you don't injure yourself, Mr Corgan."

"I'll be fine, now away with you and get some woman's work done." Keith desperately tried to dismiss his wife so that he could crouch down and brace himself against the wave of nausea rising within him.

"I'll bloody woman's work you."

Keith's fingers traced across his forehead, gathering up the sheen of perspiration that had gathered there. He affected his best Cartman from South Park impersonation and waved his wife away, saying, "Get in that kitchen and make meh some pie."

Amanda glanced over her shoulder to make sure Alex hadn't followed her from the lounge where he was sat enjoying his beaker of juice and an episode of Peppa Pig. Seeing that the coast was clear, she grinned at her husband and whispered, "Twat." And with that, she closed the door.

Keith heaved a few deep breaths, expanding his lungs fully and letting the air almost shudder out of him. He stared at the case for a long period, not knowing what to do. Call the police. Let them deal with it, he thought.

He pried his eyes away from the case lid and looked at the door to the kitchen, imagining he could see his wife through the barrier. His pregnant wife. His pregnant wife who suffered chronic bouts of anxiety and depression during the last pregnancy.

"Fucking hell," he muttered.

He reached down to the cracked brown leather and flipped the lid back once more. Keith braced himself and grabbed the bone. He rapped a knuckle against it. Is it real, he wondered. What the fuck would I know, anyway? It sounded like it could be bone. It sounded like it could be a hard plastic from some medical model.

That's it, one of those anatomical models, Keith reasoned, turning the jaw over and over in his hands. Then he focused on the discoloured teeth. And the filling in one of the molars. Fucking hell. They wouldn't put plaque and a filling onto an anatomical model.

Keith dropped the bone back into the case and eyed the other wrapped items with narrow, suspicious eyes. He crouched low over the case and steeled his nerves. His fingers found the paper and he began to tear into it like a child on Christmas morning who knew that the gifts were barbed wire and broken glass, but who had no choice but to get it over with as soon as possible.

When he had finished, he inspected the rusted pliers, the dull sawblades, the stained drill-bits and bradawls and he could not shake the feeling that these tools had become rusted and stained, like the Stanley knife, by being left covered in blood. The majority of the tools were wooden handled, rather than furnished with the comfortable rubber grips of modern equipment. He knew these items were decades old. They might have been hidden away for twenty years or more. Who was to say what happened, when, or who was to blame? Keith knew one thing, though, that with the nursing home fire, the dead family at the farm he had heard about, and the Councillor's daughter found dead in an alley, all in the space of a week, Tilwick's police were not going to give a shit about some cold case.

He zipped up the suitcase and hauled it up the ladder, shoving it back to its original hiding place. He stared at the battered case long and hard before descending the ladder once more, wondering what the fuck am I supposed to do with this?

* * *

Amanda woke to the sound of Keith coughing in the en-suite. After a moment, as she woke up properly, and her eyes adjusted to the light, which was switched on above Keith, she realised he was vomiting into the toilet bowl. She could see his rump as he knelt forward, with his upper body and head out of view.

"Keith, are you ok?" she called.

"Yeah, yeah, I'm fine."

"Not coming down with a stomach bug, are you?" she asked.

"No, babes, I'm ok. Just go back to sleep. I think something just lay heavy on my stomach, that's all."

"Can I get you anything?"

Keith flushed the toilet and stood upright, stepping into full view in the light. "No, honestly, I'm ok." He splashed cold water onto his face, gargled with some mouthwash, patted his face, chest and back with a towel to remove the water and sweat he had accumulated, then switched off the light in the en-suite once more.

Without saying another word, Keith left the bedroom, switched on the landing light and entered Alex's room, leaving the bedroom door open. The landing light illuminated Alex's bed and Keith stood over his son as he slept soundly. Keith's fingers reached out and touched the little boy's face, caressing his cheek, tracing the skin down to the jawline.

This was the third time in the night that he had repeated this action, but it was the first time Amanda had been disturbed. Keith sighed with relief, feeling the firm bone and teeth through his son's flesh. Still there.

He walked downstairs, switching lights on as he moved, checking the locks on the front door, back door, the patio door and the kitchen door leading into the garage. He returned to his bed, content that his home was secure and that his family was safe.

Out in the back garden, cloaked in the blackness of the night, hateful eyes watched Keith's every move on the ground floor until he closed the kitchen door and walked back upstairs.

"Disgusting," Amanda yelled, shocking her husband awake. He hadn't caught the word she'd exclaimed, but when she repeated it, he picked up on it and an instant wave of terror burst against him. All he could think about was the jaw.

"What is it?" Keith called, as he sat upright in bed, rubbing his eyes to ease the tight pain that had settled there during his restless sleep.

"You puked in our toilet last night, didn't you?" Amanda asked, frowning in the bedroom doorway.

"Yeah, in there. What does it matter?"

"You didn't use the main bathroom at all?"

"No, what's wrong?"

Amanda rolled her eyes up and thumbed over her shoulder in the direction of the main bathroom. "There's something weird with the plumbing here. I noticed it on the first day but thought maybe you'd used both toilets. What you flush in one... well, some of it comes back up in the other. Your puke washed through into the main bathroom."

Keith stretched his arms outward and twisted his body gently, extending his muscles a little. He slid to the edge of the bed. "Just be thankful my upset stomach was from the top end and not the bottom end, eh?"

"Too bloody right," Amanda said, turning the corners of her mouth down in disgust as the thought of diarrhoea bubbling through into the main bathroom bowl. She vanished and Keith heard the main toilet flush as Amanda got rid of the offending material. When she returned to the bedroom she asked, "What was all that about last night? Tossing and turning, sweating, checking on Alex all the time."

"Don't ask me. I'm just getting used to this place, maybe."

"All this news from around town getting you down?"

"The family on the farm is the one that gets me the most, Amanda. Christ, that man butchered his whole family and he's still wandering around here somewhere. If he could do that to his own kids, then he could do it to anyone."

"I know, Keith, I'm worried about it too, but it was a couple of nights ago. I mean, you slept fine the first night in here. It just seems strange you'd be worked up about it now."

Keith thought frantically for an excuse. One came, it was weak, but it was an opportunity to give a sly hint at how tired he was of doing chores. "I was too busy on the first day here to think about anything."

"Oh, poor Mr Corgan has worked too hard."

"Hard work always feels harder in Tilwick," Keith grumbled.

A frozen silence descended as Amanda stared at her outstretched husband. He felt her glare like a laser, seeming to sear his flesh. He propped up on his elbows and asked, "What?"

"This again?"

"What?"

"I know I wanted us to get out of Tilwick once the funeral was sorted, but things changed, okay? Deal with it. I mean, how many times do we have to go over the same thing?"

Keith sat up, puffing out his cheeks. "Listen, it doesn't matter what you say, you dragged me back here and everything you've done since then has been to trap us here."

"Trap?" Amanda cried.

"Just fucking forget it, eh?" he stormed into the bathroom and yanked at the shower cord so hard that the string almost snapped, springing violently against the tiled wall when he released his grip on it and yanked open the shower screen.

"Going to wreck the place now, eh?" Amanda snapped, standing in the en-suite doorway.

"Leave me alone, would you?" Keith moaned, grabbing the shampoo from the shelf and causing the shower gel and conditioner to clatter to the ground. As he reached down to retrieve the fallen bottles, the shower head sputtered and spat as though a large amount of air had become trapped in the system.

He heard the doorbell ring and was aware of Amanda's footsteps heading down the stairs as she went to answer. Relieved to be on his own for a time, Keith righted the bottles and rubbed his thumb over the shower head, trying to remove any build-up that might have caused the interruption in the flow.

The pressure restored once more and a hot jet of liquid splashed against Keith's face and body. He closed his eyes and rubbed his hair and face, savouring the warmth and the peace and hoped that he had avoided another argument.

Amanda answered the front door and found one of the neighbours waiting for her. She recognised the large man from around town, she had seen him at the shops on lots of occasions and on nights out, too. He was in his mid-forties, though and was not from her generation in terms of people she could remember from school; this man fell into the gap between her and her parents.

The man wore his greying blonde hair in a mullet style and in his Black Sabbath t-shirt looked every inch of him the rocker trapped in the '80s. Even though his torso comprised what appeared to be a flabby chest above a swollen paunch, the man's arms were thick and muscular. Clearly this was a man who carried out a manual job, but whose diet wasn't as healthy as it might have been. Standing at a little under six feet in height, there was just, Amanda thought, a lot of this man. He was just big, but there was an air of the gentle giant about him, too. His eyes sparkled with friendly energy and his broad face split into a smile as soon as she opened the door to him.

"Hiya," he said. "I'm Sean. Sean Fisher from just over the road." The man turned and pointed to a house only a couple of doors away from where one of her friends lived. "I was in town earlier and there's been an announcement about the Old Man of Tilwick."

"Oh?" Amanda had always supposed the resident of Tilwick Castle was not that old, at least, not as old as the local stories suggested. She expected he was a descendant of the fortress's original inhabitant, but there were groups who believed that prominent males of the Mercer family were avatars of the town's founder.

"Aye, there was an incident through the night and the master is in hospital."

"Oh dear, it must be very serious."

"From what the Council's released, it's not very good. He's in a bad way. All these murders and fires and all that, it's all connected, they reckon. Now there's been a direct attack on him. The head of the Council, Mr Forster, he was killed last night, too."

It seemed impossible that these powerful, seemingly untouchable figureheads of Tilwick, had been brought to such a state. "What do we do?" she asked.

"Well, the Council's just saying brace yourself and prepare for things like power cuts and bad weather. The Old Man's not in a position to keep everything flowing the way it normally does. The water might go funny, but they're going to keep testing the water in every ward every day until we get through this and they'll let us know if we need to boil it or buy bottled water or whatever. For the moment, they've said just carry on as normal as much as possible."

"Okay, well, thanks for the update."

"My pleasure," Sean said, turning on his heels. "I'll get moving on, I need to catch everyone I can on the estate. Oh, and welcome to the neighbourhood," he called.

"Thank you. Actually, we're having a barbecue on Saturday if the weather holds up. A few of the folks on the estate are coming over, why don't you come too and meet my husband, Keith?" Amanda offered.

"That sounds great," Sean said. "I'll try to make it. My wife won't come, like, but I'll do my best to drop by. I'll bring a few drinks if I do, is that ok?"

"Perfect. Well, we might see you on Saturday after-noon, then?"

"You might well. Take care," Sean said, giving a short wave as he left the driveway and strode off to the next house.

Amanda closed the front door and hurried upstairs to see Keith. She had forgotten the row they had begun, and instead wanted to tell her husband about Sean and his message. She gasped in shock when she entered the en-suite and saw the tiles and screen coated in thick, flowing blood.

"What's wrong?" Keith cried, seeing his wife crumbling in the doorway. "Mandy, what's wrong?"

He hit the button to stop the flow, slid the shower screen open and slipped on the floor as he stepped out, soaking wet, onto the bathroom floor. He managed to catch the wash basin to steady himself, and reached for his wife, who stared at him in horror and disbelief.

"The blood. The blood," was all she could manage to utter.

"Sweetheart, what blood? What blood?" Keith cried, wrapping his arms around her to steady her. He eased her back onto the edge of the bed. "Here, sit down. Sit down and have a rest. What blood, darling?"

Her wide eyes brimmed with tears and Keith wrapped his arms around her, struggling to comprehend what was going on as she struggled to free herself from his grip.

Amanda wiped at her hands and arms as though trying to rub dirt away. Keith looked himself over, becoming concerned that he had brought something other than water out of the shower with him and had wiped it on her. Seeing nothing, he looked back at his wife, confused and frightened by her reaction. His hands instinctively moved to her midriff, as though he was checking on the baby who he knew, in reality, was barely a cluster of cells at that point. Certainly not enough to call a baby.

"Mandy, what's wrong? Tell me," Keith cried, raising his hands to her shoulders, rocking her gently.

Tears streamed from Amanda's eyes and her skin took on a waxy sheen, turning white as she went into shock.

"What blood, Mandy? What blood were you talking about?"

"The shower. All over you." Amanda wretched, the spasm causing her head and shoulders to lurch forwards. Keith brought her head to his chest.

"There's no blood, sweetheart. You've imagined it. There's no blood there."

Amanda's reddened eyes seemed to adjust back to reality, and she recognised that Keith was simply wet from the shower. She glanced past him at the shower screen and saw that only droplets of water, gathering and tumbling down, gathering the condensing steam, marked the glass. She had imagined the scene, but it was so vivid, so horrific. Keith had been rubbing litre after litre of thick, dark red blood all over his skin, letting it tumble into his mouth, filling his eyes and slicking his hair.

"I need to get downstairs and have a drink or something," Amanda gasped, peeling herself from the bed.

"Are you sure you're ok on the stairs? Give me a moment and I'll come down with you." Keith grabbed a towel and frantically rubbed as much water from his body as he could in a few seconds before pulling on a pair of grey tracksuit bottoms. "Come on, I'll get you a cuppa. You get on that couch."

"You shouldn't have called that doctor out, Keith," Amanda insisted. "I was fine."

"Well, look, it's done now, and you just need to keep your feet up and relax." Keith left his wife propped up with pillows on the bed and passed her the TV remote. With a cup of tea in her hand, she seemed a little happier and much calmer than she had all morning. As the TV burst into life, Keith drifted from the master bedroom into Alex's room, where the little boy played with his building blocks in a room made light by two lime green and two pale cream walls, all dotted with transfers of pirates, treasure chests and pirate ships.

"Crash," Alex cried, making his voice into as savage a roar as his three years would allow.

"What are we building?"

"Not building, smashing."

"Ahhh, I see," Keith said, taking a position lying on his side with his tummy at Alex's back. "And so, what are we smashing, then?"

"The castle."

"Oooh. A castle. You must be a giant, then?"

"Not a castle. The castle. Til'k castle," Alex exclaimed, knocking another pile of blocks over.

Keith smiled, thinking that with the state of the master, according to what Amanda had heard, that it might not be too long before that old castle came down. He pondered that for a moment. What would happen to the rest of the town if the master did die? Well, what did they do every other time the man they name the master has died? Tell everyone he's taken a new body and introduce the latest member of the Mercer family, I suppose.

"Are we going to tidy that garden today, little man?" Keith asked, rubbing Alex's hair, ruffling the fine blonde strands up.

"Yeah."

"Come on then, let's get those welly boots dirty."

Keith carried Alex down the stairs, nuzzling the boy's neck as he went, causing the child to squeal in delight. Keith enjoyed the closeness of such play. He knew every ticklish site on that boy's body and took every opportunity he could, to send his child into paroxysms of hysterical laughter. "What?" he asked, feigning innocence, "I didn't do anything." This only caused Alex to laugh out louder as Keith tickled him yet again.

When he opened the door from the kitchen to the garage, Keith let out a gasp and quickly twisted away with Alex, making sure he could not see, right there on the floor, the open suitcase.

"Wait here, little man," Keith muttered, placing Alex on his booster seat at the table. "Stay there while I get your boots."

Keith contemplated the step down into the garage and glanced back at his son. The contents of the suitcase were obscured by the open lid, which had been left flopped against the shaft of the yard broom, leaning against the wall. He knew that Amanda would not have climbed up in the garage to retrieve the case, nor would she have opened it, found a human jawbone and not immediately freaked out about it.

Alex shuffled on his seat. "Want to go in the garden," he exclaimed, bored of waiting.

Keith knew he had only seconds before the boy would get off his seat and charge into the garage, where who knew what the hell he would discover in the case. He had to just look and get it over and done with. He stepped down into the garage and peered over the lid into the case. Nothing.

No jawbone. No tools. Nothing. The case was completely empty.

Keith felt a sudden wave of nausea, pulling right at the bottom of his guts. Forgetting about the boots, he turned and left the garage, locking it behind him.

"Daddy, where are my boots?" Alex asked.

"You'll just have to wait a minute, son," he replied.

"But I want to go in-"

"Just wait a minute," Keith snapped, charging out of the kitchen, along the hallway and up the stairs. "Mandy. Mandy have you been in the garage?"

"Why, is it a crime?" Amanda replied, suspicious of Keith's alarmed tone.

"Of course not... just... have you been in there? Has anyone been in there?"

"No, just you."

"Has anyone been around here?"

"No. Just that bloke over the street who told me about this thing with Mammon." Amanda paused, watching her husband's deep breathing and nervous glances. "Something's wrong, Keith. What is it?"

"Nothing. It's all right."

"No it isn't. Has something gone missing?"

"When that bloke was round, you didn't hit the garage door button on your key ring, did you?"

"No. I don't think so."

Keith's eyes widened. "Which is it? No, or you don't think so?"

"Well, no. Keith, what the fuck is this about? You're being really weird and that is the last thing I need today."

Keith stomped down the stairs, calling over his shoulder, "Just bloody forget it, would you?"

***

Keith decided that the time had come for the weeds poking through the paving slabs at the rear of the house, to meet their end. He ensured Alex was wearing his little blue gardening gloves, which made his hands look far too big for him. Keith had on his thick rigger gloves and the pair set to tearing out invading broadleaf plantain and dandelions. There was a therapeutic quality to the work, a satisfaction to the job that bypassed tedium and granted him some satisfaction.

"Look Daddy," Alex exclaimed gleefully, holding his gloves up for his father to inspect.

"Alex. What have you done?" Keith cried, throwing off his gloves and grasping his child's hands. "Are you hurt?" Alex's gloves were completely soaked through with a sticky red substance that Keith instantly knew to be blood. For the second time that week, he worked over his child's hands to find no evidence of a wound. He peered at the paving stones for clues to where the blood had come from and there, between the slabs, a dark, glistening stream seemed to bring with it more questions than answers.

"Back in the house, Alex."

"But Daddy, I want to help."

"Get back in, quickly," Keith ordered.

The sharp tone of the order was not lost on the little boy and Alex retreated to the kitchen, occasionally peering over his shoulder to cast hateful looks at his father, who had spoiled all the fun.

Keith replaced his gloves and probed the slick crevice between the stones, displacing the crimson liquid, forcing it to break over the lip of the slabs. Keith grasped another weed and dislodged it, breaking loose a clod of moss as he worked. More blood bubbled to the surface, replacing the dislodged weed. "What the fuck is going on here?" Keith muttered.

Amanda appeared at the kitchen door. "Keith, why is our son crying hysterically in the lounge?"

"Not now, Mandy." Keith braced himself as Amanda's rapid footsteps told of her angry approach.

"Never mind your fucking garden, Keith. Alex is really upset, now what did you say to him?"

Keith stood up, grabbed Amanda's hand and pressed a blood-soaked clump of weeds into her palm. "I chased him into the house because of this. I didn't want you to see it, because you've already freaked out enough, but there is fucking blood rising from beneath these paving stones."

"I'm calling the police," Amanda said, dropping the weeds. "And there's no need to take this out on us, you know."

Keith watched his wife hurry back indoors. He stared down at the blood spattered ground and felt the tide of curiosity rising within him. Moments later he was jamming the end of a crowbar under the stone, exerting force down on the metal, enough to raise the stone up on one end. One shove with his hand was enough to topple the slab and he could see immediately that the ground beneath the stone was sodden with blood.

Keith drank deeply of the wine offered to him. The bitter tang at the end of the slug sent a shiver up his spine.

"I bet you needed that," Jerry said, smiling at his neighbour.

"You're not kidding," Keith muttered.

"At least Alex is out of the way for a couple of days. And, to be honest, the police have their hands full at the moment. They won't want to disrupt you for long."

"Yeah, a couple of nights with Keith's mum will do him good. It'll do us good, too, but I don't know that we can stay there after this," Amanda said. Immediately, she glanced at her friend Jane for support.

Annette reached out and grasped her shoulder, giving her a gentle squeeze. "I wish we had enough room for you guys to stay here for a few nights."

"I feel awful for recommending the place to you," Jerry said.

"It's not your fault," Amanda assured him. "You did us a favour. I mean, if you hadn't got in touch with that landlord, we would never have been able to live on an estate this nice."

Keith looked around Annette and Jerry's comfortable lounge, glowing soft red in the side-lamp and candle light. The restored furnishings and deep red leather couch gave the place a real homely feel that made Keith decide that his own home was as cold as a grave. Every free piece of wall space was dotted with family photographs and it was clear to both Keith and his wife that the Cooper's home was a happy one.

The open blinds revealed the silhouette of their own home, backlit by the powerful police flood lights as the excavation work continued through the night.

A knock at the door announced the arrival of some more guests. "That'll be Sean and Ellen," Annette said, heading out into the passageway to let them in. "You know what Lynn's like, Mandy, she and Pete are always the last ones to arrive."

Amanda forced a knowing smile, but immediately glanced across at Keith, wondering if they had done the right thing in coming to their neighbours' place. It had been Annette's idea, with the barbecue looking like a total write-off as the police tore up the garden; she had wanted to do something to mark Amanda and Keith's arrival in the neighbourhood.

The doorway filled with Sean Fisher's bulky form, his eyes sparkling and teeth fully displayed in a broad grin. "Ahhh, the new neighbours. Heard about this strange business in your back garden."

Sean perched himself on a seat near Keith and reached out a hand. "Nice to see you again, Amanda. Keith, is it?"

"Yeah, nice to meet you." Keith shook the hand offered to him by this big, gregarious man. Keith immediately recognised that this was a man who liked to think he was some sort of 'Daddy' of the neighbourhood. As far as he was concerned, the man was nothing more than a gossip and probably just tolerated because he was so forward that he was impossible to escape.

The real surprise came when Sean's wife Ellen entered the room. In huge contrast to her husband, she was petite, with a thin face surrounded by thick, dark curls. It was clear that she had been very attractive in her younger days, but time had taken its toll on her and she looked simple tired, but well made-up. Her skill with make-up did a good job of covering up most of time's ravages.

The introductions were barely over when the remaining guests, Pete and Lynn turned up. Keith knew that Lynn and Annette had been friends with Amanda since school, and it seemed that the Fishers were here for no other reason than they were popular on this street.

The Coopers kept the drink flowing, and Keith wondered when Amanda, who was abstaining, would call time on him. He knew, of course, that she would be reluctant to do so too soon, as she had no desire to get home any time soon.

Ellen proved to be a quiet woman, who seemed to have to be tortured for information. Keith wondered if this was because Sean apparently spoke non-stop. His laughter drowned out almost everything else in the room, as though the man constantly strove to keep the focus on him.

The only time he went quiet was when Amanda turned to Ellen and said, "Sean mentioned you didn't like the house we live in. All this business has got me wondering about that. Is there any particular reason?"

Ellen seemed dumbstruck and Keith noticed Pete and Jerry shoot concerned looks at each other.

"No," Ellen said. "Not really. You know when you just have an irrational dislike of a place... the atmosphere, something like that. That's all it is."

Amanda smiled with a sadness clear in her eyes. "Well, perhaps it isn't irrational after all, eh? Depends what gets dug up around the back."

Sean cleared his throat and added his opinion, "You know, Amanda, it could just be a response to what's going on with the Old Man. Strange things happen whenever that old chap gets ill, or wounded, so the stories always say. Well, you know that anyway."

"I'll be honest, Sean, I never really went in for all that. I sort of left that behind when I moved out of my folks' place."

"Which denomination are they?" Sean asked.

Amanda smiled and said the nickname of the House of Embers, "They were mental money burners."

"Embers. You said were. Did you not keep the faith?"

"Yes, my parents are both dead now. I mean, they had me pretty late on, my brother is much older than I am."

"Ah, I'm sorry, hen. I shouldn't be so nosey."

Keith's eyes narrowed. He knew that this man couldn't survive without prying into the lives of others and now he understood why. Ellen was so repressed that it was obvious these two had no life together. That's why the lives of others seemed much more interesting. "Anyway," Keith interjected, "I don't like to talk about religion while I'm drinking."

Sean shot him a look of annoyance. "You weren't talking about religion. Amanda and I were."

Keith straightened his spine up, knowing that he was nowhere near as physically capable as Sean, but wanting to look his best anyway. "All the same. I think we should drop it." Amanda frowned at him, upset with his apparent rudeness.

"Sorry, Keith. I mean no harm," Sean said, his face returning to the ruddy-faced, grinning configuration he usually displayed. He knocked back a tall glass of Jack Daniels and coke, then got up to fix himself another. "Anyone else for a drink? Keith, much left in that beer?"

"I'm okay, thanks." Keith knew that his drink was almost finished, but some nagging sensation warned him to slow down, to keep his wits about him.

As an endless supply of coke and bourbon seemed to flow into Sean's mouth, he spoke of his band Wages of Sin and their last gig at a local bar The Silver Bonnets. This led into many tales of their drunken hijinks over the years, and theories about just why it was his band always seemed to lose their bassists. "I might as well have an advert up permanently looking for one. My brother joined us for a while, but we kept fucking fighting all the time. Hey, the Gallaghers had nowt on us."

"Does Joe still play, aye?" Pete asked.

"Well, that's a matter of opinion."

"I've never heard him practising in the house or anything," Pete said.

"What about you, Keith? You ever heard him?"

"I'm not with you," Keith said, frowning in confusion.

"Oh, you won't know. My brother Joe, he's your neighbour. We bought up a few properties on this estate years ago and did them up. Mind, we never spent much time on yours. Dad lived there for a lot of years and we never quite got around to changing as much as we did on the others. I always wanted to sort the plumbing between the en-suite and the bathroom. Had any surprises with that, yet?"

Keith forced a smile across his lips and glanced at Amanda to check if she had picked up on this revelation. *He's the landlord. He has a key.* "Yeah. I seemed to puke in two toilets simultaneously the other day."

Sean chuckled. "Oops. Look, we'll get in there and sort it out for you, okay? We'll let these coppers finish wrecking the patio, then we'll put that right and do the plumbing while our tools are in there. That sound okay?"

Keith took a long look at Jerry, who shuffled uncomfortably, staring at Pete, trying to think of another conversation he could start to move things along.

"So, I mean, I know you said you have the band, but you're what, a builder by trade, then?" Keith asked.

"Yeah, I have my certificates for plumbing, too. I used to do a lot of it, but I set the business up and brought up some apprentices to full plumbers so they could take that over. Too much of a messy job, that."

"I see. Your brother... he's a builder too?"

Sean smiled, his eyes beaming. "No. Not usually, although he is handy. I taught him everything he knows. No, Joe's a copper. In fact, he's right behind your house now with a shovel and pick in his hand."

Keith stared at Amanda with the intensity of one trying to transmit his thoughts right into her head. *Are you hearing this? Are you getting all of this? This is why I hate Tilwick. It's all stitched up. Someone was killed in that house. He has a key, and now his brother is supposedly looking for a body.*

Amanda continued in enthusiastic conversation with her friends as Keith slowed his drinking, pondering his next move. Sean seemed to be getting increasingly drunk, but did nothing to slacken the pace of his drinking. When Jerry walked through to the kitchen to gather another round of beers, Keith saw his opportunity and followed him.

Keith raised a finger to his lips and spoke rapidly, in a hushed tone. "Listen, Jerry. What's fucking going on with that house? There's something weird, why won't Sean's wife go there?"

Jerry pinched the bridge of his nose and shook his head. "Keith, keep this to yourself, ok? Sean was caught out knocking off his tenant there. We all knew he was up to something with her and it all came out. It was nasty and

Ellen really took it badly, poor cow. But she took him back and Sean ended it with the tenant, and she moved away, out of Tilwick, as soon as the shit hit the fan."

"Right, so that's why she hates the place?"

Jerry nodded. "Exactly. That's all it is, mate. Nothing spooky, he just really hurt her and apparently he controls all the money and won't move to a new house for a fresh start."

"Really? That's pretty harsh."

"Yeah," Jerry said, grabbing three beers, "but you've met the man. Is it surprising?"

Keith smiled and tilted his head, a gesture indicating I suppose not.

As they entered the lounge once more, Sean's eyes were half-closed, and he appeared about to collapse asleep on the chair. Ellen was pulling her coat over her shoulders.

"Oh, Sean's planning on a sleepover," Jerry said, chuckling.

"You're sure you don't mind, Annette?" Ellen asked.

"Not at all. The kids will do a good job of waking him up. I'll put a coffee in him and send him back to you," Annette assured her, wrapping an arm around her shoulder, pulling her close for a hug and a kiss on the cheek.

"Thanks for a lovely evening, it was nice to meet you both," Ellen said, turning to Keith and Amanda.

"Likewise," Amanda replied.

Sean fell asleep fully and began to snore loudly within minutes of Ellen leaving. "Well, I guess that's our cue to hit the road," Keith said, squeezing Amanda's knee. "Thanks for the beers, we'll have to make it up to you sometime."

"Not at all," Jerry said. "I just hope you can get the house sorted and settled soon, then you can enjoy it properly."

"We'll see," Amanda replied uneasily.

Once all the goodbyes and thanks were said, Keith and Amanda took their leave. As they walked over the road towards their home and its spectral illumination, Keith whispered, "Listen to me, Mandy, we are moving out of here tomorrow. I can't put my finger on it, but something very fucking wrong is happening here and that Sean bloke is at the heart of it."

"Where the hell are we going?" Amanda asked.

"I don't care if we have to camp in mother's back garden, we are not staying in this house. Why the fuck did Jerry not disclose that Sean and his brother are the landlords?"

"Is that a crime?" Amanda asked.

"No, but clearly some sort of a crime has taken place there. A murder. The last tenant, probably. She was shagging Sean and he got caught out and she apparently fucked off. He probably murdered her when she didn't want to call things off."

The rain came down heavier with every footstep, until they set foot through their front door and out of a full summer downpour, full of static.

"Listen to me. His brother, this copper, Joe," Keith whispered, "He's going to tell us that nothing has turned up and all the blood and all that, it's going to be passed off as what's happening with Mammon."

"So you're a believer now?"

Keith wiggled his jaw from side to side, letting the tips of his teeth grind together. "Listen, I'm not saying that.

But I'm saying he is, and everything he has to say on these disturbances is based on that."

A knock at the front door made them both jump in fright.

Keith answered to find a policeman waiting for him. He recognised the broad smile immediately – this had to be Joe Fisher. "Evening, Mr Corgan. I'm Joe, by the way. I just live next door to you."

"So I understand, nice to meet you," Keith said, offering his hand. "And call me Keith." He put on his best neighbour act, thinking, I'll play the game, you bastards.

"Great, Keith. Listen, this rain's making a bit of a mess out back. We're going to call off until tomorrow morning and we'll see what the weather does then, ok? I should add, though, there are no signs so far of anything untoward, so I'm tempted to think it may all be to do with the Old Man getting smashed up."

"Could well be. I think we'd all hope that rather than anything else, eh?"

"Too bloody right. Anyway, try to sleep well, and I'll check in with you in the morning, but if anything should happen, if you think you need help just feel free to knock on my door, all right?"

"Thank you so much."

"Stay safe."

Keith closed the door and waited, his hands pressed against the hard white PVC. He turned the handle upwards, engaging the locks, before twisting the front door key, fixing the locks in place. He breathed deeply, trying to force his spiralling mind into a sense of calm, a state in which he could form a cohesive plan.

"Keith," Amanda cried from the bedroom.

Keith hurried up the stairs to find his wife lying flat on the bed. "What's up?"

"I've got this pain in my left shin. Would you take a look for me, please?"

Keith leaned in close and guided Amanda's left leg, encouraging her to bend her knee. Amanda had not closed the curtains when she had entered the room, but even the light pollution from the floodlights in the garden was not enough for Keith to see clearly. He reached for the bedside lamp and turned it on. "What the hell is this?" he asked, pointing a finger at the pea-sized fleshy bump a third of the way down her shin.

"I don't think it's a bite. It's not itchy, it's just sore."

"Hard to tell what the hell this is…" Keith prodded the lump with his fingertip, eliciting a sharp gasp of pain from his wife.

"Jesus and Mammon, Keith."

"Tender, eh?"

"What the hell is it?" Keith muttered, nudging the solid little lump aside.

Amanda hissed through gritted teeth.

"Mandy, if it's that sore, maybe I need to get you to A and E."

"What? After all you've had to drink?" Amanda's front teeth pressed down hard against her lower lip.

Keith glanced up at his wife. "Did you do anything over at Annette's? Can you remember bumping anything? You might have driven a splinter in and it got infected."

"It doesn't look infected, though. It's not red."

"No, you're right. It just looks... normal. I want to get a pair of tweezers at it. So tempting just to squeeze it and see if it bursts." Keith wore a playful grin, the mischievous look of one who enjoyed inflicting a little pain under the pretext of helping.

"Fucking dare, Mr Corgan and I'll take an eye."

"Just rest it up, that's all you can do. Want some parac-etamol?"

"Yes please."

"Let me get a slash, first."

"Oh, Keith I hate it when you say that. Can't you have a piss like anyone normal?"

Keith chuckled and wandered into the en-suite. "Who says I'm normal? Oh, bloody hell."

"What is it?"

"Don't come in here," Keith said, staring into the toilet bowl.

"What the hell is it?" Amanda cried, inching toward the edge of the bed, teeth gritted against the pain of the mysterious growth in her leg.

"I said fucking stay there. You can't see this. Stay away."

Amanda ignored her husband and limped to his side. "Christ and Mammon," she screamed, staring at the tangle of white, shrivelled fingers in the bottom of the toilet bowl.

Amanda staggered backwards and, turning, she fell against the side of the bed, scraping her shin. She howled as the wooden lip around the bedstead caught the small growth, unleashing fresh, searing pain through her body.

"Fucking hell, Mandy."

Amanda rolled onto her back, clutching her leg. "Keith, it's agony. Have I ripped it open? I can't look."

Keith grasped his wife's foot and inspected the raw skin, sheared in the fall. Blood leaked from the bump. Keith probed the wound with his fingertip and pinched a tiny thread he found, highlighted by the tiny blobs of blood clinging to the fibre. "Stay still. This may hurt."

Keith teased the fibre away from Amanda's leg, finding that it doubled in length, sliding from the bleeding flesh. "It's a hair. I think it's a hair."

"In my leg?" Amanda gasped.

"It's really dark, though. It isn't your hair."

"Are you kidding, Keith? This isn't the time to take the piss."

Keith kept drawing the hair from the wound and noticed that it was threaded through Amanda's flesh around the bump. As he continued to draw out the hair, the flesh began to open, like stitches being picked from a garment.

"Keith, it's agony. Stop what you're doing," Amanda screamed, grasping at the bedclothes hanging over the bed above her.

"Just stay still, it's almost open."

The skin peeled open to expose the interior of the bump, where Keith saw a reddish brown lump. "What the fuck is this?"

"Leave it alone."

"No way." Keith dug his fingernails into Amanda's flesh, slipping over the tiny item, and he adjusted his grip until he managed to get purchase once more. "Try not to move. I have this."

"Don't, Keith. Please," Amanda cried.

Keith tugged the little bump free, finding that it led to a longer shaft, about six inches long. Amanda screamed until the entire nail was dislodged from her flesh.

"A nail? How the hell did that get into my leg?" Amanda screamed.

Keith unravelled the black hair, which was wrapped around the nail a dozen times. "How the hell did this hair get in there? And whose hair is it?" He straightened the fibre out and saw that the hair was almost two feet long.

Amanda pressed down on the hole in her leg, trying to stem the bleeding. "Pass me a towel, Keith, would you?"

"Sorry, here." Keith stood up and grabbed a towel from the rail above the small radiator in the en-suite.

Amanda pressed the towel down and glanced up at Keith to see him staring out of the window. "What now?"

The rain looked like a blizzard, cut out sharp in the hard light, each drop a white-hot spark against the blackness of the corners of the garden beyond the burning bulbs.

"There's someone down there."

"What?"

"I'm telling you, there's someone in the garden. She's looking right at me."

Keith raced down the stairs, through the kitchen and slammed the key into the back door lock. In moments stood on the soft earth among small mounds of paving stones, squinting in the floodlit glare. "I saw you. Give it up now," he shouted.

His night vision ruined by the floodlights, Keith peered into the darkness, shielding his eyes from the raindrops. He strained his ears to hear above the rising wind and staccato impact of the rain all around him.

He grasped the nearest floodlight and wrestled the black plastic handle, twisting lamp around, casting the intense beam around to previously pitch-black areas of the garden. His heart leapt and he found the impossible urge to run away when the pale face and black eyes peered out from behind a bushy honeysuckle.

"Tell me what the hell is going on," Keith demanded, stepping forwards.

The woman shied away into the shade of the thick bush.

"Get back here. I need answers. I need to know what the fuck is going on here." Keith hopped up onto the terrace above the ruined patio, only a few feet away from this strange woman. He had noted her thick, black hair. It seemed impossible that this was not the same hair as that found in Amanda's leg.

A throaty hiss emerged from the mouth of this mysterious woman. Keith braced himself; the noise seemed somehow primitive, feral even, and he expected an attack any second. Instead of a sudden rush, however, the woman emerged from the cover of the honeysuckle slowly.

Keith closed his eyes when the light caught her face and her disfigurement became apparent. The whole lower portion of the woman's head was a ravage of tattered flesh and bruise. Her tongue lashed around beneath her upper palette, but the lower lip, gums and jaw were entirely gone.

Despite himself, Keith staggered back as the woman reached for him with both hands, revealing hands devoid of fingers and thumbs, and forearms encrusted with nails driven right through from one side to another. The woman's entrance into the light revealed ever more brutal damage. Holes had been bored into her temples, her kneecaps had been hacked off, and lower than that, Keith noted in utter disbelief that she made no contact with the ground. She was upright, but had no feet and seemed to levitate above the sodden grass.

Terrified, he turned to flee, caught a fleeting glimpse of a broad smile, heard the clang of metal on bone and felt the momentary agonising pressure inside his skull before all went dark.

***

"He wants you. He wants you. Bitch. Fucking bitch. I saw how you looked at him. How he looked at you."

"Ellen, please. Please, Ellen, listen to me. I don't understand."

Keith heard his wife pleading before his vision sharpened. She was terrified. She was in terrible danger.

The light hurt his eyes as he blinked into full consciousness. He made to stand up but his arms refused to move and his torso could twist no further. The handcuffs kept him locked to the radiator. He was in the lounge. Amanda was still upstairs and her begging drifted down the stairs and through the open lounge door. Keith grasped beneath the radiator, tugging it up against the hooks that pinned it to the wall. The radiator seemed to be stuck, but Keith persisted, yanking upwards again and again. Eventually, the dried paint cracked and the radiator shuddered upwards. Keith pulled at the pipe, bringing the right side of the radiator free of the wall, bending the soft alloy hooks at the other side.

He yanked and heaved at the copper pipe, feeling the satisfying give of the soft metal as he pulled, but he could only go so far. The solid body of the quick-cuffs prevented him from wrapping a chain around the pipe where he might have been able to bend it and eventually snap it. He fought and fought, but the metal would not give. He felt as though his bones might, though. He braced his forearm and tried to twist into a position where he could snap his wrist.

<hr>

Amanda stared at the rusty tools in the battered suitcase and the deranged, elfin woman stooped over them. She had seemed so slight, so vulnerable earlier at the Coopers' place. Now she knew otherwise. This woman was pure insanity.

Ellen brandished the short, pointed bradawl, hovering over Amanda's legs. "Ooh, you have a nasty hole there already, I see."

"Please, Ellen. Please, if you put that thing down and just go... just go home... Nobody would know. I wouldn't tell a soul, I swear it."

The point hovered over the opening where an hour earlier, Keith had drawn out the nail. Amanda fought against the length of rope that fastened her to the bed. Ellen used the rusted tool to gentle probe the tiny wound. "I wonder if I can do this without touching the sides, you know, like that game where it buzzes when you touch the wire. Do you know the game I mean?"

"Please..."

"Do you know the game I mean?"

"Yes. Yes, I know the game you mean."

Ellen slid the tip of the bradawl into the opening of the wound. "I was never much good at the game, and whenever it would buzz, I used to just hurry all the more, buzzing all the way to the other end. You get what I mean?"

"Yes, I know. Please," Amanda screamed when the metal point bit into her flesh.

Ellen chuckled and said, "Oh well." She rammed the bradawl to its hilt, feeling the spike scrape against shin bone. Amanda screamed and kept on screaming as Ellen withdrew the tool a little and jammed it in again, over and over. Eventually she pulled the bloody point clear.

"There, that was a little taster. What shall we do next? I like your legs. I think he likes your legs. He liked her legs. She had long legs like yours. Just like yours." Ellen reached into the suitcase and produced the thick, dirty tenon saw. "Long legs just like yours until I shortened them for her."

"Oh Christ. Ellen, please. You have to believe me. There is nothing going on. I've only just met him."

"She only just met him. Just met him again and again and even though I begged him, he would not stop shagging her. He promised he would, but I saw him sneaking in here night after night. Making a fool of me. They all knew. They all knew. I should have visited them all. But he never looked at them the way I saw him look at you." Ellen brought the saw blade up to Amanda's right kneecap. "And that slut, she let him come in her again and again. He couldn't get me pregnant, oh but he fucking made sure she was."

"Ellen, you have to listen to me. Ellen. You've got this all confused."

"Confused? I am not confused. I know exactly what I'm doing. Just like she knew what she was doing, just like you know what you were doing. Did you think I would let you just move in here and let him pick up with you where he left off with her?"

Keith yelled in frustration and agony as he twisted his wrist to its extent. Sweat mingled with the damp from the rain, all over his body, running down his face in rivulets as he squatted over his crooked hand. "Fucking hell, fucking hell, fucking hell."

An impossibly long scream came from upstairs. Keith cried out in response, and forced his knee down, throwing all his weight into the movement. His cry of exertion turned into his own howl of agony as the bones of his wrist separated with a sickening, wet crack.

"Wake up. Wake up," came the voice.

The light of the lounge bled into the darkness as Keith's eyelids peeled apart. His thoughts stumbled about inside his pounding head as he tried to make sense of the screaming from upstairs and the pain in his left arm.

"There you are. Nice to have you back."

"Sean fucking Fisher..." Keith murmured, his head rolling around on his neck, impossible to control.

"Wrong brother," Joe chuckled. "Not a bad try, though. Sean's wife, she's upstairs, getting to know your wife much better. Inside and out, you could say."

The screams upstairs increased intensity once more and Keith cried, "What are you doing to my wife?"

"I doubt very much that good-looking wife of yours was actually looking to shag my brother, but by God and Mammon, when Ellen gets something in her head... well, let's put it this way, when the last tenant, Michelle, was running around with Sean, you have never seen a woman laid so low... she just fucking imploded. The only release she had, came after years of knowing my brother could not leave that slag alone. Only after all that humiliation did she finally explode. And my God did she. She even used my dad's old tools from up in the garage to do the job."

"What a... lovely family..." Keith snorted.

Everything had become quiet upstairs. Keith's eyes rolled to the doorway, where he could only see the white spindles on the staircase.

"Don't worry, Keith," Joe said. "She's not dead. Ellen will make this last hours. That gives us a bit of time to talk. It's not like I can just talk about this with anyone. I can't even discuss it with Ellen, for fuck's sake. After tonight, it will be like this never happened. She'll go back to my useless lump of a brother, cook him his bacon and eggs, and carry on terrified that he's sticking his cock into some other woman. He, on the other hand, will believe that another tenant has made a hasty exit from this messed up haunted house, but really, you won't leave. I've already made a good start on the garden."

Keith hung his head low as the impossibility of the situation became clearer. His shoulders juddered with each sob. From the bedroom, a new wave of screams rang out and Keith strained against the radiator, trying to tear his shattered hand free.

Joe sat in his uniform, watching on, amused and casual, as though the tortured screams of an innocent woman did not fill the house around him.

"What the fuck do you get out of all this?" Keith moaned.

"Ellen has her thing, and I have mine. See... Sean wasn't the only Fisher to stick it up Michelle. I was in there too... except I did it after Ellen had finished with her. Your wife is next on my list. She's a bloody good-looking woman, Keith. I reckon she'll be the best-looking bit of dead fanny I've ever had."

Keith's teeth grated against each other until he felt they would shatter any second. An animal howl escaped his lips and for the first time since seeing this house, he wished he was in a semi-detached property, where the neighbours would have heard him. He remembered something about the sound of Joe playing bass not penetrating his house, and it was implied he didn't play it quietly. With a desperate heave, Keith yanked his left hand out through the cuffs, hearing the snap of his thumb as it crushed beneath the solid metal.

He toppled as the cuffs fell away from the radiator, but he quickly corrected himself. Joe leapt to his feet and caught him with an agonising punch to the jaw. Keith staggered aside, his vision blurring once more as the screams persisted from above. Keith had only one idea in his daze. He had to get to his wife, but Joe was too strong for him. There was only one thing he could try.

He charged at the policeman once more, his fist drawn back. Joe expertly knocked the blow aside, smiling at the ease with which he turned the attack away, but Keith had some momentum built up and the two slammed together hard, knocking the policeman off-balance and onto the couch. Joe grabbed Keith's hair and smacked his left temple with two rapid blows. Keith clung to Joe's uniform but slipped away to the floor.

"Not much of a fighter, eh?" Joe sneered. "I wonder what would happen if I took you up there to see her? Would you have a bit more fight in you then, eh?"

Keith curled into a ball on the floor, desperate to make a dash upstairs to Amanda, but knowing he had no chance to do it with this monster looming over him. Instead he crawled. Inching his way across the floor as the screams echoed down the stairs anew.

"Go on, then," Joe mocked. "You're a right knight in shining armour, you are. Go up there and fucking save her if you can." He rose to his feet and kicked Keith's rump, knocking him flat. "Get up you cowardly little bastard."

Keith crawled out to the passage, hearing Amanda's screams transform into the sound of crunching wet gravel. He heard retching and spitting as his wife vomited between cries. His shattered hand reached the bottom step.

"Nearly there. So close, Keithy. Go up and fucking save your wife. You do it. If only your laddie could see you now, he'd be fucking ashamed of you. Crawling on your belly like this... absolutely ashamed of you."

Keith made it halfway up the stairs and stopped. His limbs burned with furnace intensity. His left forearm felt like a water balloon about to burst in an explosion of blood and bone. Amanda's cries came anew, and Keith fumbled at his chest.

Joe heard a click and a familiar squawk and beep, and a panicked despatch operator was heard to shout, "PC Fisher, respond. Can you hear me? State your location."

Keith shouted the address and added, "It's an emergency."

"What the fuck have you got there?" Joe snatched Keith's ankles and dragged him down the stairs until he crashed to a halt at the bottom. He grabbed Keith's shoulders and heaved him over onto his side to find Keith grinning through his cracked, bloody lips. His hands clutched the radio he had stolen from Joe when they collided.

"They've heard the screams, Joe. They'll be here looking for you any minute."

Joe grabbed the radio and slammed a fist into Keith's nose, breaking it across to his right cheek. "You sneaky little cunt." The policeman thought for a second. There was no way he could hide the scene. No way he could cover this up before his colleagues arrived.

"Ellen," he shouted. "Ellen, wrap it up we've got to get out of here."

Joe knew that his words had gone unheard. Ellen was too busy enjoying herself.

He took a moment to stamp on Keith's chest before turning to run out of the front door.

As soon as the door opened, Keith caught a glimpse of the blue flashing lights out in the cul-de-sac. Through his tear-scorched eyes he made out no faces, only the shapes of his neighbours spilling out of their homes and onto the street, drawn by the sudden police presence.

"He tried to kill me," Joe cried. "That bastard tried to kill me."

Keith rolled over onto his front once more, leaving the police to hear out their colleague as they tried to ascertain the situation and understand why his radio call had been filled with the sound of his threats and a woman's agonised screams. Keith crawled up the stairs one by one and heard the calls of the police who had entered his home.

"Stop where you are."

He ignored them.

A policewoman's voice rang out below. "Stop where you are, right now."

He pushed on until he crawled over the top step and collapsed on the landing. His limbs had finally taken enough punishment. The adrenaline was all gone and the last vestiges of strength had been sapped from his being.

The bedroom door stood open and Keith saw Amanda tied to the bedstead, on the side nearest the door, where she always slept, where she could respond to Alex's cries in the night.

Amanda's attacker stood over her, arms working busily, the woman totally unaware of Keith's presence. She hummed as she worked. Amanda's screams had dried out into a hoarse, cracked rumble.

Keith felt hands pulling on him, rough, strong, vengeful. But only for a moment. "Dore, in here," the male police constable shouted.

Dore, the police woman, stepped over Keith and both constables filled the bedroom doorway.

Ellen finally recognised that she had been caught in the act. Keith caught fleeting glimpses of the gore-stained woman, whose face was caked in drying clots of his wife's blood.

Too drained even to cry, Keith spotted Amanda. Through the blood, it was difficult to ascertain what he was looking at, as the police struggled with the manic woman. Ellen snapped her teeth and struck out with the bradawl, puncturing the palm of the male officer, who cried out in pain. She pushed, driving the tool up to the hilt.

Dore took the opportunity of that moment, when Ellen left the bradawl jammed in the man's hand, to swing her baton, knocking the woman against the cream-coloured wardrobe doors.

Ellen reached for another tool even with her bloody cheek squashed against the wardrobe door. Dore was not having that, however, and stomped on the back of the woman's left knee, sending her down to the floor. Dore cracked the baton across the woman's forearm, smashing her hand away from the toolkit.

Dore knocked Ellen flat to the floor and Keith heard the caution being recited. The policeman groaned as he slowly drew the long, slender bradawl from his palm.

It was then, as the policeman ducked aside to deal with his own injury, that he caught a full look at his wife's face and could finally make sense of the scene. Her left eye was obscured by a brown, rectangular object and blood covered the left side of her face from her hairline to a point above her nose. Keith now knew that this was the tenon saw, embedded in his wife's head, where Ellen had been in the process of sawing through her skull. Her cheeks were a ruined landscape of deep gouges and punctures, her upper set of teeth hovered above a crimson gulf where only a savaged tongue hung, ragged and slick, in an open space where once her perfect mouth had been. Her jaw was missing. It was then, as he tore his eyes away from the sight of her destroyed face, that he noticed her legs poking out from beneath the bed, both with a wrecked half kneecap hanging from tattered flesh.

Keith closed his eyes and felt the swamp of exhaustion consume him once and for all. The house seemed to grow full with the heavy stomp of boots as more police officers rushed in. Screams broke through the darkness once more, and after a second, Keith realised that this time, the horrific shrieks did not originate from the lips of his wife. They were the screams of a man. They were his screams.

"That should settle everything for you now. There will be peace in this house."

"There will be plenty of peace. I'll never let another person live in it," Sean said, staring at the small wooden shrine the specialist had just installed in the overgrown garden. The structure itself was similar in size, to a birdhouse, but with some personal artifacts placed within and holders for incense and candles on the outside.

"I understand, but... well, life goes on. You may feel differently in a while and I just want you to know that if the next occupant honours the dead with that shrine, they should find peace in the house." The specialist took one last look at Michelle's hairbrush and necklace, and Amanda's compact mirror and the picture of the little boy and the father who had left Tilwick a few days before.

"Malcolm, wasn't it?" Sean asked, staring blankly at the shrine.

"Yes," the specialist replied, pulling his leather jacket back on.

Sean offered his hand. "Thank you for setting this up for me."

"You're welcome. It was a horrible business all of this... but you can't blame yourself, Mr Fisher. You weren't to know." Malcolm had read the news at the time and had, of course, heard all the rumours of Mr Fisher's psychotic wife, who had dismembered a new tenant in this very house. He had heard of the widower who had spent months in Tilwick Psychiatric Hospital, receiving treatment after the whole horrendous experience had caused a complete mental breakdown.

"Do you mind seeing yourself out? I think I'd like to stay here for a little while."

Malcolm patted the large man on the back and took the narrow path along the side of the house, using the weather-beaten gate to make his exit. As he closed the gate, he caught sight of Sean Fisher kneeling on the grass, shuddering as grief and guilt claimed him once more.

10

— · —

ABOUT 'HARD MAN'

Don't you just love a good dive bar? I do. I enjoy a trendy bar, or a hipster joint, but there is something about a really shitty bar that I love. In fact, I know what it is: it's the company.

Some of the original inspiration behind my old Matt Carsun stories came from one particular pub in Alnwick that is long-gone. Demolished and replaced with flats now. It actually wasn't a bad boozer either, just old, full of character. And full of characters. I loved to finish my Saturday nights there, after I left the club (really club should be in inverted commas - it was one of *those places*) and I'd stay for a lock-in and leave as the sun came up. At that point I'd nip along to a cafe that stayed open all night, and grab some food, then sleep through most of Sunday. During those lock-ins, I was drinking next to drug dealers, and someone reckoned this bloke over in the corner there raped a woman. There was the guy who found a dead body in a storm drain. Apparently, that other one over there is the man to see if you need a body to disappear. I didn't know

156

which stories were true and which were just urban legends, but they stayed with me, because who doesn't love a good story?

There's a family of three tough blokes, three hard men, back in my home town. Two of them are a bit naughty, shall we say? They went to school with my Dad and my uncles. They love my Granda, the loved my Great-Granda, and when they have a few drinks in them, they like to tell a few little tales, memories of when they were kids and they were wowed by the hard-working, hard-drinking elders of my family. It's nice to see their features soften, their guard come down, and for them to share a genuine moment with you, where they reveal that even though I don't buy what they're dealing, we are connected in a small way. Over the years I've listened to stories of their capers, and their stories of being in prison on those occasions where the capers went wrong. Their stories are always touched with a little bit of self-deprecation that comes from a lifetime of knowing people won't fuck with them. They don't have to *act* invincible, when it is well known they *are* invincible.

One of their sons and one of their close friends had been drinking together and were both beaten up badly when a young, rival dealer decided to step up his campaign. He soon realised his mistake of course, and fled the town right away. He was known for being a sneaky bastard, hitting people with clothes irons and shoving them down flights of stairs as they walked away, things like that. A sneak, not a hard man. The family's reaction to these beatings, the fury that you could practically feel as they roamed the pubs night after night, hoping to catch a glimpse of the culprit, is something that will stay with me until the end of my days.

I remember thinking: this is what it looks like when you go up against these guys. They are relentless. They don't care about prison. Somebody has crossed a line and they are going to be crossed off, if they show their face again. It made me very pleased that my interactions with them never strayed beyond exchanging pleasantries in the pubs that served as the border between their world and mine.

And one day I peered back into their world, and wrote about a...

11

HARD MAN

They always called me a hard man, and around Tilwick that's the sort of reputation that sticks. Win a few battles, take a beating occasionally and laugh it off, and people start talking. That's how it starts, anyway; bruised knuckles and beer – sometimes the beer with the bloke who just tried to knock my lights out. That meant people knew I really didn't give a fuck about fighting, that I just think of it as just another thing to do.

I have rules though. What's life without rules?

I only have two rules. There's not much I wouldn't do, but I keep to these rules no matter what. First rule: never throw the first punch. Self-explanatory, isn't it? I know they call me a hard man, but they don't call me a trouble-maker. Well, not that kind of trouble anyway. Second rule: the floor is the last thing to hit them. Once they're down on the floor, they're beaten, so leave it there.

With those rules I've made it this far, a kick in the arse off sixty. I'm in decent shape, I've had more wins than losses and I've kept most of the friends I had when I was in my twenties. And that last one, I'm not so sure is a good thing, but there you go. So, I think you know, I'm Eddie Garfield, and since you asked for the truth about what happened, what I'm going to tell you is all true. I wouldn't lie about it, and when it's over, well you can think what you want about me and that'll be that, and you can do what you want.

I suppose the start of all this shit was a pretty normal Tuesday night. I was out up the moors with my middle brother, Tony, and our mate, Tiny Tim. You probably think Tiny Tim's real name is Timothy, right? Wrong. He's called Steven, at least by his mother, but nobody else. We all call him Tiny Tim from that long-haired fucker, weird looking bugger from years ago, and he sang that song where it goes Tiptoe, through the tul ips... Well, Steven – Tiny Tim, he likes the odd tiptoe through a window, and back out of it again with a telly under his arm, or a bit of jewellery in his pocket, and that's how he got his nickname.

So anyway, me, Tony and Tiny are up on the moor, pitch-black darkness, except for the little fire we had going. Thick black smoke looked dark grey in the clash of firelight and night and the unmistakable, choking, chemical smell of melting plastic stung my eyes and nostrils so much I backed away.

Tiny laughed at me, he'd wrapped a bandana around two thirds of his face. "Can't stand the heat, Eddie? Should keep your nose and gob covered, man."

"No thanks, I'd rather choke than look like you do right now."

Tony chuckled and fed more railway cable into the fire. "Aye, he looks like the world's shittest cowboy, doesn't he?"

"Fuck off, you two. I'm not the one crying for the thousandth fucking time of doing this. You think you would learn instead of breathing these fucking fumes in every time."

"Shut your fucking mouth, Tiny, and draw that fucking copper out the fire, would you?"

Tiny did as Tony told him. He was okay for a bit of banter, but he knew where the line was, and he knew we don't lose a payday for the sake of having a laugh. The thick strands of copper, glowing orange, would bring us a pocketful of money and because Tilwick is... shall we say... off the beaten track, as well you know, the British Transport Police have no idea where we vanish to when we raid the East Coast line. We move about a bit, but the Ashmouth and Amblington areas, they're the best, because we can nip back to Tilwick quicker than from anywhere else on the line. Anyway, that night we'd worked a bit further south of there, between Widdrington and Morpeth. Can't hit the same spots all the time, of course.

It was all going fine, as usual, when we heard this engine approaching. We were up among the hills, so we only had to turn towards the town to see the headlamps.

"Copper. It's got to be," Tony growled.

"Put that fucking fire out."

Tiny threw soil onto the fire to extinguish it. I joined him, using the side of my boot to rake up the dirt and shove it on.

"Hurry up, lads," Tony called, the van keys jangling in his hand as he unlocked the door and prepared for a hasty exit.

"Is it a paddy wagon, or just a Panda, or what?" Tiny called.

"Height of the lights it looks like a Panda."

Me and Tiny had the fire smothered, and the smell of baking earth filled my nostrils. I liked the smell. I associated it with excitement. I have to add, if you ever decide to do a bit of cable burning, the size of the fire is key. Too big and you can't put it out if you spot the pigs – and on that subject, make sure you're on high ground so you can see approaching vehicles - too small and you'll be there all night melting the plastic, increasing the chances of someone coming by and spotting you. See? There's a bit of an art to it. And remember to let the copper cool properly before you carry it off. I've seen some nasty fucking burns given out when lads have handled the copper too soon.

"Come on, let's throw it in the back, fuck it," Tiny whispered.

I shushed him and moved to the front of the van, watching those headlights speed closer and closer. "Means fucking business. Tiny, fuck the cable, get in the van."

"There's too much to walk away from."

"Fuck it man, get in," I shouted.

Tony started the van up and his Moody Blues CD came on, Nights in White Satin started up and we were off, the van bouncing along the dirt track. Tony kept the lights off and took us out onto the main road, just as the police car came up to the rise of the hill.

"Hold on, lads." Tony flicked the full beams on to dazzle the bastards, and he floored it.

Well, the daft fucking copper only tried to block the van with his car, pulling into the middle of the road. One of the doors opened and a stupid twat started climbing out onto the road. I knew straight away that this was just a young copper, a new one. Had to have been. Only a green copper would try to be a hero in Tilwick.

I don't know what I shouted to Tony, I can't remember what it was, but what I can remember was the van swerving, and it felt like we were going to roll. Tony twisted the wheel back and we struck the edge of the open car door, slamming it shut on the copper, whose head, fingers and leg were already out.

Tony slammed his foot on the brakes. Tiny screamed for him to keep driving, but the van had already skidded to a halt, and I jumped down from the cab, running back up the road a little way.

The other door of the police car swung open, but Christ, I didn't even look at the copper climbing out, just the young one on the floor. His helmet lay on the ground a few feet away from his crushed face. His nose and everything were gone, from his eye sockets down to his chin, it was like a big, deep puddle of blood, glistening in the car's interior light. I saw a couple of fingers lying there next to him, and one of his legs was snapped almost completely through.

Tiny shouted something from behind me, and I heard a grunt and a sort of whoosh, and that was the moment I thought about the other copper who got out of the car. The smack he gave me on the back of the head with his truncheon nearly sent my eyeballs flying out of my skull, I swear to God and Mammon. I fell forward and smacked against the side of the car.

While my head felt like a spinning top, Tiny and Tony had come to my rescue. The copper's head banged against the back of the car and as I got to my feet, those two were giving the fucker the kicking of his life. He curled into a ball and protected his face with his arms. Tiny was really going for it; you'd think he was taking a penalty kick with the copper's head. They don't have the same rules as I do.

"Cut it out," I shouted to them both. "Get back in the fucking van, you idiots."

Tony turned to me as he drove hell for leather down into the town. "Is that the thanks we get for saving your fucking arse? Calling us idiots. That copper would have had you away in the back of that car, and nowt's so sure."

"All right, just leave it fucking out, would you?"

"How's yer heed?" Tiny asked.

I dabbed at the back of my skull with two fingers, to find my fingertips coated in a sticky wetness. I didn't have to look at my fingers to know what that was. "I'll live."

"Let's get a drink, eh?"

"Are you fucking kidding, Tiny? Tonight was a bloody disaster. We've come away empty handed and I think we killed a copper." I shook my head in disbelief.

"Empty handed? Doesn't have to be that way. Tony, turn the van around, we'll stick that pig in his own car boot with his handcuffs on him and we'll get the cable. It'll be just about cool now."

And do you know what? I didn't get out of the van, but before long at all, one type of copper lay bleeding and handcuffed in a car boot, while another type of copper lay in the back of Tony's van.

I woke to the sound of someone hammering on the front door and when I answered, it was Tony. His eyes darted all over the place and he kept pulling his jacket zip up and down. I made us both a cup of coffee while he told me about a visit he'd had that morning from Inspector Pitt. Hilton Pitt is a fairly reasonable copper. He's a tough bastard, mind. But he uses his brain before he lifts his hands, and we all grew up with him, so he knows our game.

"He told me a copper died, a young, fresh-faced probationer, and another was hospitalised. He fucking knocked on the door at nine this morning. He wasted no time going anywhere else. He knows it was us."

"Has he seen the van?"

"No, I hid it in the yard last night. Tiny's heading down there now to crush the fucking thing."

"That poor young lad, killed for a few quid."

Tony shrugged. "If we'd kept driving, he'd have been killed for nowt, so what do you prefer?"

I ignored the question and asked one of my own. "Did Pitt say anything else?"

"He framed it like he wanted me to keep an ear to the ground, but I swear he fucking knew the situation. There's no two ways about it. He'd asked if we were up there burning cables recently, said it looked like someone was out there doing it last night and he knows we sometimes use that spot."

"What'd you say to that, then?"

"I told him we're out of that game."

"Did he ask you where you were, want an alibi or anything?"

Tony shook his head.

I banged my mug down on the coffee table. "Why the fuck did that lad have to get out of the car? Silly bastard. Why did he put the car into the middle of the road? He could have just turned it round and chased us for a bit."

"Probably watching too many films, man. That's all it'll be. Probably been watching Dirty Harry or something."

Tony craned his neck and checked the back of my head. "Still looks nasty. How's it feel?"

"Rough. Bloody rough. My head's pounding."

"Take a couple of painkillers, you fanny," Tony snorted.

"Fuck off man, this would have killed you."

"Well, I'd better get a move on." Tony stood and tipped the last of his coffee into his mouth. "I'm going over to Amblington to pick some toot up. Coming out tonight?"

"I dare say so. Nag's?"

"Aye I'll be out about seven."

So later on, I was sitting in the Nag's with a pint of Castle Keep stout in my hand and I couldn't wait to see Tony with that toot. Best painkiller there is.

This was a Wednesday night. Strange night to be out dealing, you might think. Well, not really, and for a couple of reasons. You know Tilwick's a pretty drunken town, with all these bars and not a lot else to do in the evening, you get a lot of drinkers out most nights of the week. Secondly, students don't give a shit what night it is if they've got money in their pocket. Finally, Tony spends Wednesday afternoons cutting the coke a bit. Not much, either. It's still the best gear in town. He keeps the very best stuff for our noses and some samples, then the touched stuff goes out on sale. Our big buyers, little dealers, they tend to meet us on the Wednesday and pick their gear up, so they have a couple of days to do some cutting of their own and stretch it as far as they can, ready for the weekend.

I took it easy with the beers and after being there about an hour, a text arrived from my son, Gavin. He wanted to know if I was out, so I told him where to come and find me, but I remembered thinking it was weird, because he knows what Wednesday night is, and in the past, he'd come to join us. Anyway, I didn't think about it anymore and before long he was sat next to me, with his girlfriend Gemma sat by his side.

Gemma's a nice lass, she always gives me a cuddle and a kiss when she sees me, she's one of those kids with an old head on young shoulders, a bonnie little thing, too. Wears her blonde hair in big curls hanging down to those young shoulders and she has the face of a model. Delicate, smooth as marble. She's the kind of lass that makes this old bloke feel a bit younger when she's around.

I bought them each a drink and Gavin kept looking at the door every time anyone came up the stairs. "Are you expecting someone, son?"

"No, why?"

"You keep twisting your head around like that lass from *The Exorcist* every time you hear footsteps on the stairs."

"Oh, I just feel a bit pumped, you know?"

"Did you fall out with your barber?" I asked.

Gavin rubbed a hand over his hair. "No. What do you mean?"

"I haven't seen you with your back and sides that long for ages. You're usually a grade zero man."

"Just tell him," Gemma said, resting her fingertips on the back of Gavin's hand.

Gavin let out a long sigh and I reached over and gave his shoulder a squeeze. "Come on, son. Tell me what's wrong."

"I owe a month's rent. Landlord says he'll kick us out if I don't settle up by next week."

"Christ son, you had me worried there. So, what is it? Two months' rent next week?"

"Yeah."

I took out a roll of notes from my pocket and flipped through them under the table. "Here's a grand. Pay the man and get plenty of shopping in. Fill the cupboards up." I stuffed the money into his hand.

"Dad, I can't take all this."

"Yeah, you can. I had a win on the horses the other day."

Gavin slipped the notes into his pocket and smiled at me. His cheeks flushed red with embarrassment, but his eyes glistened with... well, I don't know what. Relief? Gratitude? Either way I knew he appreciated my help, and the fact that I didn't ask any questions before I gave it. Maybe that was my mistake.

Maybe if I'd asked him some more questions, he might still be alive.

A few months ago, when that maniac Geordie Sketcher was killed off, Tilwick's naughty types jostled for position. I include myself and Tony in that, and Tiny Tim, of course. We had to knock out a few teeth to make sure we could carry on working out of the Nag's Head. The Grahams got their claws on the lion's share of the drug trade in Tilwick, but there was no fucking way we could face them down. Even with one of them in prison at the time, it wasn't worth the hell that would break loose when he got back on the street, so we had to sort of turn our eyes the other way as they took what they wanted.

Then of course, there's all the up-and-coming, wannabe gangsters out looking to make a name for themselves. Some of those little dealers from our Wednesday night trading sessions had taken themselves up a peg or two, but there was one particular lad who had become a bit of a nuisance. If I'd known the trouble he was going to cause, I would have killed that little fucker and stuck him into a peat bog before he had a chance to wipe his arse.

On the Saturday afternoon I had a couple of drinks on my own and watched the races in one of my favourite pubs, the Sun, Moon and Stars.

Anyway, the horse I'd backed, Conquistador, took a bad fall. Tough little fucking horse, though. They showed some footage after the race was over. They'd kept a camera on the accident as the race carried on, and the injured animal seemed to position itself over the fallen rider, like it was protecting her from getting trampled by the other horses. It was a hundred quid down the drain for me, but I had to admit, I admired that horse. It showed more... I don't know what the word is. It's a better word than pity. Pity isn't the right word. Anyway, whatever that word is, this animal had some bloody courage. It was a hard fucking horse.

Now, this little fucking dealer I was telling you about, a lad called Craig Bettaney, he came into the pub before I left. He wasn't alone, it was him and his whole bunch of pals. Loud, cocky, taking the piss... all except Craig himself. He sat quietly with his back to the window. You know that feeling that you're being watched, and you can see this face in the corner of your eye. Well, I had that, and a couple of times I turned to face him, but my eyes aren't as sharp as they used to be. I probably need glasses really. Either way, it was the third time I looked at him that I realised he was actually staring right at me.

I didn't know what to do at first. I was that surprised.

He's twenty-odd, a young buck, and me? I'm in my late fifties. I don't like threatening young lads without good reason, but that little fucker was burning holes into my head with his eyes. My jaw tensed up and I finished my pint, placed the glass back on the bar and walked over to Craig's table, slowly, calm-like.

"I know I'm good-looking, son, but you're not my type," I told him.

"Sorry, Eddie, I just like studying a bit of history, that's all."

His friends all fell silent as I planted my fists, knuckles down, on the table in front of that cocky little prick. "Son, you're not the height of my cock and maybe you've had a few too many, so I'll just leave it today. Speak to me like this again, in fact, even look in my direction again, and I'll smash your fucking head in for you."

The younger Carsun lad, James, was behind the bar and he shouted over, "Problem here, lads?"

"No problem, young 'un. Just reminding this little lad to respect his elders."

"Fuck off, you silly old twat," Bettaney said.

And the place fucking erupted.

One of his little arse-lickers swung a bottle and it smacked the back of my head, same place that copper got me. The pain... I've never known anything like it. It dropped me, like. I bashed my chin on the table as I fell and just as I did, Bettaney tipped the table over and me with it, straight onto my back. I had stars in my eyes and almost passed out, but I managed to hold on, and thank fuck I did because the way he'd flipped the table over onto me, the edge almost crushed my windpipe.

That moment, when I realised I could snuff it any second, I got a massive belt of adrenaline in my chest, and I shoved the table aside. I had boots and trainers lashing out at my head, my arms, my back, everything, as I rolled over and picked myself up. Now, after a kicking like that, my head pissing blood out all over the place, and me getting back up on my feet, every single fucker in the bar wanted to be second in line, so I had my pick.

I popped the nose of the closest of Bettaney's little plastic gangsters and knocked him straight over a table, glasses smashing off the floor, bottles tumbling everywhere. Another of these pricks fell and I was nowhere near him, that's when I saw young Carsun mid-swing with that baseball bat of his. Bang. He dropped another one.

I know the Carsuns. The whole family. This one's dad, Cameron, he's a tough fucker, but his two sons never struck me as scrappers, like. I'd never seen them laying on before, but the young 'un wasn't shy with that bat. What do the Yanks call it? A home run? He knocked a few fucking home runs that day.

I sunk my fist into the gut of the next lad, doubled him over, grabbed his hair and took my knee up into his face. I shoved him over into the next one. Something bit into my side and as I turned, I felt my skin tearing away.

Bettaney flashed a screwdriver, dripping with blood. My blood. Then he stuck it into me again, in almost exactly the same spot, down under the ribs. It wasn't cold that time, though. It burned like red-hot coals. A glass shattered over the back of my head and again I dropped to my knees. Bettaney kicked my face and that was it, I went over onto my back. Chunks of that broken glass bit into my scalp and slid into the gash that had already opened up again when I was hit the first time.

I threw up. It was like a disgraceful brown soup of beer and chips, and my chest felt like someone was pushing a fist against my heart as Bettaney's gang continued to break my second rule.

The next thing I knew, I woke up in hospital.

"Now then," I called, seeing that my older brother Peter had decided to pay me a visit.

How can I describe Peter to you? You won't have seen him out on the drink much; he tends just to be a birthday, weddings and wakes kind of bloke. Remember that big fucker on the James Bond films, Jaws? He's like him just with a load of false teeth instead of metal teeth. Big fucking jaw on him, you couldn't knock him out in twenty tries. And he's as gentle as a lamb.

Peter lifted a plastic carrier bag onto the bed and took out some grapes and a copy of the racing paper.

"No flowers?"

"What? You think I'd be seen carrying flowers around for you?"

"What's going on, then? Am I missing much?"

Peter drew the curtain around the bed, screening us from two old grey men with the oxygen tubes up their noses who shared my room, and plonked himself down on the high-backed chair next to my bed. Sat as upright as the chair forced him to, he looked very uncomfortable. "No, not much."

"Where's Tony? I thought he would have been along to see me."

"Put it this way, I've come to you from him."

I frowned, wondering why it was so significant that he'd seen Tony before coming to see me. "Right..."

"He's in intensive care."

"He's fucking what?"

"He's been beaten to a fucking pulp. Gavin reckons it was an off-duty copper who got him on Sunday night on his way back up home." Peter sighed. "Any idea why an off-duty copper would do that?"

I shrugged, but an idea took hold of me in that moment. I couldn't shake it. Pitt would have arrested us if he had evidence, unless someone had paid him not to. Even then, he wouldn't let one of his men hammer Tony unless someone had told him who was driving the van. We had a grass in the ranks.

"Just tell me you two idiots had nothing to do with that copper who was killed up on the moors."

My eyes widened. "Of course not. Jesus Christ, what do you think we are, like?"

"Well... I just had to ask. Hey, your Gavin wouldn't have had anything to do up there, would he?"

"Why the fuck would Gavin be up there?"

A nurse poked her head around the curtain. "Can you watch your language, please? There are other people around you."

"Sorry nurse," I said.

Peter winked at her, and she tutted, slipping out of view once more.

"You know he's running around doing jobs for that young Bettaney lad, don't you?"

"He's what?"

"Brilliant, so you don't know? Christ... I'm the one who stays in all the time. How come I know before you?"

"Well, I know now. What the hell's going on? It was Bettaney's lot that put me in here... oh, hold on a minute. Gavin was at me for rent money the other night. I bet it wasn't rent money at all, was it?"

Peter slowly shook his head. "Nope. I bet every penny was for Bettaney. I heard something a couple of weeks ago, that Gavin owed him some money for some dope. You know when Gavin was off work when he hurt his back?"

"Yeah."

"Well, Bettaney didn't give him money; he gave him a load of dope to sell. It was supposed to be enough to make about five hundred on, and give two-fifty back to Bettaney."

I didn't need to hear any more. I was off the bed and within quarter of an hour, I had dressed and discharged myself, all to the background blethering of Peter and a doctor protesting that it wasn't safe, and I could have a second heart attack. I couldn't listen though, not interested. My boy was in trouble. I didn't even visit Tony. He was safer in his hospital bed than Gavin was out on the street.

"I can see you're taking no notice, so I might as well give you a lift into town," Peter said, a few steps behind me in the car park. "The car's this way."

I turned and followed him to the blue Astra. "Have you got Gavin's number on your mobile?" I asked him.

"Yeah, here." Peter passed his phone to me, and I caught it, but I almost dropped it and had to snatch the bloody thing to my chest fast, or else it would have probably cracked off the tarmac.

"See? You're not right, man. Your reflexes are fucked. You should have stayed in there."

"Leave it, man." I pressed the phone to my ear as I climbed into Peter's car. "No fucking answer."

"Leave him a voice-mail. Tell him to call you on my phone as soon as he gets the message."

I did as Peter suggested and hoped that Gavin would call soon, so I could tell him to get out of sight fast.

"Where do you want to go first?" Peter asked.

"Take me to Gavin's. He's probably not in... he never fucking is, but I might as well see, just in case."

The beauty with a place like Tilwick is also, in some ways, the biggest problem with it. Generally speaking, in my old neighbourhood, the same families grow up and stay in the area. We went to school together, played football together, went out together. You knew who was riddled with the fucking clap, and you knew who could keep a secret. All very useful. Problem was, they all knew about you, too, so when you're on the up, you're never short of an open hand wanting something from you, and when you're on the downside... well, some fuckers are like sharks, aren't they? They smell the blood from three fucking miles away.

I ran up the steps to Gavin and Gemma's front door and rang the doorbell a couple of times. I turned around to look over the street and sure enough a couple of blinds and curtains twitched. Nosey bastards. I turned back to the door and was just about to push the button for the bell again, when Gemma appeared, a massive smile on her face. She wrapped her arms around my neck and give me a big kiss right on the lips, bless her.

"You should be in hospital, Mister."

"None of the nurses were as bonny as you, so I broke out. I can go back now, a happy man."

"You'd charm Jesus off his cross, you would."

My smile must have slipped, because she knew straight away that something was wrong. She invited me in, and I waved to Peter, who sat in the car with the engine running. I held up two fingers and mouthed two minutes.

"Gemma, listen. I know Gavin's in trouble, and I know it isn't with the landlord."

She dropped to the sofa as though her legs had suddenly turned to jelly. Her eyes fixed on a spot on the carpet and her face drained to chalk white.

"Don't worry, sweetheart. I want to help him. I can get him out of it, but he needs to get back up here and out of sight. Do you know where I can find him?"

"He's out with some of his mates. He said he was going to the Nag's."

"Right, keep trying him on the phone, tell him I'm coming to pick him up."

Gemma already had her phone in her hand as I rushed out the front door. Just as I climbed into Peter's car, I noticed Hugh Graham walking up the street, his usual carefree look on his face, shoulders rolling as he walked. It was clear that the Bettaneys of the world didn't bother him at all.

"Hugh looks like he's on holiday," I said, giving Hugh a wave. We were technically rivals, both making a living slinging coke and weed, but there were plenty of customers and we were old school. We were friends first and foremost. We knew not to get in each other's way. I was tempted to get Peter to pull over so I could ask Hugh about Bettaney and see if he'd had any run-ins with him. I didn't have time, though. I had to get to the Nag's.

"Hugh's been on a fucking permanent holiday since about 1995," Peter said. "Lazy cunt."

"He's not lazy with them fucking fists of his."

The Nag's Head was only a couple of minutes away, but of course, being up a lane, you can't park outside it, so I had to run up from over by the market place. The way my chest tightened, and my breathing rasped, I thought I was up for another heart attack, so I slowed down and walked into the pub. I knew where he would be sitting, as usual, upstairs, where we carried out business on Wednesday nights.

The relief when I saw him sat with a couple of his mates and Tiny Tim, safe and sound... I'll never know relief like it again, I can tell you.

"Come on, get up. We're going."

"What's wrong?" Gavin asked.

"I'll explain later, come on, we're moving." I reached over the table and gripped Gavin's jacket collar. "We're going now."

"He's all right with me, Eddie. I'm keeping an eye on him."

"Tiny, if I fucking see you near any of my family again, I'll kill you, right?"

Tiny stood up, palms raised in objection. "What's this about?"

I grabbed his pointy nose and banged his head back against the wall. "You fucking know what. I'm telling you now, you little fucking grass, you'd better get out of town or you're fucking finished, got it?"

When I released him, blood trickled from his nostrils. I knew I should have put a pint glass into his throat then and there, but I needed to get Gavin away to safety so I could fathom out my next move.

"What the fuck was that about, Dad?" Gavin asked, almost tripping over an uneven paving slab as I ushered him along the street towards Peter's car.

"Just keep moving. I'll explain on the way."

And so I did. I told Gavin about what happened on the moor, and how Tiny must have grassed on us to some of the lads on the force who like to get things done out of uniform, or that he must have at least told Bettaney about it. With my head kicked in and Tony hospitalised and it being a matter of time before either the coppers made us disappear or got some actual evidence to connect us to the death, Bettaney would easily take over our business. "And I don't trust that he's going to just leave you alone. I want you and Gemma to stay in, doors locked, until I get back to you."

Gavin climbed out of the car and leaned his head back in through the door. "Where are you going, Dad?"

"I need to make sure the van's gone. I can't assume Tiny crushed it. If he's held onto it to stitch us up, the coppers'll have what they need if they do come looking for an arrest. Might be his bargaining chip with the coppers. Might use it to get himself off the hook."

We left Gavin at his front door, and Peter motored across town, taking us along the back roads rather than through the town centre. In five minutes, we arrived at the scrap yard. The gate hung open and I smiled. Tiny had saved me the trouble of finding him again later. He must have left the Nag's straight away, jumped into his car and belted down here before I could.

I pointed to the workshop. It looks like a small plane hangar. There's a big retractable door that lowers from the roof, like a big garage door. I told Peter, "Drive past the shop, he's probably down in the yard going for the van."

Peter did as I said, but as we passed the workshop, I realised I was wrong. Through the open door, I saw Tiny's car parked at an angle in the workshop, like he'd raced in there and dumped it in a hurry. I glanced up the metal staircase to the office and saw him in there through one of the windows. It looked like he was in the middle of an argument.

"What do you want to do?" Peter asked.

"Stop the car, let me out. I'll see what's going on up there. You find Tony's van and blow the petrol tank, right?"

"You're going to have to tell me more about that dead copper."

"It's a long story, Peter, and we don't have time now. It was an accident. A bad one. Just trust me. Get this settled and I'll have time to talk about it later."

As I jogged to the foot of the stairs, fire flared up in my chest. I grabbed the handrail and fell onto the first couple of steps. I rolled onto my back, bending my knees and pointing my toes upwards. I'd heard it somewhere that you need to make that sort of shape if you think you're having a heart attack.

I slid down the steps and waited, rubbing my chest, breathing deeply, hoping I could get my pulse to slow down. That was when the glass shattered in the window directly above me. Bits of glass sliced through the air and in among them fell Tiny. I heard the crunch of his forearms shattering when he hit the floor, even over his screams, and fuck me, he was doing plenty of screaming. I heard teeth scatter across the floor like dice.

The office door opened and that's when I heard Bettaney say, "Well look here, signed, sealed and delivered. I thought we'd missed the chance, with you in hospital. Looks like we get to finish the job now."

"Well, you'd fucking better. Because if you don't, you're dead, son."

Bettaney and three of his lads stepped over me and stood there, cool as you like, watching me rub my chest, desperately trying to get my ticker to behave itself.

Tiny moaned and Bettaney told one of his lads to, "Shut that fucker up."

Two of Bettaney's cronies hauled Tiny to his feet, dragging him up by his broken arms. The man screamed like a wounded animal. He'd betrayed me, but I felt genuine pity for the bastard. I would have killed him, but he wouldn't have felt it. Well, not much anyway.

The third man walked over to the compressed air gun, laughing as he pulled the nozzle up off its hook, the hose trailing behind him as he returned to Tiny. Tiny was squealing by that point, crying, begging me to help him, not that I could make out many words with all that blood pissing out of his mouth.

"Shove him over the bonnet," the guy with the air gun said.

"Ooh, it's on now," Bettaney announced.

They pinned Tiny face-down over the car bonnet. They dropped his pants and forced the end of the air gun up his arsehole. If I thought the screams of him being dragged up were bad, they were nothing compared to when that air started inflating his guts. He kicked his legs out and thrashed his head about, but the men held him good and tight. I could see his back rising as he filled with air. Next thing, he just went quiet, and he stopped struggling. When the bloke with the air gun pulled the nozzle out of Tiny's arse, the air escaped and forced a thick mass of blood, chunks of gut and shit out, like a horrendous wet fart.

"What did yeh think of that, Eddie?" Bettaney asked, his mouth curled into a smug grin. "I hope you liked it, because you're next."

They dumped Tiny on the ground and came for me. I backed up on the staircase, no longer worried about slowing my heart rate down. My pulse throbbed in my ears. It felt like my veins were going to blow and blood was going to burst out of my head. On the stairs, they could only come at me one at a time and when the first approached, I rammed a long triangle of glass down into his shoulder, just behind his collarbone. It sliced the fuck out of my fingers, almost to the bone, but I got that cunt a blinder, snapped the glass off and he collapsed back onto his mates.

Then there was an explosion out in the yard.

"What the fuck was that?" Bettaney ran to the front of the workshop as I knocked his three cronies tumbling over each other, and chased after him. We collided and fell into the yard.

My blood-soaked fingers slipped over his face, so I couldn't get a good enough hold on his head to smash it against the floor. I should add, my second rule doesn't count when I'm down on the floor with the other man. It's all fair game when we're both down there. He growled with effort or anger, I don't know which, but he clawed at my face and tried to get his fingers into my eye sockets. I bit one of his hands and tore a piece off the fucker, spitting it aside as he screamed and drew back, covering the wound. I head-butted him and broke his nose.

Only two of his lads were in any shape to fight and they had caught up to me. They dragged me off their boss and when Bettaney stood, he had a knife in his hand. It was like a little pen-knife thing. Well, it might have been little, but when he jammed it into my right shoulder, it hurt like a bastard all the same.

He pressed the blade to my throat, and that's when Peter roared over with his car. He caught a glimpse of me and snatched the steering wheel aside just in time to avoid running me over, but that meant he missed Bettaney, too. Instead, he took out the bloke to my right, who flew over the bonnet, across the roof and hit the ground like a rag-doll.

The next thing I knew, my head smacked the ground. I didn't even feel myself fall. I was standing one second, and on the deck the next. Peter grabbed my jacket and shook me, shouting in my face... fucked if I know what he was saying, but it woke me up and I took his hand, and he helped me back to my feet.

Bettaney had escaped with one of his lads, the ratty-faced little fucker who had killed Tiny. We left the last two cunts bleeding to death, and Tiny's body along with them.

From the backseat, I told Peter to get the ciggie lighter burning. When it clicked out, he passed it back to me over his shoulder. The tip glowed like a cowboy's branding iron, til it disappeared into the hole Bettaney had opened with the knife. The smell of my flesh and blood cooking almost knocked me sick. The smell, or maybe the pain, I'm not sure which it was. By fuck, it hurt.

Little did I know, it wasn't the last time I'd smell flesh cooking that day. I leaned back on the car seat and the ceiling seemed to spin around. It felt like I was going down a plughole, swirling around the edge, about to slip away for good.

Peter said something about Bettaney getting a phone call, before he drove off. He said Bettaney told the person on the phone to keep him there. Whatever the fuck he said after that, I don't know. The chest pains took over, creeping up past my burning shoulder, and that was me out for the count again.

<hr>

I woke when the engine stopped, and Peter helped me out of the car. He supported me under my left shoulder and dragged me up the steps to Gavin and Gemma's front door. He knocked and it sounded like a machine-gun going off inside my head. The key rattled in the lock, and the door just fucking flew open. I had a split second to glance up and then I heard this twang noise and a soft thump. It took a second for my eyes to focus, but once they did, I saw one of those bastards from the scrap yard standing on the staircase, with a crossbow in his hands.

Peter became a dead-weight, and I turned to see a short bolt sticking out of his left cheek. He fell down the stairs and I had no choice but to let him fall, or else I was going over with him and we'd both be fucking dead then.

One of them had to be behind the door, to have opened it so fast and let the cunt with the crossbow take his shot, so the first thing I did was barge in, smacking the door back hard against the man hidden behind it. I say man... these are fucking kids compared to me. I slammed it again to be sure, but I had to contend with the crossbow kid straight away.

The thing with these younger ones and their obsession with weapons instead of using their hands is that it makes life a lot easier. While he couldn't seem to get a bolt into place quick enough, I was on him. I knocked the crossbow up into his face and threw my whole weight onto him. I snatched that bolt out of his hand and jammed it down into his left eye, bursting it and driving it back into his skull, right back into his brain.

I swung the crossbow round into the face of the twat who had hidden behind the door. He had just stepped out in time to catch the full force, smashing his nose sideways. I jumped back down the stairs, knocking him against the front door, and slamming the door shut behind him. I grabbed his throat and squeezed, but the sneaky little prick got hold of my little finger and bent it back, twisting until it snapped. The pain was like lightning, but worse still, with that fucking slice I'd taken through my hand with the glass in the workshop, well, there wasn't much left to keep the thing on once he snapped the bone. So that was me less a finger right there.

Have you ever had pain so bad that you get this whistling in your ears? No? Well, I have. A few times in fact, and that was one of those times, but I knew if I stopped, I would collapse again and maybe I wouldn't get up. I smashed my knuckles into this little prick's windpipe and crushed it. I let go of him as he tried his best to get a breath, but once he hit the floor, as much as I would have liked to finish the fucker, you know my rules. I think he was the ratty little bastard who killed Tiny. I wanted to finish him, but I had to move on to find Gavin and Gemma.

It was then that I noticed the smell. Singed hair, burning skin again... through the whistling in my ears I heard this sort of a... like a dry, rasping cry, but it was muffled. It wasn't a proper scream, but you could tell the person was trying to screech, but for some reason they couldn't get the noise out properly. Then the noise got louder, but not much louder... there was panic there.

I knew something else, too. I knew it was Gavin.

I reached the top of the stairs and another of Bettaney's lads rushed me, this one from out of the bathroom. That smell of cooking flesh made my stomach turn over, as the lad got a good jab onto my jaw and my teeth clashed together. White lights floated about in front of my eyes, and I almost fell back down the bloody stairs. I grabbed a picture frame off the wall. Couldn't tell you what the photo was, but I smashed the frame off this lad's head and jabbed him two, three times with the jagged wood and glass. His cheek split apart, flashing all his teeth right up the left side. I dropped him with a perfect right cross.

That's when I stormed into the bathroom. The whole fucking place was drenched in blood. All over the floor. Right up the tiles. Gavin was lying in the bath. They'd wrapped the shower curtain around his head, but I knew it was him. Newcastle United tattoo up on his left arm.

Bettaney stood over him, pointing that little penknife pointed at me. I glanced down into the bath. Bettaney had used that knife to saw right into... he'd fucking gutted him.

Gavin. My lad. My little lad. There were no rules anymore. What was the point? These young 'uns have no rules. Why should I?

The sneaky little cunt lashed out with that knife at the same time I threw a punch. The blade slid into my fist, and I nearly lost two more fingers, but the blade slipped up over the bone and snipped the tendons. Might as well have chopped the fucking fingers off, they're useless now. I got my left hand to him, gave him a cross and his head smacked against the wall. I grabbed his hair and smashed his face against the tiles, again, again... I couldn't tell you rightly how many times I smacked his head on there, but the tiles cracked away and I kept going, smashing a hole into the plaster. After a while, I changed tack and banged his head down onto the sink. The sink collapsed after a few smacks, so I turned him onto the toilet bowl, and I just kept going.

I ruined that sneaky little bastard. His skull sounded like an eggshell when it finally cracked open. When I flushed the toilet, one of his eyeballs, and it must have been about half of his evil little fucking brain, got washed away.

I crawled out of the bathroom and into the main bedroom, where I thought I might have found Gemma, but she wasn't there. I tried to follow that smell, the smell of burning skin and hair and I dreaded what I was going to find. All I could think about was them raping her and torturing her, while I was unconscious at the yard.

Someone else had been in the house while Bettaney was at the scrap yard dealing with Tiny. One of them might have gone in just after I last saw Gemma. Maybe I delivered Gavin right to them. Maybe they'd started on Gemma before Bettaney even got up there. Bettaney had only told them to keep him there, when he spoke on the phone, after all. He'd wanted to do Gavin himself.

The door to the little spare bedroom was open. This was the room they called Gemma's walk-in wardrobe. The lassie had so many clothes and pairs of shoes, they needed their own room. It was where she kept her make-up. It was where she kept her hair dryer and all that shit.

My heart was already broken with what I'd seen in the bathroom... but I think the last threads of my sanity went with what I saw in that bedroom. Her legs wide open, tied to the clothes rails on the left and right, hands tied behind her back. A pair of socks stuffed into her mouth so hard her front teeth had smashed out. I saw things on that lassie I was never meant to see... they'd ripped her top open. Bruises and bites all over her tits. They'd stubbed tabs out on her, the bastards. They'd stuffed one of those curling wands up her fanny, switched it on and left it. They'd fucking cooked her.

It must have been the same one who did Tiny in... he seemed to like sticking things up people. I remembered I'd left him at the bottom of the stairs. He had to go.

Staggering to the stairs, my legs swayed and buckled like I'd drank about twenty pints on an empty stomach. The little rat fuck took one look at me, then ran out the front door, just as my legs finally gave out. I threw up, clinging to the banister, trying not to topple down the stairs as my second heart attack got into full swing.

It was Inspector Pitt who cleaned it all up. Harold Fenwick will have been looking over his shoulder from the council offices, wanting it all as hush-hush as possible. Not that you could keep all that mess quiet, but they did their best. I took a bit of time in the mental hospital, rather than prison. That was the bargain struck to keep the peace.

They got the crossbow bolt out of Peter's face easily enough. He was never a looker anyway, but now he's less a few teeth and his left eye isn't much good. His wife and kids won't speak to me anymore.

Tony healed up eventually. Got out the hospital. He went to the Nag's with Peter one Wednesday night and found one of Hugh Graham's sons sat there dealing, with Hugh sitting in the corner, keeping an eye on everything. Tony knew better than to say anything, he and Peter just turned round and walked out.

Shows you where Bettaney got his stones from, doesn't it? Old Hugh has his back the whole time, or at least he loaded the bullets and let Bettaney fire the gun, if you like. The Grahams run the whole weed and powder game in Tilwick now. The coppers say nowt. Must be getting plenty money for the Christmas party if you know what I mean.

I had prayed to Mammon every night when I was in the nut house, that when I got out, I would have the strength to put all this right. But if there is a Mammon, he's smiling on the Grahams. All that money running through their hands. All the blood.

What fingers I've got left, I don't have the guts to lift them against the Grahams, although every now and then I feel like saying "fuck it". I could just go down swinging. For now, I'll keep quiet, bide my time, have the odd pint.

And when the time comes, I'll show them what a hard man really fucking is.

12

— · —

ABOUT 'GHOSTS OF CHRISTMAS PAST'

I've already told you a little bit about my work in the care industry, and here again is a story that stems from that connection. The mind, complex piece of machinery that it is, can do some scary things as it breaks down. Various conditions grouped under the term *dementia* can result in the afflicted hallucinating. Sometimes the visions are innocent enough, traces, perhaps of old memories intruding on the present. Other times they are upsetting. And sometimes, they can be confused for the supernatural, and downright terrifying.

I remember one lady who told me about the drummer boy she kept seeing in hospital. A little boy, she told me, in a blue and white uniform, dirty from the battlefield. She said the boy had a kind, innocent face, and though she saw him move around her hospital bed, she never heard his voice nor ever heard him beat the drum. Convinced he was a benign, peaceful spirit, she took enjoyment from his visitations.

The old lady even connected it to her condition. Not that she was hallucinating a character she probably saw in a movie, or on the side of an old biscuit tin, but that she had never been able to view departed spirits until dementia took hold. To challenge her would have been futile. Why should she not have the belief that her inescapable, debilitating illness makes her somehow special? My job was not to feed her fantasy, but it also wasn't my job to challenge it. This woman was not going to get better, so I couldn't see the harm in letting things lie, since she was suffering no distress from her belief.

Some would ask, what if it wasn't just a hallucination? What if she was right? But then, why did she only see that one spirit, and only in that one place, the hospital? A modern hospital, at that, and one not on the grounds of say, a field hospital in the Peninsula War? Because that's where, it seemed, her vision was rooted. She had probably been watching *Waterloo* or an episode of *Sharpe.*

But one can't escape the notion that while she had a vision locked in her mind in that hospital setting, what if the vision had been malign? What if that menacing vision appeared within her home? How terrifying it would be, to be plagued by an inner demon in the truest sense - a spirit whose energy has no anchor in the outside world, where it could perhaps be exorcised or bargained with, *appeased,* perhaps? What if the only escape was further brain damage, or even death, the two things everyone around you is trying to prevent. That, dear reader, is a true horror.

Or let's look at the fanciful notion that dementia enabled her to tune into the dead and see some horrific spirit. How do you escape something your brain is now rewired to see? And would those around you believe your experience? Would they not dismiss it as a hallucination, a symptom of your failing health?

We might lose a lot before the end, folks, but if your luck is in, you'll remember happiness, love, good times and hopefully only guilt and grief will slip away. With this in mind, I invite you to visit with...

13

GHOSTS OF CHRISTMAS PAST

"Bloody hell," Teddy shouted, flinging the cushions across the sofa. He glanced at the clock on the mantelpiece and tried to calculate how long he had spent searching for his keys. Rubbing a hand over his thinning grey hair, he turned his head, scanning the room, trying to spot a likely hiding place for the mischievous little bastards.

He glanced at the clock again. There was something to go to. Something he needed to hurry up and get to. It's 10 O' clock, he thought, cheerfully. Time for a cuppa.

He rinsed out his mug, shuffled to the fridge, opened it and reached for the milk. But it was gone. "Where the bloody hell is the milk?" he muttered.

He found it, almost immediately. There on the table, next to two bowls. One full of soggy cereal, another empty, having already been eaten. The scene was all at once familiar and alien to him. "Elsie," he muttered, staring at the full bowl.

Can't be, he thought. Elsie's gone. How long has it been?

Next to the empty bowl sat the keys he had spent all that time searching for.

Here all along. "Well, Elsie. You tricked me again, old girl." Teddy had taken to doing that since Elsie's death. When he was lonely, it filled the silences. Not full conversations, but the odd few words here and there, just in case she happened to be watching over him.

He picked up the keys and turned to admire the view of the garden through the window in the upper half of the back door. This was his view every mealtime. He plodded out to the coat hanger next to the front door and grabbed his thick coat. He pressed his feet down into his dark green wellington boots and returned to the back door. Fumbling with the keys, he tried to unlock the door, but the mechanism would not budge. He tried another key, but that did not even fit into the keyhole.

"Bloody thing," he mumbled, returning the first key to the lock and rattling it back and forth. He snatched at the door handle and the door mechanism withdrew, allowing the door to open. Wasn't locked in the first place.

He looked back at the bowls of cereal. Who else has been in here? Someone's let themselves in. Been helping themselves to my food.

From the corner of Teddy's peripheral vision, he detected movement, just a shift of light and shadow, as of someone peering in at the kitchen door, then darting back into the passageway once more.

"Who's there?" Teddy called. He tried to freeze the shadow's shape in his memory, determined to make sense of it. The shape was fast-moving, small, about the height of a child. "Get back here, you little sod."

Probably one of the neighbours' kids playing a prank.

Teddy clumped across the kitchen floor in his wellingtons, hoping to catch sight of the little bugger so he could determine which room he was hiding in.

No footsteps on the stairs, no doors opening or closing... Teddy reasoned he must be hiding in the lounge, and stepped through the doorway to see. He assumed it was a boy he was chasing. Girls tended not to do this sort of thing.

"Come out, and I'll let you go without telling your parents. If you make me chase you, I'll be very cross and march you over to your mum."

There was no response. Teddy crept along the back of the sofa, trying to peer over the arm at the end closest to the lounge window, but he could not get a clear view from that angle, so he kept stepping forward as quietly as he could, hoping to give this child a good scare that would make them run out of the house and not bother him again.

Must be a bloody small boy, he thought as he got closer to the end of the sofa and still could see no sign of the child. He suddenly bent down, leaning over and around the end of the sofa, exclaiming, "Got you, you little bugger."

But there was nobody there.

A door slammed in the passage. It was close to the front door, but with no letterbox flap rattling, it could only be the door to the toilet installed years ago to save he and Elsie traipsing off up all those stairs every time they needed the loo.

Moments later, Teddy slapped the palm of his right hand against the locked toilet door. "Come out. Come out. Unlock this door at once."

He paused, listening for a response or some sound from little room's occupant. Nothing.

"Come out at once, you little bastard," he snapped, slamming the underside of his balled, bony fist against the door. "Come out now."

The front door handle wiggled, immediately to his left. Puzzled, he snatched the black handle and shouted, "Got friends coming to terrorise me now, eh? Well they're not getting in here."

The front door locks withdrew and Teddy fought against the force being applied to the door handle from the other side.

"Get away, you nasty bugger. I've got your friend trapped in here."

A familiar voice from outside called to him, "Dad, what's going on? Who's in there with you?"

Teddy released the front door handle and stepped away. "Carol?"

"Let me in, Dad," Carol replied.

"Okay, I'm clear of the door. There's one of the neighbours' little bastards in here, trying to frighten me."

The front door opened and Carol's face appeared, creased with concern. "Are you sure, Dad?"

"Try the toilet door. The little sod's locked himself in."

Carol pressed the handle down and the door opened immediately. In the room, all was as expected – more or less. The toilet and small washbasin occupied the room as they should, but what struck Carol was the dirty streaks in the toilet bowl, and yellow splatters of dried urine on the white plastic toilet seat. The washbasin was badly in need of a clean, too, with limescale and grime marks coating the porcelain, and a growth of mildew around the tap heads and plughole.

Carol's green eyes moistened as she turned back to her father, who stood with his eyebrows raised.

"Well, who's in there?"

"Nobody, Dad. It's empty."

"Can't be. I was locked out."

"Look, Dad, we'll talk about it in a minute. Why don't you go and put the kettle on?"

"Carol, someone's playing silly buggers with me. Trying to frighten an old man, and I'm not having it."

Carol sighed and stepped up to him, wrapping her arms around him and giving him a squeeze. "Give us a cuddle, Dad. Just calm down. Let's have a nice day and we'll get your decorations up, eh? I thought we were going to have a lovely time putting that tree up?"

"Christmas tree? Elsie, the kids are all grown up."

"Carol, Dad."

"What?"

"Never mind. Anyway, my kids aren't grown up."

"Well, I never see them," Teddy moaned.

"Edward McIntyre," Carol said, dropping her voice an octave or two, adopting the role of parent, "I'll have you know that Miley was round on Sunday to see you and she was here twice more during the week. I know the boys aren't great at dropping by, but what can I do?"

Teddy grinned, his eyes narrowing with pride as thoughts of his mischievous teenage grandsons filled his mind. "Chasing girls, I'll bet."

"You're not wrong. Now listen, I'm lucky I'm not dying of thirst here. You stick the kettle on and I'll find that nice Christmas CD, eh?"

"Alright," Teddy replied, his voice drenched in mock reluctance. He loved it when Carol got her take-charge head on. He would never admit it, but it had always helped him to focus on what needed to be done.

In the kitchen, Teddy opened the olive-green, vintage Ringtons tea tin and dropped two teabags into the kettle. He pressed down the button to start the boil, making sure the little blue LED came on, as sometimes he had a habit of not making the button click into the on position.

He took two mugs from the little wooden mug tree next to the chrome toaster, then turned to find the milk.

On the floor, a boy of eight years old lay outstretched, breathing bubbles of blood in deep, rasping gurgles. Ribs poked through his shirt and his left arm and leg lay twisted around to an impossible angle. The child's face was coloured a ghastly bluish-grey, highlighted with deep, purple welts.

Carol raced into the kitchen, hearing her father's scream and the clatter of him falling to the floor, his head striking the handles of the kitchen drawers on his way down. She found her father laid out unconscious on the cold linoleum, twitching and muttering.

She cried out, snatched the telephone from the charging stand in the kitchen and called for an ambulance.

"Shaun, I thought you'd want to know... he's getting out today," Carol said, bracing herself for Shaun's reaction to her call.

"Why would you think I'd even care?" Shaun asked.

Although she could not see him, Carol could imagine that impatient, tight-lipped look on her brother's face. "I just thought that maybe... well, maybe the kids should see him."

"And maybe not. I don't want that miserable old bastard having any influence in their lives."

"Shaun, that's not fair. He's an old man. I don't... I don't think he has much longer left. I thought he'd had a stroke, for Christ's sake."

"Well, turns out he didn't, so why don't we just deal with the facts instead of what you thought might have happened?"

Carol gripped the phone ever tighter. "Shaun, there's no need for you to take it out on me. Whatever passed between you and him shouldn't make me the villain of the piece, just because I still love him."

"Even after he drove Mum to her grave?"

"We don't know that, Shaun."

"I bloody well do know it."

"Oh, Shaun... he was good enough for Mum to stay with him all those years so just give it a rest. For all we know it was that fight you both had in front of her that finished her off."

"Oh, so I killed Mum, now? Fuck off Carol."

Carol stared at the receiver in utter disbelief, as though this thing represented her brother and he would see her expression. The dial-tone droned. Shaun was gone.

Carol's husband, Pete, appeared at the kitchen doorway. "No joy, then?"

"He's so unreasonable, Pete. He hates him." Carol clenched her jaw and tried to keep the tears burning in her eyes, but her efforts were soon overcome and fat, hot tears streamed down her cheeks.

Pete lunged across the room to be with her instantly. His muscular arms wrapped around her shoulders and he pulled her head onto his chest. The fluffy woollen fabric of her jumper grated against his stubble with a series of tiny snags as he nuzzled into her neck. "He'll come around. He just needs some time to think on it."

"He won't, Pete. He just wants him dead and out of the way and that's it."

"I'm sure it isn't as simple as that," Pete said, rubbing her back, soothingly.

His hands had the rough, dry texture common among plasterers, but his heart was as soft and as warm as almost anyone Carol had known. "I love you, Pete."

"I love you too, little woman."

Carol's back arched slightly, drawing her head away from Pete. He released his grip. Her moment of vulnerability passed, and now she was returning to her usual state of having everything in order and nothing getting to her. She sniffed, then wiped the tears from her eyes and cheeks with the heel of her hand. Next came the smile. It was a weak smile to begin with, but Pete knew exactly what she would do next, and she did it. She puffed out her cheeks, squeezing her lips tight and let air escape from a tiny gap until her cheeks deflated. By the time she set foot in the lounge, her face, flushed with tears at first, had begun to calm and return to Carol's normal tanned complexion.

"Wow, you got that up fast," Carol exclaimed, staring at the tattily dressed Christmas tree. The distribution of the decorations was lopsided and the tree looked to be heavy on the right side. The white fairy lights seemed to favour the right side too and so half of the tree was in darkness.

"Well, you fuss on with it too much. It doesn't have to take all that long."

"And I'm about to fuss on with it again. You're a lovely, smooth plasterer Pete, but you know sweet bugger-all about dressing a Christmas tree," Carol said, chuckling. "Bless you for trying, though."

"And I don't feel patronised at all," Pete replied, smiling. He had, after all, never thought for a moment she would leave the tree as it was. "I suppose I should just put the packaging back in the cupboard, then?"

"That'd be a big help, love. A huge help." Carol had already begun untangling the tinsel and lights. "I just want it all to look lovely for him when he gets back, you know? I want it to look just like when Mum was still alive. It might just keep his brain… I don't know… present, you know?"

"Have they said it's Alzheimer's?" Pete asked.

"No, they haven't diagnosed anything, but I think it is. They've only this morning ruled out diabetes. They thought it might have been a UTI, he was so hysterical on the ward when he went in, but it's not that, either."

"I'm not an expert, but it's not sounding too good, is it?" Pete added.

"They'll only say it's dementia if they know it's absolutely nothing else. I mean... hallucinating... I heard people can do that at late stages, but wouldn't we have noticed him struggling sooner?"

Pete shrugged. "My uncle had Alzheimer's, and nobody knew until he was at a quite advanced stage. He must've known something wasn't right and he was either hiding it, or frightened to talk about it, or whatever. Downstairs in the house looked okay, but like you found with your dad, it's upstairs where all the problems were."

"Keeping up appearances," Carol said. "I couldn't believe it when I came in though, Pete. He was wearing his raincoat and wellies, but over his pyjamas. He would never go out like that if he was well."

"Teabags in the kettle and all that. Breakfast made for your mum." Pete sighed and shook his head at the catalogue of symptoms of his beloved father-in-law's mental decline.

Carol turned away from the tree and looked at her husband. "For Mum, or he forgot he'd eaten it and made himself two breakfasts. What worries me is, what happens if he does that with his tablets?"

"Jesus, I didn't think about that." Pete started to scoop up the cardboard and plastic boxes for the baubles and festive ornaments. "Are you sure he won't come and stay with us? Can't we just tell him it's for over Christmas?"

"Then what? Keep him locked in? If it is dementia, which obviously it looks like, it's better for him to be here, where his surroundings are familiar and all of his possessions are."

"Fair enough," Pete accepted. "I just hate the thought of him sleeping here on his own. It sounds like old Teddy was really frightened last week. I can't even imagine him like that – I know he's your dad and all, but I've known him a long time. He's a tough old sod."

"He's the worst one in the world for accepting help though, Pete. You know what he's like."

"As stubborn as his daughter."

"Cheeky bugger." Carol tutted and sighed. "Did you deliberately put this fairy on backwards?"

"I never did, did I? I was sure I had it the right way around."

"Don't say you're getting it, too?"

"Ooh, Christ. Don't say that, Carol. Just take me out to the woods and shoot me if I ever get that."

Every inch of Teddy's body trembled as he walked slowly, gently up the path towards his front door, Carol and Pete on either arm to support him. "I wish I could just hurry up. I don't want the neighbours to see me like this," he muttered, wishing that the darkening mid-afternoon was a little darker still, to mask him from prying eyes.

Neither Carol nor Pete spoke, they simply kept moving, concerned by the tremors vibrating through them from the bony arms of their burden.

Teddy's eyes snapped onto the master bedroom window and he stopped in his tracks, no longer seeming to care about the neighbours seeing him. His thoughts had overridden his embarrassment.

"What is it, Dad?" Carol asked, following the line of his vision, trying to ascertain what concerned him so suddenly.

"It's nothing."

Carol applied a gentle pressure to her father's arm, urging him to take a step. "Let's get inside where it's warm, eh?"

"Okay," Teddy said, but his heart was not in it. He glanced at the front door, then back to the upstairs window.

When Teddy stepped forwards again, Pete was not prepared and apologized, quickly shifting his feet to match Teddy and Carol's movements. He kept glancing up at the window, too. Teddy had not said it, but Pete thought he knew what the old man had seen. He noticed a shape moving between the vertical blinds, too.

Once inside, Carol took her father's coat and prepared his slippers as he unfastened his shoes and took them off. "Thanks, Carol," he said, speaking quietly, as though afraid to disturb someone, perhaps someone asleep in the house.

"I'll get the kettle on, eh? Get us all a hot drink," Pete offered, desperate to have a moment alone to gather his thoughts.

"Wait one second, Dad," Carol said, holding up a finger, a playful, happy look across her face. She slipped into the lounge and emerged once more a moment later. "Come on, then. Come and see Santa's Grotto."

Teddy allowed a thin smile to play over his lips at the sight of the Christmas tree. The white light reflected off the tree ornaments, sparkling purple, red, green and gold. Tartan bows hung from the ends of the branches and little ornamental buildings formed a tiny village on the coffee table, upon which was draped a white runner, suggestive of a blanket of snow. Apertures within the village buildings allowed flickering light to escape from within, creating a scene of cozy cottages and a village church. Tiny ornamental villagers wrapped in winter dress, grouped as couples, and choirs of carol singers, a vintage car and snow-covered telephone box made the scene complete.

"Oh, this is a lovely surprise," Teddy said.

"And don't worry about the little buildings, there are no candles in there. I found these great little flickering lights that fit in perfectly and they're on calculator batteries, so no risk of a fire."

"Ahhh," Teddy said in wonder.

"So there's no excuse for not putting them on, right?" Carol insisted.

"Aye, Captain." Teddy raised a bruised hand to his battered forehead in a mock salute.

"So... what do you think?"

"Well, I still think it's for children, all this Christmas malarkey, but you've done a lovely job yet again, Elsie."

"Carol."

"Eh?"

"Carol, Dad."

"She's asleep upstairs, Elsie. I didn't want to wake her."

"Come and sit down, Dad," Carol said, leading her father to his favourite chair. "Just relax. It's Christmas Eve. I've got a nice bit of cottage pie for your dinner, and then tomorrow, Pete's going to pick us up and take you over to our house."

Teddy frowned. "This is our house, you daft woman."

The rattling of spoons and mugs on the tea tray announced Pete's arrival before he could be seen. "Here we go," he said, setting the tray down at the end of the coffee table.

"Which one's mine, Shaun? And which one's your Mum's?"

Pete glanced at Carol wide-eyed, showing the palms of his hands to her, with an expression that said *what do I say to that?*

Carol recalled somewhere hearing that you should try to orientate people with dementia back to reality if possible and so she reminded her father who they both were.

"Well, where's your mother?"

"You don't remember what happened to Mum? It was eight years ago, Dad. Can't you remember?"

Teddy frowned, then said, "She died, didn't she? Shaun shouldn't have told her about that boy."

"What are you on about, Dad?" Carol glanced nervously at Pete.

Teddy looked at Pete and his eyes narrowed with a sudden fury. "You shouldn't have told your mother about that boy, you little bastard."

"Teddy, it's me. It's Pete."

"I know who you are, you bastard." Teddy pressed his hands down into the arms of the chair, shuffling his backside closer to the edge, preparing to launch himself upright. "And you killed your mother, right? You should never have opened your big, stupid mouth and it wouldn't have worried her."

"Come on, Dad. Calm down. That's not Shaun, it's Pete. Your son-in-law. My husband. You remember?"

Teddy frowned again, staring into Carol's eyes like a lost child. "The plasterer?"

"Yes, Pete the plasterer."

"He's a good bloke." Teddy relaxed back into the chair and smiled at Pete, calm once more. "You're a lovely dad to those kids, Pete."

"Thanks, Teddy," Pete said, breathing a heavy sigh of relief as he sat down. He reached for the first mug of tea. "I'll be mu- I'll just get these... Here, Teddy, this one's for you. Just how you like it."

Carol sat down on the sofa, where the arm of her seat almost touched the arm of her father's, so she could be seen and heard by him more easily. "Dad, I do think we need to talk about you getting a bit of help in, you know."

"I don't need a babysitter."

"I know you don't Dad, but can you remember what happened?"

"What do you mean, what happened? To the boy?"

"To you, Dad. Can you remember why you were in hospital?"

"I had a bloody fall, didn't I?"

"That's right. But I think you fell because you were very tired. I think the house is getting a bit much for you."

"You think I'm still drinking, don't you?" Teddy growled. "Come on out and say it."

"That's not it, Dad. I believe you."

"Not a drop in five years," Teddy announced.

"It's longer than that, Dad. It's about eight years. You've done really well, haven't you?"

"I didn't need all these meetings and that Alcoholics Anonymous. Did it myself. I tipped the last bottle down the sink and said goodbye, and that was that."

"You did, Dad. I'm proud of you."

Pete had tuned out of the exchange. He had spent his entire time in the house wondering if he should explore upstairs. He knew it was next to impossible that someone could be up there, and that was what made him think something unnatural was going on. It was not helped by Teddy's random outbursts about his dead wife and a boy, he had to admit. The whole situation was creepy. Sometimes the old Teddy was sat there in front of him, and sometimes it was like a different person, wearing Teddy like a suit of clothes.

A creak on the stairs caught his attention. He turned and stared at the lounge door. "Did you hear that, Carol?"

"Is someone in here, again?" Teddy asked.

"Again?" Pete asked.

Carol rested a placating hand on her father's arm. "Dad thought someone was in the house the other day, before his accident."

"They were here, alright. That boy was running around in here, playing tricks on me. Moving things and locking the door."

"That's enough, Dad. I think we should finish these cuppas, and you can come to ours." Carol turned to Pete and lowered her voice as she said, "Look, I'll stay with him, I'll be able to calm him better than you can. Could you grab that overnight bag in the passage, throw the clothes in there into the laundry basket, and whatever you take out, replace it with fresh and that'll do him for a couple of days?"

Pete glanced at the lounge door again. "No problem."

"What's wrong, Pete?" Carol asked. "Is Dad's story spooking you out?"

"No, don't be daft." Pete placed his mug back on the tray and stepped out into the passage. He scooped up the navy blue cloth and leather overnight bag and switched on the staircase light. The bulb illuminated for only a second before the light clicked off again. "Not the bulb," Pete muttered. He pressed the switch again and the light returned. "Oh," he said, chirpily. He was three steps up before he realised that if the bulb had not blown, then the light must have been switched off from the landing.

Don't be bloody stupid, he thought. He pressed on up the stairs. As soon as he stepped onto the landing, he heard a crunch and felt something snap underfoot. He found the fairy from the top of the Christmas tree crushed, with its left arm and leg twisted around at impossible angles and sharp shards of plastic jutting out of the white gown it wore. "Brilliant," he muttered. Like everything else about Christmas in this house, since her mother died, the ornament had sentimental value to Carol. He knew he was going to get it in the neck for this one.

In the lounge, Carol placed the used mugs on the tray and said, "Dad, I'm just going to wash these up and then I think we'll head over to our house."

"I'm fine where I am," Teddy replied.

"Dad, just... trust me."

"Do I have to spell it out, Carol? I don't want to leave. This is my home and I want to spend bloody Christmas in it with your mother."

"But she's gone, Dad."

A tear slid down Teddy's cheek. "She's not, Carol. She's not to me. I talk to her when I need someone to talk to. I don't want to be at your house, you'll think I'm away and senile. You'll think I'm talking to myself, but I fancy she can hear me still."

"Dad-"

"Don't Dad me, Carol," Teddy snapped. He shuffled forwards to the edge of his chair once more and rose to his feet on shaky legs. He grabbed a picture of his wife from the mantelpiece. "She's here, Carol, and I want to be near her and it's nobody's business but mine what I want to do."

Teddy stared at the Christmas tree and somehow the scent of a roasting turkey came to his nostrils. He saw Elsie carrying baby Carol into the lounge and Shaun's cowboy hat peeking over the top of the sofa, where he hid, ready to ambush his father with his new cap-gun.

"Don't frighten the baby with that gun, Shaun. Don't frighten your sister with it," Teddy said.

Carol reached out and touched her father's hand. "Dad? I'm right here."

Upstairs, Pete pushed open the bedroom door and immediately felt the temperature drop. The hairs on his arms stood on end, desperately trying to retain his body's warmth. A tingling sensation crept over his scalp. It felt like a hand, but a hand constructed purely of static, pressing down on him, stealing his energy, causing his legs to buckle. "Carol," he cried, "Carol, get out of here."

Carol heard Pete shout, but could not make out the words, just the distressed tone. She raced from the lounge, leaving her father to his imaginings. Bounding up the stairs, calling out to her husband, the broken tree fairy caught her attention for a second and she tutted just before she rounded the newel post and stopped dead at her father's bedroom door.

It took her brain a few seconds to register the particulars of the scene before her, but the certainty was that Pete lay unconscious on the floor. What her mind struggled to reconcile was the air above her husband. A small, black, human-shaped figure, seemingly constructed of mist or smoke, stood with legs apart over Pete's body in a posture suggesting victory over him. With each passing second, the figure's form dissipated, like drops of ink in water, swirling and diluting until no trace remained.

Carol crouched at her husband's side, calling his name, shaking his shoulders as some of the first aid training she had sat through at work came back to her. She placed her ear at his mouth and immediately both felt and heard his breaths. Satisfied that Pete was going to survive, she manoeuvred his right arm and leg, rolling him into the recovery position.

She glanced up at the bedside cabinet and saw the telephone there. She snatched it up and was about to dial 999 when the phone rang, and she answered the call. Carol recognised Shaun's voice immediately.

"Listen, are you still at Dad's?" Shaun asked, his tone friendly and much calmer than in their conversation that morning.

"Yeah. Shaun, I have to go. Something's happened to Pete... I can't explain it. There's something really wrong going on in this house."

"I know."

"What?"

"I know all about it. It's the little boy, isn't it?"

"How the hell-?"

"Just stay there. Don't go anywhere. I'm coming over."

The line went dead. Carol checked Pete over once more, he seemed to be in a deep sleep, so she pulled the duvet from her father's bed and draped it over him. She made an unspoken promise to check on Pete every couple of minutes and if he seemed to deteriorate, she would call for an ambulance immediately, whether Shaun was there or not.

Her father's cries from the lounge drove her back downstairs.

Teddy stared at the tiny, illuminated village and the car parked in the snow. He saw a tiny model boy twisted and bleeding before the vehicle. Crimson leaked into the white table runner, so much blood for such a tiny body.

"Dad, what's wrong?" Carol asked.

"I had to have a drink with them. It was the done thing back then. It was Christmas... I was the shop steward. And I told them, I told them it was just the one."

"Dad, what are you talking about? What happened?"

"You had to. They called you a queer if you didn't drink with them. Didn't matter if you had family or not. I wasn't having them calling me that every day. I told them just the one, and I'd get 'em in. But then they brought another round over and another one."

"What is this, Dad?"

Teddy seemed not to hear his daughter. His mind was elsewhere, in another time, another Christmas Eve.

"I only had to drive a mile and a half, I thought I would be all right."

"Dad, did you hurt someone?" Carol asked, placing a hand on her father's shoulder.

The front door opened and Shaun strode into the lounge. "All right, Dad, let's get you upstairs into your bed."

"Wait a minute, Shaun. He's telling me something."

"He needs a rest. The ramblings of a demented old man aren't worth the trouble of him being tired." Shaun wrapped an arm around his father's shoulders, guiding him from the room. "Where's Pete?"

"He's upstairs. Something happened. He collapsed or something. He's in Dad's room."

"Okay, well we need him out of there. Go and see if you can wake him," Shaun suggested.

Carol hurried upstairs, frustrated at Shaun interrupting her father's story.

"What are you doing here, Shaun?" Teddy asked.

"I've come to help you, Dad," Shaun replied.

"Mum will go mad if she knows you've come here... Playing pool? Don't give me that... You're here to get a sly drink. I was your age once too, you know. I know all the tricks."

"That'll do, Dad. Let's just get you upstairs."

"You can have one. One drink with your old man. One drink for Christmas."

Shaun hurried his father up the stairs, making him stumble. "Come on, back up. Up on your feet, Dad." He called up to Carol, "How's he doing, Carol? Can you get him moved?"

"Just a bloody second, Shaun. You're really throwing everything into disarray here. I had this under control. He was trying to tell me something that's upsetting him."

"I know exactly what it is. I know what's upsetting him and I'll tell you, but first, let's get him upstairs and tucked into bed." At that moment, Shaun's eyes fixed upon the broken fairy ornament. The pose looked so familiar. "No," he cried.

"What is it?" Carol asked, appearing at the bedroom door.

Shaun shook his head, as though trying to loosen and free the images that had become lodged in his mind's eye.

"Imagine the Christmas his mother and father had," Teddy muttered. "Poor buggers. That poor little boy. I couldn't go to prison, though. It would have killed your mother."

"Shaun, what the hell is he talking about? Why's he on about prison now?"

"You were too young to remember, Carol. There was a boy who lived a few streets from us. He was run over and killed on Christmas Eve..."

Carol's jaw dropped and she stared at her father's red, tear-streaked face. "Oh God, no. Don't tell me... don't tell me that Dad..."

Shaun nodded. "I'm afraid so."

Pete moaned and began to stir. Carol turned to him immediately, encouraging him back into full consciousness and awareness. "Pete, come on. Let's get you sat up."

"I should never have given you that drink," Teddy said. "I should never have encouraged you to..."

"That's okay, Dad. It was only a drink. I enjoyed having a drink with you," Shaun said, patting his father's back.

Carol's eyes narrowed in suspicion. She turned to see her brother and father shuffling over the landing.

"Is everything alright with your Dad?" Pete muttered, rubbing his head with both hands, trying to clear the ice-cold headache from deep within his skull. "Oh, Shaun's here."

"Hi Pete, I just need to get Dad into bed for a rest. Could you just come out of here, please?"

"Shaun... why are you suddenly so concerned about him?" Carol asked, her jaw firmed and eyebrows knitted with apprehension.

"It isn't fair me leaving you to deal with him when he's going downhill like this. It's for you, not him, Carol. Now why don't you go and put the kettle on and I'll tell you all about it when I get down?"

"Come on, love," Pete said, encouraging Carol away from the bedside.

Teddy flopped onto the bed and Shaun helped him to settle into position, propping his head up on a pillow. He spread the duvet over his father's body and sat by his side. He shrugged off his coat and pulled out a long, narrow cardboard box he had kept hidden within the garment.

Teddy stared up at the ceiling, no longer seeing plaster and paint and light-fittings... in his mind, he stood staring at the dented car bonnet and the mangled child, shivering in the snow as his life ebbed away, blood bubbles bursting on his lips with every ragged exhalation from his punctured lungs.

"Pull away, son," he snapped.

"Shhhh, Dad."

"Pull away. Now listen to me. I'll tell your mum I bumped a car in the car park at the Red Lion. I'll tap the dent out tonight."

Shaun opened the cardboard box and began unwinding the clear plastic cling film.

"We can never tell anyone about this. Not your mum, not anyone. You can only ever talk to me about this. We'll both be in trouble, son, if anyone finds out."

"It's okay, Dad," Shaun said, stroking his Dad's cheek. "We'll keep it a secret."

Down in the lounge, Carol told Pete what she had put together from what she had heard so far. "I'll bet that's when the drinking started. I'll bet that's when he started to get handy with Mum."

"It makes sense... but I can't believe old Teddy would do that. Hit and run? He's such an honest bloke, or so I thought."

"He was drunk driving, Pete. He obviously wanted to keep himself out of prison. That poor little boy. His family... Can you imagine that, Pete?"

"It's terrible, Carol. It doesn't even bear thinking about, does it?"

"Christmas Eve, Pete. That little boy's parents would have been waiting for him to come home and his presents would have been wrapped up, ready to go under the tree. He was probably running home to hang his stocking up... maybe he stepped out onto the road, or Dad was driving too fast, or was too drunk to hit the brakes in time."

"And bang. He's gone," Pete whispered.

"I think I have to call the police, Pete. I think the truth has to come out. His parents could still be alive. They should have the answers to what happened."

"Let's wait and see what Shaun has to say, eh?"

Teddy clawed at the plastic. Shaun gently moved his hands away, not wanting to leave a mark on his father's arms if he could help it. But, since his arms were covered in marks from his fall anyway, he was not too concerned if he had to get more forceful.

"Shhhh, Dad. Just give in now," he whispered, unsure if his father could hear him through all the layers of cling film wrapped around and around his head. "Won't take long now."

Carol called from the foot of the stairs, "Everything alright up there, Shaun?"

"Yeah, we're just having a little heart-to-heart, sis. I'll be down in a few minutes."

Those minutes seemed to take an eternity as his father trembled and bucked, desperate to draw breath. Shaun repeated over and over, in a soothing tone, "Shhhh, shhhh, shhhh. Almost there."

When his father lay still, Shaun carefully unravelled the cling film and stuffed it into his coat pocket, concealing the original box and roll within the garment to hide it when he went downstairs. He carefully, methodically checked his father's fingernails for any traces of skin or plastic, but found he had done a good job of keeping his hands away. Prying his father's lips apart, he peeled some tiny traces of plastic from between his dentures, where he had attempted to gnaw a hole through the cling film. No breaks. No bruises. A job well done.

He stared down at the face of the man who had made him keep a terrible secret all of his life. So many times as a child, Shaun had wanted to tell the truth, just so he could relieve himself of the weight in his chest, hoping that perhaps it would stop his dad from drinking and stop him from hurting Mum. Eventually, he accepted that secrets and hiding were to be part of his life, forever, just as they dominated his father's existence. But dementia... that presented a problem. The old man could no longer be trusted to keep the secret. He was better off gone.

Shaun stepped out of the bedroom and stopped to consider the tiny, mangled ornament at the top of the stairs. Fingers of static penetrated his skull and he was there again, in the snow, his drunk father beside him. Shaun could feel the steering wheel in his hand and the buzz from the half pint of beer his dad had allowed him to drink. He could hear the laughter as his dad gave him the rushed driving lesson that gave him just enough information to carry them to the warmth of their home. Then he heard the screech of tyres, felt the sickening sensation of the car wheels sliding on the ice and snow and the climactic bump as the little boy, who had been out singing carols with his friends, crunched under the wheels.

Bump. Again. Bump. Again. Bump. Again. *Bump-bump-bump-bump-bump-bump-crash.*

Carol and Pete burst out of the lounge, to the bottom of the stairs, where Shaun lay motionless, his left arm and leg twisted to impossible angles, his head split wide open, a dark, crimson stain leaking across the floor.

Carol screamed and Pete tried to pull her away from the scene. Had Carol just looked up to the top of the stairs, she would have seen two faces, one of them most familiar. Her mum stood hand in hand with a pale little boy. She smiled, seeing the end of the terrible secret that had overshadowed every Christmas in her home for years, the secret which had killed the little boy by her side, and which had, in time, stilled her own heartbeat.

The spirits faded, no longer tethered to the world around them, no longer weighed down by grief, no longer bound by the guilt of the living, free to move on to the realm beyond the physical. To the warm embrace of a Heavenly peace.

14

— · —

ABOUT 'MY LAST EASTER'

I was invited by Matt Shaw to make a submission to an anthology he was putting together under the title *Easter Eggs and Bunny Boilers*. Pleased to be invited to anything at all, I jumped at the chance to collaborate with him and the great line-up of talented indie writers taking part.

As a kid, I loved those rip-off eggs that come with a little pod inside. You split the pod open and usually find a shitty little plastic toy car you have to build, or sometimes a little ornament from a collection of friendly terrapins or lions doing sports and stuff. You know the ones, yeah?

Well, I came up with a different kind of surprise egg for this story. One which, if you open it, contains a hell of a lot more than a plastic toy.

I also threw in a load of *easter eggs* relating to the works of many of the other contributors in that anthology (so if you've read work by Matt Shaw, Matthew Hickman, Stuart Keane, Kyle M, Scott, and others, you might make some connections) I love a good easter egg in a movie, game or book, don't you? So it was fun placing a whole bunch of nods to my contemporaries in...

15

— • —

MY LAST EASTER

The first Faberge eggs were produced by Peter Carl Faberge and his company between 1885 and 1917. The most famous of these were made as exquisite gifts for the wives and mothers of Tsars Alexander III and Nicholas II. Each ornately designed piece contained finely-crafted jewels and trinkets and they were produced every year except in 1904 and 1905 during the Russo-Japanese war. Two additional eggs were believed planned for Easter 1918, but never delivered due to the Russian Revolution.

A legend persists that Peter Carl Faberge lost a beloved nephew in the revolution and, sick with grief, created another egg in secret, one not intended for any Tsar, but imbued with mysterious properties that he believed could bring about an end to all conflict. Forever.

Tommy Pritchard stifled the disappointment well. No chocolate egg from Grandma Somerville this year. His heart had dipped inside his chest when she'd told them. His sister Charlotte, older than him by two years, ever the ten-year-old suck-up, climbed onto Grandma's bed and gave her a big hug.

Tommy kept his distance. She's too sick to go to the shops to buy Easter eggs? Then she's too sick to cuddle me. He hated the idea of climbing up there with her. He felt like there was this film over everything in Grandma's house and it seemed to stick to him every time he visited. Largely, this feeling came from the smell. The warm, welcoming smell of chocolate cake baking in the oven had long been replaced by a more clinical, plastic smell and sometimes a strong smell he recognised as being pee.

As his mum and grandma chatted, with Charlotte pretending she was an adult between them, Tommy gazed at a black and white photograph in a little brown wooden frame, propped on the dressing table. The man in the picture, Grandma had told him, was her Dad. His great grandfather Katovich. Never having met the man, in Tommy's mind's eye, his great grandfather had taken on some sort of legendary, mythical quality – great meaning he was a great size, a great warrior, a great man. He certainly looked impressive in the picture, in his thick coat with buttons that fastened right over on one side of his chest, instead of down the middle, and a flat cap, that Tommy knew was an army hat. A thick moustache curled up at the corners of the man's mouth. He looked important. Grandma said he went to a bolshy party, whatever that was, and Tommy remembered her saying the man called Lenin, was a friend of his. Tommy imagined that the old band his dad liked, The Beatles, must have played at that party.

"Give your Grandma a hug, Tommy," his mum urged, breaking his daydream.

"Don't want to."

"Tomm-eeeee."

He knew that tone, and he didn't have to look at his mum's face to know exactly how it looked. She could make a dog shit itself with that scowl. Shoulders slumped, bottom lip stuck out and his eyebrows knitted into a frown that matched his mum's, Tommy trudged over the mint green carpet and leaned over to give his grandma a fleeting hug. He retreated to the chair in the corner once more, immediately, as though afraid he'd catch leprosy from her.

"Tommy, sometimes you are such a rude little boy," his mum huffed.

"Yeah," Charlotte chimed, "you are such a rude little boy."

"That will do, madam," Mrs Pritchard warned, raising a straight finger to her pursed lips.

"Yeah, leave me alone."

"All of you leave him alone," Grandma Somerville commanded. "He's a little boy, he doesn't want to go around cuddling old women like me."

"No, he wants to cuddle Freya at school."

"Do not."

"That will do, you two."

"Yes you do, Thomas."

"Well, you want to cuddle Jeremy at school."

"You two. I have had enough of your bickering. Go downstairs and amuse yourselves, so your Grandma and I can have some peace."

Charlotte barged Tommy into the wall right before the top of the staircase.

"Watch it, you nearly pushed me down the stairs," Tommy yelped.

"Watch it yourself," Charlotte said, stomping off ahead. "I can't help it if you're blind."

Tommy knew better than to keep it up. Either Charlotte would turn around and smack him, or their mum would come down the stairs like a tank, and give them both something to cry about.

Charlotte snatched up the TV remote and plonked herself down in Grandma Somerville's favourite seat. Tommy knew this was his sister claiming superiority in the room. "I wish Grandma had Sky," she muttered jabbing the channel up button, flicking from boring show about cooking, to boring show about houses, to boring show about antiques. "There's never anything on normal telly."

Tommy ignored her and peered out of the window, watching raindrops chase each other down the glass. No eggs 'til we get home, and that'll be ages now that Mum and Grandma are gossiping, he thought – his inner voice as gloomy as the weather. He glanced over his shoulder to see that his sister had settled on CBBC and that programme about the kids in the care home. He hated that show.

As he turned his attention back to the window, the china cabinet caught his eye. Long had he yearned to slide aside the glass panel and inspect the treasures within, but Grandma never let him even stand close to the cabinet for fear he would trip and smash everything and hurt himself

(Tommy often wondered what her order of priority was on that particular matter).

Tommy pressed his thumb into the gold-painted plastic ring nested in the glass and applied pressure to the right, hoping the glass plate wouldn't stick in the runner and make a noise to get him caught.

"What are you up to?"

Tommy's cheeks flushed and he snapped his hands back by his side. "Nothing."

"You were going to steal from the china cabinet, weren't you?"

"Was not."

"Were so and I'm telling Mum." Charlotte crossed her arms over her chest and scowled at her little brother.

"Do what you want. I can't get told off for looking." Tommy turned his attention back to the cabinet. He saw crystal animals that looked dark without sunlight, or the cabinet's built-in lamp shooting rainbows through them. Ballerinas stood on pointed tiptoes, lifeless and dull. These things held no interest for Tommy, however. There was a specific piece that had captured his imagination ever since he had first clapped eyes on it.

A tripod of gold fixed a golden belt in place, within which sat an egg about as tall as his Batman action figure and at its fattest section, about as wide as the span of his thumb to the tip of his forefinger. He reckoned he could fit about four Cadbury Crème Eggs in it at a push, or maybe only three and he could eat one. Staring at the ornamental egg caused him to lick his lips even though he knew the piece was anything but edible.

The exterior of the egg was painted, but the decoration was elaborate and included a finely painted scene of the grown-up-baby-Jesus with his beard and the little towel around his rude bits, and he was hanging on a cross. Tommy rubbed the palms of his hands, when he remembered the gross story about the nails going through the middle of his hands, and through his feet. The story reminded him of that bit in Home Alone when the robber stands on the nail and you see it go right into the middle of the soft bit of his foot. He could never watch that and hid his eyes from the screen every time it came on.

At the foot of the cross, bright orange flames lapped at the wood and shadowy, horned figures seemed to prance and dance around, long tongues poking out between their sharp teeth.

They looked like bad-guys. They looked like Green Goblin, but shadows. And it looked like they were happy that the grown-up-baby-Jesus was in pain up on the cross. The picture looked like the baddies had won, and it made him feel very strange, because the bad guys were always supposed to lose.

"You like the egg, don't you?" Charlotte asked.

Tommy nodded, never taking his eyes off the piece.

"I touched it once. I held it."

"No, you didn't."

"I did. I got it out and touched it, then put it back before anyone could see."

"Liar."

"Want to see me do it again?" Charlotte asked.

"No," Tommy murmured. "I'm going to do it."

Right then the floorboards creaked as their mum moved around in Grandma's room. Charlotte's eyes turned skyward, but no more sounds came. When she levelled her gaze at her brother, her jaw fell open.

Tommy slipped his thumb into the plastic hoop once more and pressed his free hand against the glass, sliding the pane aside. He reached up and snatched the egg, whipping it free of the golden stand, which toppled as he had not the height to lift the egg free in a direct upwards movement, it was more of a drag. The stand collided with a crystal squirrel, which fell from the open front of the cabinet, to land on the thick burgundy carpet with a soft thud.

"Look what you did," Charlotte gasped, pointing at the angular little squirrel.

"Look what I did," Tommy exclaimed, holding the egg inches in front of his nose like Indiana Jones with a hard-won treasure. Turning the egg, he saw that the scene was repeated front and back, but now, able to see the piece from all angles, he noticed a hinge embedded in the back. "It opens, look." Tommy showed his sister the discovery.

Charlotte pounced, snatching the egg away from her brother. "I want to open it."

"Give it here," Tommy yelled.

Charlotte stopped in her tracks, holding the egg high above her head, where her little brother couldn't reach it. "Shhhh," she hissed. "If you bring Mum down here, neither of us will see what's inside."

Tommy seethed, knowing his sister was right. He nod-ded his acceptance of the situation; his need to see the surprise inside this expensive-looking Kinder Egg outweighed his need to be the one to actually open it.

"Who is queeeeeeen?" Charlotte crowed.

Tommy rolled his eyes up.

"Who is queeeeeeen?"

"You're the fupping queen, okay?"

"Oooh, swearwords. Maybe I should just put this egg back in the cabinet and tell Mum about your foul mouth."

"Then you don't get to see what's in there, either," Tommy said, his wide eyes seeming to glow with this little victory.

Charlotte grasped the top and bottom of the egg and applied gentle pressure. The top portion tilted on the hinge and a blue glow was cast across Charlotte's face, turning the whites of her eyes into pools of sapphire light.

"Wow," Charlotte gasped.

"Let me see it," Tommy cried.

Charlotte lowered the egg so that he could share the view. Within the outer, painted egg, was a glass egg which housed some sort of swirling blue mist, crackling with contained lightning, like a tiny storm trapped in glass.

"Maybe it's like a snow globe," Charlotte suggested, shaking the piece with such violence that the inner egg dislodged and fell from the outer shell. She gasped, waiting for the crash.

Tommy pounced and caught the orb in his right hand. Both he and his sister breathed a sigh of relief. He perched the orb on his fingertips and stared into the glass in awe.

"Look at this," Charlotte cried, holding up the painted outer shell, revealing that the colours had bled away, blurring like a watercolour in the rain, revealing a skin of black porcelain beneath.

"Mum is going to kill us."

"It's your fault, Tommy," Charlotte yelled, dropping the outer shell to the carpet. She lunged at her little brother, but Tommy tucked the egg close to his chest and barrelled into her, shoulder first. Charlotte crashed to the floor, winded.

Tommy glanced back at her, stopping in the corner to inspect the orb. The swirling clouds contained within had a mesmerising effect, he found it incredibly difficult to focus on anything else. He could hear his mum's footfalls on the stairs. He knew that trouble was on the way, but he could not move. The orb seemed to thrum with a tightly contained power – he could feel it, it was like the feeling he got on his tongue when he licked the top of one of those square batteries, but in his fingertips.

"Give that here," Charlotte snatched at the orb, knocking it from Tommy's fingers, but her own grasp failed her. The orb shattered against the wall with an ear-splitting crash.

"Look what you did," Tommy screamed, his face turning red, cheeks burning with rage. His fists squeezed into tight balls and he turned, ready to pound his sister's face.

"What the hell is going on in there?" their mum cried from the stairs.

Charlotte stared over Tommy's shoulder. "Look."

Tommy turned to see that the storm from the orb was no longer contained. Blue lightning flickered outward, like impossibly fast tentacles, snatching at the curtains, the carpet, the door handle. The clouds swirled and stretched – a vortex of impenetrable darkness forming in the heart of the miniature storm.

"Fupping hell," Tommy squealed.

"Telling on you."

The skirting board's white paint lifted and splinters of bare wood gravitated to the growing clouds. The corner of the carpet tore free of the staples that pinned it down, its threads unravelling, sucked into the vortex like dark red spaghetti.

Tommy backed away as his mum entered the room. "Right, you two, we're going." She paused, taking in the destructive cloud whirling in the room. "What the hell have you two done?"

"Charlotte did it."

"Tommy did it."

The lightning forks snapped at the doorframe and wallpaper peeled away from plaster and splinters of wood darted through the air into the nothingness.

"Out. Get out," Mum cried.

Tommy stood mesmerised as Charlotte ran to her mother's side, hugging tightly to her hip.

The curtain tore free, snapping the curtain pole as this new gravitational force refused to let go. The windowsill split and disintegrated into the darkness.

Tommy's mum grabbed his wrist and yanked him out of the lounge as a low rumbling sound filled the air. Lightning arcs flashed, blinding and ferocious in their wake, the force of their discharge thudding into the walls and furniture. Tommy could smell a metallic, burning tang in the air.

The three of them burst through the front door, into the chilly rain, in time to see the storm eating through the brickwork of the house – only a couple of bricks at first, but blades of grass rippled, standing on end, pointing at the threat. A dozen bricks collapsed inward, with more peeling away every second. The vortex seemed to gather strength with every passing moment and the lightning flashes in the lounge created a strobe effect so intense that it could even be discerned outside in the daylight.

"Keep going," Mum ordered.

"What about Grandma?" Charlotte cried.

"I'll get her, just keep away from that... thing."

"Don't do it, Mum," Tommy warned. "Don't go back in there."

"I have to, Tommy. Grandma needs help to get out of there."

"You won't make it. Neither of you will make it."

Tommy's mum ruffled his hair and cast him a sympathetic look. "She needs me."

"We need you too," came Tommy's response, a lump rising into his throat.

Tommy watched his mum race to the front door as the storm sucked away bricks only a few feet away from her. Daffodils and gravel whipped up from around the lawn, and a lightning flash chopped a chunk out of the turf, leaving a smoking, steaming hole in the grass.

Charlotte screamed as she saw their mum stride through the front door and stop in her tracks.

"Mum," they both cried in unison.

A bolt of lightning shot through their mother's forehead, neatly punching a tunnel through right through her skull. She fell to her knees, steam rising from her white-hot wounds. She toppled forward and, unseen by the two children, another part of the storm must have crept closer to her, as her hair rose on end, tearing free of her scalp, pulling chunks of flesh away. Skin peeled off in layers, down to fat, the muscle, then bone as gradually, another fringe of the storm drifted into view, consuming her body.

Tommy sat on the pavement, hands over his eyes, rocking back and forth. Charlotte raced to the doorway, seemingly oblivious of the fact that what happened to her mum was bound to happen to her.

Amid the blue glow in the lounge, flickers of orange appeared as textiles, paper and wood caught fire at the force of the lightning strikes. The window frame buckled inward, pausing as the fixing bolts held fast.

Tommy found that he wasn't alone on the street. His grandma's neighbours had come out to see what the fuss was about. "What the hell is that thing? Some sort of gas cloud?" one of them cried.

"Is Hanna still in there?"

"Tommy, where's your mum, son? Can anyone see Justine?"

"Quick, fetch your Dad. I think it's a fire. I think old Hanna's trapped."

Jonathan, who lived right next door to Tommy's Grandma, grabbed Charlotte and dragged her away from the doorway. "Come on, sweetheart. You need to get away from there. It's too dangerous, my petal." The old man wrapped an arm around Tommy, pressing the siblings close together. He turned to the others gathered around. "I saw Justine, I think. It's hard to tell... she's gone."

Charlotte seemed to crumble, squeezing into Tommy's huddled form, knowing Jonathan's meaning – knowing this meant she wasn't dreaming - other people were seeing this, too. It meant that she had killed her mother. It meant that she had brought about this destruction. It meant that no matter what happened next, it was all, every bit of it, her fault. The crushing weight of this truth rendered her dumb. She didn't want to see any more. She didn't want to hear any more. She didn't want to know or accept any more, but the truth rushed in around her from every direction at once, like that toon-ami that hit Japan, guilt lifting her off her feet and dragging her along with its current, drowning her.

The window frame finally collapsed, dragging with it the lintel, bricks aligned with the first floor timber and a huge portion of the lounge ceiling. The front door vanished as the vortex expanded to fill the door-frame. More brickwork collapsed inward, the whole front of the ground floor almost exposed. Three more lightning flashes drove the crowd of onlookers back across the road.

"I've called the fire brigade."

Jonathan turned Charlotte's head away from the scene and wrapped his arms and the thick woolly jumper sleeves thereupon, around the children's heads, trying to cover all four little ears at once. He hoped to muffle the shiver-inducing screams of their terrified grandma, as the unyielding cloud ate through the lounge ceiling and in turn, the bedroom floor around her.

As the vortex expanded upward and outward, so too did it grow downward, swallowing the ground, tearing at the foundations of the building, feasting on the water pipes, the electrical cables, the gas pipes, which snapped and hissed and rumbled beneath the ground, as they, much like the threads of the carpet had, slid like spaghetti into a hungry mouth.

The fire engine sirens came, distant, but growing and Tommy knew that it was pointless. He had seen into the eyes of this beast. This was something great in every sense of the word. Something huge. Something powerful. Something unstoppable. He knew that this nothingness, this storm, would eat and eat, forever, until there was nothing left.

This is the end. This is how it ends. This is how everything ends.

I've had my last hug from mum.

The lightning bolts smashed through the roof tiles, sending sharp, grey shrapnel raining down onto the street. The crowd broke for cover. Jonathan leaned over the two children, shielding them with his old, bent back.

I've already had my last kick of a football with Dad.

Lightning thudded beneath the ground.

I've had my last chocolate egg ever. My last Christmas, my last birthday, my last Easter.

Grandma's roof collapsed.

I won't see Batman fighting with Superman, or Iron Man fighting with Captain America at the cinema.

The front of Jonathan's house began to crumble.

I should have given Grandma a better hug.

The lawn was half-eaten and Jonathan pushed the children back, further down the street.

I never told Freya the Valentine's card was from me.

Toby, Jonathan's black Labrador raced around the house from the back garden, streaking towards his master. Tommy reached out and stroked the animal who whimpered and nuzzled into Jonathan.

Tommy turned to face his sister. "Charlotte?"

Lightning thudded underground, sending shock-waves through the pavement. It felt as though the ground would cave in at any moment, a notion amplified by the cracks tearing through the tarmac and paving slabs.

"Charlotte, I love you."

Gas hissed through growing cracks in the tarmac. The neighbours in the crowd babbled louder in a jumble of concerned remarks and warnings.

"What?"

"I said I love you."

The sickly sweet smell of gas everywhere. Lightning thudding beneath their feet. Panicked cries. Screams.

"What?"

"I said I-"

16

WELCOME TO LEEDS

I moved to Leeds when I was 26 and fell in love with the place immediately. My friend Andy was working there and when I'd quit a lousy job, he managed to get me a spot working for a bank, with him. I loved in particular the area close to the train station, where dark bars and a rock club nestled in the dingy arches of railway bridges along the banks of the old canal.

If it weren't for Leeds, I wouldn't have my two wonderful sons, as that was where I met their mum. I met some great friends there and have fond memories and a strong connection to that city. Leeds feels more like a hometown to me than my actual hometown of Alnwick. It was in Leeds that I gained a new confidence I had never had as a boy. This was the place and the time where I struck out on my own, knowing only one person in the whole city, and started a new life almost from scratch.

Even as I write this, in a time more personally and emotionally challenging than any other I've ever faced, I don't yearn to be in Alnwick, it's Leeds where I want to be. I feel a need to draw up some of that old heat from the forge in which my adult self was created. I know the minute I step off the train and set foot in Leeds, I'll feel the energy of the place rising into my body, soaking through my pores, and I will be replenished, ready to face all challenges.

I think everyone needs a special place like that, a true *home*. And Leeds certainly felt and still does feel, like mine.

Leeds is a wild fusion of a thousand different races and religions. Its city centre is encased in layers of towns that butt up against each other in continuous waves of brick and concrete, each with a distinct character, from Afro-Caribbean Chapeltown, to student haven Heading-ley, and on to dicey Middleton. There's traditional Hors-forth (the birthplace of the actor Malcolm McDowell from *A Clockwork Orange* - I regularly drank in the pub his parents used to run). There's hipster-chic Chapel Allerton and dozens of places in between. I absolutely love that city and miss it terribly.

I have, at time of writing this introduction, written about Leeds only twice. Both of these stories I have includ-ed here for you, each with its own introduction, but I felt I needed to acknowledge the city itself and my connection to it.

Without doubt, Leeds will feature in my stories again.

17

—·—

ABOUT 'ANTI-TERROR'

The first of my Leeds stories, I feel, needs a little bit of explanation before you get stuck in. It was born of an invitation from Stuart Keane, to join him, Kyle M. Scott and Angel Gelique in a collection called *Carnage: Extreme Horror*. Extreme horror wasn't a subgenre I'd considered before then, but I decided I could rise to the challenge if I could make that subgenre work for me. Any story I produced for *Carnage* was going to be very different to stories like *The Seance* or *The Cabinet of Doctor Blessing*, so I had to find my own angle, my own way into the extreme.

I recalled a certain feeling I had, a couple of years after London's 7th July 2005 attacks and the shooting, only days later, of a man named Jean-Charles de Menezes. Some of the London bombers had been found to have connections in West Yorkshire, around Leeds, and some other terror attacks had been traced and prevented. Seeing the police on high alert, carrying firearms (very unusual, here in the UK), standing sentry at concrete barriers outside the train station I used for my daily commute, made me feel like all hell could break out any moment. The prospect of an attack was real. The precautions were in place. *Everyone* was a little nervous. And if some commuter wandered into that station with a secret plot, there was nothing anyone could do about it.

Every time you saw a commuter running in the station, you immediately felt your nerves bristle as your suspicions rose. You could see police and security locking in on the commuter, weighing up the threat of their actions. Are they going to blow us all up? Or are they just late for the 17:13 to Bristol? Remember, when Jean-Charles de Menezes was shot, it turned out he was an innocent man, but his behaviour in the station, his failure to stop when being hailed, his rush down to the platform and a packed train... the rest is a sad little piece of history.

A story came to me, but I felt like I couldn't tell it in my usual way. I needed to look at it from a different angle, or many different angles. What makes violence and horror *extreme*? To my mind, it can only be defined by the person *perceiving* it. So I perceived it from many different angles and presented the story as a set of interviews with people who witnessed the events described within. I had enjoyed a book by Chuck Palahniuk, called *Rant,* with a similar structure, referred to as an *oral history*, and I felt like experimenting. What's the point in being a creator if you can't test yourself once in a while?

Look out for another cameo appearance from a character you've caught a glimpse of elsewhere in this book. No clues this time, but do tweet me if you spot it.

I enjoyed writing this story and approaching horror from a new angle, but the only person who can gauge if it is entertaining, dear reader, is you...

18

— · —

ANTI-TERROR

Excerpt from the West Yorkshire Evening Chronicle, Saturday 12th August 2006

An explosion ripped through Leeds City Train Station at approximately 6.00pm yesterday evening as a suspected terrorist attack killed at least 104 people, plunging the West Yorkshire city into chaos.

West Yorkshire police confirmed 103 deaths in the blast, and a further fatality on a station platform. A further 40 people are in a critical condition in Leeds General Hospital. The West Yorkshire ambulance service said it had treated 40 people with serious or critical injuries, including burns and amputations, and another 100 people with minor injuries. A controlled explosion was carried out at 8.00pm on a suspected explosive device within the platform area of the Leeds City Train Station, but this was later confirmed to have posed no threat to the public.

245

Police also said that there was no intelligence that any further bombs were on the rail network.

The Prime Minister said it was "beyond a shadow of doubt" that the blast was the work of terrorists. He said neither the police nor the intelligence services had been given any warning of the attack.

Reports have emerged that the man shot dead by police on the platform was not carrying the explosive device used to perpetrate the atrocity.

The Independent Police Complaints Commission has launched an investigation.

Note from Stuart Scott

I decided to compile this oral history, using the above news article as a starting point. See how the reporter made a bland report of such an explosive event. Living in Leeds at the time of this shooting, it took only days for the rumours to reach me, that there had been a massive cover-up. Cover-up? I had wondered. What kind of cover-up is it when Police admit to wrongfully shooting a man in a train station in peak time?

The rumours came thick and fast, though, and with each new rumour came a new twist, a new detail, a new inaccuracy. I tried to chase these rumours down, tried to get back to the source. I needed to meet someone who was on that platform, but at every turn I was shut down. My interest faded. It was simply a tragic shooting distorted with paranoid fantasies, which had faded into the annals of urban myth.

Then I received a letter around the fifth anniversary of the shooting. A man had become aware of my past interest in the case. He had known of some of my better-received journalistic endeavours and realised that I might cast light on the shadowy conspiracy of silence he had come to know over the years.

This man, Alan Keane, wrote of his son, Kyle Keane, whose fascination with conspiracy theories made him something of an online celebrity, with a blog page receiving thousands of hits a week.

Kyle had been there, in the station, when these events took place. Kyle saw things before he was rescued by the police. Kyle saw things that scarred his psyche forever. But, Alan informed me, that was nothing to the cruel damage inflicted on him by certain members of West Yorkshire's constabulary who were not happy with Kyle's lines of enquiry.

From Alan's letter I was able to assemble some of the fragments Kyle had managed to discover. I was able to locate and meet with others who witnessed the events that led up to the shooting of Russell Fischer, and the horrifying aftermath. These others would often meet in private, never daring to bare their knowledge in public for fear of the repercussions. Many of them thought that they would be sectioned under the Mental Health Act for repeating their stories. Many of them feared death at the hands of those who wish to keep the true events secret.

I regret that I never got to meet Kyle. So distraught was he left by this grisly affair that he sadly took his own life two months before I received the letter from his father. Kyle had placed his head on a train track near York and waited for the next train to pass. I tell you this purely because I want you to consider how afraid a person must be, to lie there stock still as the grinding metal wheels scream over the rails towards their face. You must understand that this terrifying exit from the world seemed a better alternative to him than living. This work is to honour him, adding to his legacy; a beacon of truth in a world obscured in a fog of spin and denial.

You should also note that during the transcripts, my questions appear in *italics*, interspersed with the interviewee statements.

Vicki Beadle (waitress): I saw him, like, when I were in't main waiting area. I were minding me own business, like, trying to mek out the screens to see when the next train to Castleford were.

An' I knew there were something wrong wi' 'im as soon as I saw 'im. He were sweating, I mean really sweating. His skin were tanned dark, but his cheeks looked red, like he had been running. Panting away he were. Nowt unusual in that, I suppose. He's late for his train, I were thinking. But then I noticed he were looking over his shoulder all the time, and it were then I heard him muttering... it sounded like a prayer or summit.

He went past me an' I saw his backpack and his dark skin and I noticed his hand was tucked up inside his jumper, like he were hiding something. I thought, "Hello, he's one of them.

He walked over to the Body Shop and he kept looking all around him like he were afraid of summit or summit like that. I thought, mebbe he were afraid of being caught, like. Afraid of being stopped.

That's when I told the coppers I were worried about him, and I thought to me'sen', "Fuck this." I got out of there and paid a bloody fortune for a taxi ride back home.

Glad I bloody did, an' all.

David Conlan (former Chief Superintendant West Yorkshire Police): Now listen, it's all well and good everyone blaming the police for what happened. Look at all that in London, all those people killed and maimed. I stood by our lads at the time and I stand by them now. It was a clean, good shooting. The suspect failed to stop when challenged and was running across a heavily populated platform and a full train in rush hour.

I defy anyone in that same position to make a different decision. There was a choice to be made. A split-second, horrible choice. One life, or hundreds. Who could have predicted in that split second, how it would turn out? There was no intelligence to suggest an accomplice. And that's what he was, an accomplice. They were well known as close friends in London, those two. And that's all there is to be said on it.

PC Val Neeson: Wayne always had a great... instinct as a police officer. He had that even temperament, you know?

A clear head, always such a clear head. I mean, they don't just let anyone get into Armed Response, as I'm sure you know. He had pulled the trigger before, I mean in a situation, but he had never ever taken a life before.

And yes, it did haunt him afterwards. Of course it did. I mean, it obviously did; that's why he never came back.

He didn't return to policing?

Well, I suppose I mean that, too.

Wayne Cross (former West Yorkshire Police Constable): All they were interested in was poor him. Poor Russell Fischer. Poor Russell.

You don't feel any sympathy for the Fischer then?

Of course I fucking do. But I had to do my job. How was I supposed to know he had a mate already on the train?

What do you mean?

All those people. Jesus Christ. They were killing themselves all because of him.

Andrew Irwin (PPI salesman): I saw him, yes. He was kind of hovering about outside W H Smith. I was in there, killing some time until the train for Newcastle got in. I was looking through a couple of Tom Clancy books and I noticed the blokey, the one who turned out to be this Fischer.

I just thought he was on a hands-free call at first, and I remember thinking that he looked really stressed out. He looked about this way and that, and he must have turned right around at one point because I noticed he had no earpiece in, no headphones, nothing. But his lips kept moving.

You get all sorts in the station, to be fair. The heroin addicts I've seen gibbering away and screaming and throwing themselves on the floor. I didn't give him a second thought.

Think about him all the time, now.

Do you need a tissue? Here.

Not a day goes by... Not a single day goes by.

Lisa Sandberg (Solicitor at Sandberg and Sandberg, executors of the Morgan Hamilton Estate): The item that had been taken from the Leeds City Museum has been returned to a secure location. That is all that I can share with you.

Could you tell me something about the item itself?

I have said all that I am permitted to say.

Come on, it's been eight years. Let's unravel some of the mystery.

There is no mystery, Mr Scott. The item is quite safe and secure.

The mysterious object, which you refuse to describe, has no mystery attached to it? Come on.

Our time is up, Mr Scott.

Why did he take it? What value does the item hold?

Our time is up, Mr Scott.

Where was the item kept before Hamilton died?

Please, Mr Scott, our time really is up.

Where was it kept?

Escort Mr Scott off the premises, please.

People died for this object, Miss Sandberg. Don't you think that's rather strange? Don't you think the story needs to be told?

There is no story to be told, Mr Scott. There is no story that has not already been told. A poor, deluded man resorted to theft and made a fatal error, resulting in his tragic death. And now a poor, deluded man is going to be thrown out onto the street. Leave things well alone, Mr Scott.

Lisa Wood (marketing consultant): He pushed his way through the ticket barrier. I got an elbow in the ribs as he went past. I was winded so I didn't even get a chance to shout at him or to protest and he was away. He moved like... I don't know, like a ferret or a scared rabbit or something. I heard him whisper, "Allah," I'm sure it was.

I looked back into the station concourse to see if anyone was chasing him and there were a few men hurrying towards the gate, but people are late for trains, you know? They get stuck in a bar and before you know it they've got a few seconds before their train arrives.

Rosie Ost (Russell Fischer's former partner): Did I know about Russell's fixation with the occult? Christ, that's what attracted me to him. The things he knew... the places he had been. The first night we met, he fucked me in Highgate Cemetery.

We had broken in just before midnight. Thank God he didn't get a stop and search beforehand; he was carrying his favourite ritual blade. That blade he held to my throat when we fucked on Karl Marx's grave. Don't ask my why Karl Marx, it just seemed like the right thing to do.

I was on my period, but I was really sensitive and I was excited, too. He fucked me urgently, forcefully. I came quickly and when he had come inside me, he made me lie there, with come and blood running out of me, onto that cold, damp grave. I have to admit, I became scared, I didn't know what was going to happen. He held his knife over me and started his incantations.

I thought Karl Marx was going to burst out of his grave. But nothing happened. He told me he thought he may have been too late and that we were probably finished fucking just after midnight meaning the ritual wouldn't work.

After I'd been seeing him for a few weeks, he admitted to me that it had been a con. He told me he had been desperate to fuck me and would have said anything to get me to do it. Knowing I was into the occult, but a bit of a newbie to it, he knew a ritual in a graveyard would get me wet.

He had been right. He was really romantic like that.

David Conlan (former Chief Superintendant West Yorkshire Police): Yes, I did hear the rumours afterwards. Yes, I heard what people were saying happened. Do I believe the rumours, though? No, of course I don't.

What do you think happened?

There are reports and statements stacked up to the height of Bridgewater Place, for Christ's sake. I will say this, though: I don't believe in ghost stories. Full stop. Now, this interview is over.

Mark Johnson (former security guard at Leeds City Museum): I'll never forget that day, I mean, how can I? That wath when I got thethe fucking thcarth all over my faith. Every time I look in the mirror and thee what that bathtard did to me... every time I have to hear my own voith and hear thith fucking lithp, I remember hith faith. Both thothe bathtardth faitheth.

My wife left me, you know? Thed I thcared the kidth. Ain't theen the kidth thince. Why would they want to thee me?

Do you need a moment? To gather your thoughts...

No. No, I'll be fine. I jutht feel tho thtupid thometimeth when I get thith upthet. It'th tho pathetic, but thothe cunth took everything I love away from me. I athk mythelf why did I take that extra thift? And I think, why didn't I jutht let them run off with the bockth and let the poleeth deal with them? The twatth could have thcrapped it out themthelveth and one of them would have been thtabbed inthtead of me. All thith and you know what wath in that bockth? A fucking bone. Eh? A fucking dog treat and I got thtabbed becauth of it.

Such sad circumstances. I know.

Eathy for you to thay. Whatth your name, again?

Stuart Scott.

Yeah, eathy for you to thay. And the wortht bit ith, I can't even thay the name of the bathtard who thtabbed me. Thimonath Thit-thin.

Rosie Ost (Russell Fischer's former partner): Russell had been really excited about his trip to Leeds. It was a hastily planned trip. I knew that he and his friend, Simonas Sitchin... has anyone mentioned Simonas to you?

Yes, his name sort of came up.

Russell had learned of some millionaire in Leeds, who had died, leaving some artefacts to a museum up there. One of these items had him really excited.

Did he say what it was?

Yes. He told me it was an unholy relic. The bone of a demon, he told me.

Mark Johnson (former security guard at Leeds City Museum): Tho theeth two cunth walked into the mutheum. Came thtraight through to the cabineth of curiothitieth and they jutht looked like any other tourithts or cuthtomerth. I wath in the gift thop, thatting to Thuthan and I heard thith mathive thmath. I ran through to the cabineth and there wath glath everywhere. Thothe two fuckerth had run round the back of another cabinet and got patht me while I wath trying to make thenth of what had happened.

I thtarted running after them ath they patht the gift thop and I tried to get thum help on the radio but they were almotht at the door, tho I thped up and couldn't get a methadth to the other guardth.

Thith wath when one of them hit the other with the bockth, jutht thmacked him right over the head with it. I think he hoped to put him down tho ath I would cat-th that one, but I have to admit the little bathtard recovered quickly and thathed after hith partner.

When I got out of the front door, thothe two were rolling down the thtairth, punthing the living thit out of eath other. The one who got hit over the head with the bockth, he wath on top and he took the bockth off the other one, thmathed him right over the nothe with it and thtarted running again.

I thought I had betht cat-th one of them, tho I thprinted down the thtepth.

Bathtard wath waiting for me, though. He had hith knife ready. Thtabbed me right through my theek. The blade thmathed thickth of my teeth out and the blade got thtuck in my dthawbone, I mean literally thtuck... embedded in my dthawbone. He grabbed the handle of the knife and tried to pull it back out again, but my head wath attatthed to it and he couldn't get it free, couldn't take me with him. Nearly cut my tongue off, the fucker. Then he ran after the other one.

Wayne Cross (former West Yorkshire Police Constable): This Russell Fischer had made a woman suspicious while he was hanging around in the train station. After everything that had happened in New York, and especially with what happened in London, people were scared and paranoid. I mean, nobody expected that to happen on British soil, right?

And after all, there were only armed coppers in the train station as a direct response to London. We had the concrete barriers outside and all that in case they tried to stick a Land Rover full of explosives into the main concourse.

Our presence, with the guns and armour and everything, it had people on edge. They read that as though a direct threat had been made. If I had taken the time to reassure every nervous person I saw, I would have been so distracted that Osama Bin Laden himself would have been able to walk in and level the place, so I had to just let people stare and worry and shuffle off to wherever they were going.

So that suspicious woman came over and I detected the smell of alcohol on her breath. We'd had so many alcoholics coming out of the station bars, making hoax allegations and all that; I have to admit, I was dubious at first, but this woman, she'd just had a couple of post work drinks, by the looks of her.

Then I saw him, the guy she was on about. He was wrapping something in his hooded top, like he didn't want people to see it, but it was also like he didn't want to touch it with his hand it was weird. He was visible flustered and kept looking this way and that. I could see he was sweating. My first fear was that his sweat might trigger the explosive, you know, something unstable like gelignite.

I thanked the woman for her vigilance and advised her to get out of the way. By that point the suspect was moving towards the platforms.

PC Val Neeson: I know you've been to see Wayne. Look, whatever he says, and I say this with deep love and respect for the police officer he was, but you can't believe him now.

What he went through would change any copper and it certainly changed Wayne. Every time I've seen him since, he's waving that crucifix around and talking to me about quotes from the bible.

The only signs of religion he had before were when he blasphemed.

Let me tell you a story about him, though, so you know I'm not just being critical of him. I love Wayne dearly, I do, I really do.

We were posted on Headrow when the EDL decided to put on a protest to coincide with the Vaisakhi procession, which as you know stretches all the way down from the Sikh temple at Chapeltown Road, down to Millennium Square. Generally speaking it was a peaceful day, you know, as in, we contained the situation well and kept people moving. The EDL didn't really get any satisfaction. The Sikh procession had passed on when the troublesome EDL elements were pissed up enough to stir any real bother up.

There were thousands of people out there in those crowds, though and Wayne could see hundreds of EDL supporters from his position. Through all of them, he spotted two former customers of ours, a man and a woman who were still wanted for questioning in connection with a brutal assault on a Polish man.

Wayne was over the barrier in an instant and battled his way through a storm of protestors, with only his baton out to help him create a bit of space. Those two had no idea the cause of the commotion was a copper walking among them. He got the cuffs on the male suspect and caught the female by the arm as she turned to escape. He read them their rights, of course and pulled them out through the crowd.

Now, any one of those protestors could have tried to stop him, but they all wanted to be the second in line, if you get my meaning. Wayne just had this look about him. He meant business. I knew it, his two prisoners knew it, and all of those protestors knew it that day.

He made two arrests, nobody was hurt, and he was given a verbal warning for putting himself at risk. Bloody fine copper to watch. You see that lot on the telly and in films, Bruce Willis and all that lot? Wayne Cross is the real Mc-Coy, I'm telling you. Was, anyway.

Wayne Cross (former West Yorkshire Police Constable): My colleague, PC Mullins, and I began to advance on the suspect who had made it as far as the ticket gate. We wanted to keep a safe distance so that he wouldn't panic and make his move in urgency. Our plan was to let him get round to the platforms where we would be able to close some ground on him and stay low in the crush of commuters by the gate.

We reasoned that if he wanted to detonate the bomb anywhere he would just do it in the main concourse and get it over and done with. Lots of people, lots of glass, lots of damage. We could assume then, and did assume, that he wanted to be on a train, or at a certain location while on a train.

Justin, PC Mullins, I mean, he drew my attention to another party who ran across the concourse from the right, over by the ticket offices. He was really moving, hands bloody. A right mess. We had no way of knowing if this individual had something to do with our suspect and nothing had come over the radio about any attacks at that point, but it was too much of a coincidence these two clowns turning up at almost at the same time.

This second one, he was totally oblivious to our presence even as we crossed the concourse and he caused a stir as he pushed into the crowd at the gate. Both of these men made it past the guards without tickets. The guards had moved forward to give chase to the second man, doubtless pissed off at the first one, Fischer, who got past them; they must have wanted to catch the second one to make up for it.

PC Mullins shouted the guards back and people cleared out of our way as we pushed through the gate. Mullins was telling the commuters to turn back, to get out. Well, you can imagine the panic that broke out then, I'm sure.

In my earpiece something came through on the radio about a stabbing at the museum. I responded and told them we had the suspects in sight. I wondered how many knife attacks they had committed on their way down to the station.

Andrew Irwin (PPI salesman): There was another one, you know? Another bloke. I had just got through the ticket barrier. I double-checked the screen on that side to confirm the platform hadn't changed. It hadn't, so I went up the escalator with my bag.

I heard guards shouting behind me, back at the gate and I looked down to see what was going on. This bloke had pushed through. He looked a bit of a mess. Blood all over him. I thought again, "Here we go, more junkies have been fighting" and sort of left it at that. I thought the two of them, him and that other bloke, had fallen out full of drink or drugs.

I just hoped to hell they weren't getting on my train, but it was then, from the overhead concourse, that I noticed on the other side of the first sets of tracks, there was the first man I had seen, pushing his way down the stairs towards platforms 9, 10 and 11. Just my bloody luck, he was heading the same way as me.

This other one, the second one to get through the gate, he must have seen the first guy, because he jumped down from platform 8 and scrambled over the tracks. Well, I thought nothing was as sure as that idiot getting crushed by an oncoming train. I didn't dare look.

Lisa Wood (marketing consultant): I was standing in the queue at the Costa on the bridge and just killing a bit of time because as soon as I got through to the platforms, they announced my train was delayed. So when the guards started shouting at this other man, and the armed police appeared at the gate, I knew it had something to do with the first guy. The "Allah" guy.

I remember the buzz of the crowd down at the gates. People were pulling each other and turning around, going back through to the main entrance. I got really frightened. I asked this man next to me, some random guy in a suit, if he knew what was going on. He said no, but he didn't take his eyes off the scene.

The second man who had caused trouble down there was in the process of running over the tracks. A train was coming in up ahead. The train's horn blasted and there was that screaming sound of brakes as the driver brought it to a halt further up the track. It wasn't even close, because he was obviously coming to a halt anyway, but still it was scary. Who just does that, jumps down and crosses the track? Especially just to go and get into a fight with someone.

Caroline Gebbie (department store assistant manager): At first I didn't know there was a man on the tracks, I just wondered why the train was stopping at the far end of the platform. When you think something might be wrong, you think of your kids, don't you? I did anyway, and pulled them in close.

It's so weird. It was all sort of happening at once. The train stopped and people were pointing over at the track and there was a man picking his way over the rails, but then I heard people shouting from the gates, so I immediately thought the man hadn't bought a ticket, but then there was this other man running down stairs towards the kids and I.

My daughter, Tilly, stepped forward, pointing at the man on the track. I just grabbed her arm and pulled her back. I told her off. Well, you never know who these nutters are at the station.

I mean, one of the last things I got to say to her... and I was telling her off.

Rosie Ost (Russell Fischer's former partner): I think that maybe there was some rivalry between Russell and Simonas, yeah. Simonas was more comfortable living the life of the occultist, whereas Russell tended to… not hide it, so much as just not wear it like a badge.

Simonas wanted everyone to know. He was knowledge-able, though, it has to be said. At least I thought he was knowledgeable. Russell used to say he was just regurgitating someone else's spiel, but those were the days when Russell was pissed off with him. The next day he'd be in love with him again and Simonas would be the best thing since sliced bread.

That's just how it was with them. But they did love each other. They were rarely apart. They lit up around each other. I think they needed each other, but at first it would appear that Simonas could be on his own, like he didn't need anyone outside of an occasional fuck-buddy. But I know that wasn't true and I realised it especially when I moved in with Russell.

Simonas would come round for at least two meals a day on most days. He would cook, or bring food with him, he wasn't incompetent, wasn't a cheapskate. He wanted the company. I think he was incapable of having a proper relationship, but wanted to be part of one, even if he was a spare part.

Nobody else got to see that side of him, that vulnerable side. When we were out together, he was in the centre of everything. Bragging, showing off. Only occasionally did this all piss Russell off, because he liked being there for the ride, I suppose, but he didn't have to be the instigator. He could just unleash Simonas the entertainer and sit back.

Working as that sort of double-act, they got many young men and women who wanted to follow them, wanted to be part of a séance, or to take part in a ritual. Their regular hangout was the Green Goblin in Camden.

Simonas was notorious in there, with the ladies, I mean. He was more immediately good-looking than Russell. Took more time over his appearance. I thought Russell was the most handsome, though. More rugged. But those Goth-girls just couldn't keep their hands of Simonas.

"Willing victims," Simonas used to call them.

There was one night when they rowed and other than, you know, day to day bickering, that was the only time I'd ever seen them argue for real. Simonas and Russell were members of a cult known as the House Grandier. Russell tired of House Grandier. He felt that it had become... I don't know if commercial or popular would describe it, but, well, he said there were too many hangers-on. There was also something about a scientist who had risen to the position of High Priest, and who believed that through the use of DNA or genetic engineering or something like that, they could create a true Leviathan. He didn't want just one, though; he wanted to make a male and a female. A breeding pair. Russell dismissed it all as a bunch of crap and wanted out.

Simonas wanted him to stay, of course. Simonas had been rather successful with the ladies in that cult, too. On top of that, he was in favour with this High Priest, whereas

Russell had diminished his own visibility in the cult and had not caught the Priest's eye.

Russell was adamant that he was leaving and eventually he and Simonas were at logger-heads. He actually snapped and chased Simonas out of the house; I thought he was going to hit him. Simonas must have thought so too, because he ran out of there.

Professor Vincent Dover (High Priest of the House Grandier): Yes, I knew both of the boys very well. Both of them had been affiliates at the House Grandier.

How long were you acquainted with them?

I knew them for approximately three years. I had been only an affiliate myself when they came to join us. Russell was a quiet young man, very introspective, but very serious about our work.

Simonas was an extrovert, but willing, hard-working and showed much potential. He had the sort of charisma that would have made him an excellent Priest or High Priest in our organisation, with time and with a guiding hand.

Your hand?

Perhaps. But then they both left. I had known that Russell Fischer was unhappy for some time. He did not agree with some of my strategies, as is his right. Nobody is forced to believe or to follow anything or anybody here at House Grandier. He made his choice, but I can't help believing that it was his influence that caused Simonas to leave.

So Simonas left because of Russell?

After Russell announced he was leaving and subsequently left, I neither saw nor heard from either of them again. Simonas never did explain his departure and I was not afforded an opportunity to ask him.

Andrew Irwin (PPI salesman): The train had managed to stop in good time and the bloke got himself up onto the platform. Again, my theory about the junkies having a fall-out seemed to be about right, because right there in front of everybody, they just started fighting. I mean, they were really going for each other. I have to admit it, I watched. I thought it was funny. I mean when it comes to scum like that I usually think whoever loses, society wins.

I'm sorry, I know that's not a nice thing to say, but that's what I was thinking at the time. I didn't know what else I was going to see... Didn't know I would... it would get so...

Lisa Wood (marketing consultant): People gathered up to watch these two fighting down on the platform. What had been pretty scary at first seemed to turn into a bit of entertainment. A bit of amusement, you know, watch these two drunken idiots fight it out. So long as nobody got too badly hurt I don't think anybody there cared.

Then I saw two armed policemen making their way up the stairs. They were pointing back at the gates as they met people or passed them and I knew something more serious must be wrong with them. I just thought "Terrorists" and that was that. Suddenly that first one muttering about Allah seemed to make sense.

I made a move off the bridge towards the stairs and the policemen met me at the top. One of them just said, "Make your way out of the station as quickly and calmly as you can."

I didn't hesitate for a moment. I practically jumped down those stairs.

Caroline Gebbie (department store assistant manager): I pulled my son and daughter along the platform as soon as that man climbed up from the rails. Jesus Christ, I was so terrified. He looked insane. He looked... violent. He was covered in blood. When he saw the other man at the bottom of the stairs, he just leapt at him.

I kept trying to cover Tilly's eyes, and Jay kept trying to watch the fight and he slipped out of my grasp. I had to pull Tilly back towards the scene and all these disgusting people who stood around just gawping. Some of them were laughing like this was some sort of sport, something fun to watch.

Jay, being a boy of ten, well, he found this fascinating, but I don't even let him watch that obnoxious wrestling on the TV.

I glanced at these two grown men, rolling about on the floor. I shouted at them to stop and screamed for anyone to break them up. I could see that one of them was trying to take something from the other, but then I saw the knife.

The blade caught the light; I just saw a flash at first and one of the men screamed.

I grabbed Jay and turned his head, forcing him to look away but I know I was too late because his cheek was covered in speckles of blood from the one who got cut.

Malcolm McNight (occultist and author of 'I Love Lucifer'): What do you mean, do I know the whereabouts of the rod? I thought you called me here because you knew where it was.

That isn't what I said.

Well, you certainly fucking implied it. So you don't know where it is?

No, I was hoping you could tell me about it.

I came here thinking you had it for me, or could tell me where to get it. Wait a minute, is that fucking thing switched on? Switch it off.

Wayne Cross (former West Yorkshire Police Constable): It was mayhem down there on the platform. You see, people had noticed us coming over the bridge. Some of them had spotted the other commuters making their way towards the exit. Add to this the people already streaming across the bridge for the exit from other arrivals.

Beyond this, the driver of the train that had arrived on platform 9, well he started to move forward with the track now clear, getting ready to let the passengers disembark.

PC Mullins and I, we could see this fight had broken out on the platform, but we hadn't been able to see who was involved as when we were coming over the bridge and directed commuters to the exit, we lost sight of both of the suspects just for a moment or two.

As we reached the top of the stairs down to platform 9, we could see the fight and all the rubber-neckers there and we could see at that point that the fight involved both of the suspects we had been following.

Let's slow this down, though.

Two men, two suspicious men, have charged through a train station. One of them is acting very nervously, one of them shows signs of having been in a struggle. A member of the public has said one of them seems to be hiding something up his top.

The platform is busy; there is a rush-hour, intercity train pulling in, ready to drop off dozens of passengers and collect the dozens more who are at ground zero.

One of these men, it appears, has a bomb and all he has to do is think, that's all. He just has to twitch his thumb, or pull the pin, or let go of the handle, or whatever was going on under his top. In a moment, he would incinerate and maim hundreds of people; depending on the power of the bomb, he could even do worse.

The second man could be an accomplice, who now wants to stop the plot, or the bomber may have lost his nerve and the second man wants to make sure the bomb goes off as planned.

The perfect resolution to any situation is one where nobody even gets injured let alone loses their life.

I was halfway down the stairs, with Mullins behind me. I don't know at that point what he makes of the situation. We didn't have time to confer.

I shouted to try to clear the way, to disperse the crowd, hoping that the two men were too involved in fighting each other to notice that we were closing in. The train pulled past them, going ever so slowly and I just prayed to God it would keep moving, pick up speed and get clear of the station.

The train stopped.

The crowd was not dispersing. I did not have a clear shot, which means Mullins certainly didn't. What were we meant to do? I could see children down there.

I had to get closer; I had to get more people out of my way. I had to get that clear shot. If someone has to die, I have to make sure it is the right person.

I got a few steps further down and a little boy turned around. He had blood on his face. I felt my grasp tighten on the grip of my Glock 17 pistol. This was it, the situation was about to erupt, and I knew it.

Caroline Gebbie (department store assistant manager): As they fought, the one who had run down the stairs, this Russell Fischer, whatever he was chanting, it got louder. I didn't hear it properly, but I know someone said they heard him chanting about Allah.

His voice grew louder, and he was the one holding the knife, but he had something else tucked up inside his clothing. He was trying to hold it, but it was strange, it was like he didn't want to touch it directly.

What makes you say that?

The thing slipped down in the struggle, it was metallic. I saw that much. And when he tried to get it under control again, he sort of pulled at his clothing first rather than just grabbing it with his hand.

I think at that point we were all starting to think the same thing. Backpack, chanting. We all thought we were about to be blown up.

Now, this Fischer man, he slashed wildly with the knife. He cut the man who had been on the track, tore him right across his chest, but his arm kept swinging. And that's when... That's when he... That's when Jay...

Wayne Cross (former West Yorkshire Police Constable): Fischer was shouting his mumbo-jumbo even louder and swinging with that knife of his. That little boy I mentioned, he turned back to see what was happening and someone pushed his mother and she pushed into him. They were all starting to panic down there. They thought the same thing as us, I suppose.

Well that boy ended up with the knife slashed right across his face. Both his eyes burst open. I've never seen anything like it before, that stuff, the jelly, just running out over the kid's face. The bone at the bridge of his nose had snapped and was poking out. His mother went insane at that point I suppose. She was just screaming and crying. There was a little girl... the lad's sister. She was screaming, too.

The train had stopped, to make matters worse, there were even more civilians on the scene. There was no clean shot available.

I still couldn't see Mullins as we weren't in position and to be honest I didn't dare take my eyes off what was happening on the platform.

The other lad, this Sitchin one, he had blood pouring out of his chest. Fischer, poor fucking Russell Fischer, was still swinging that knife around. I saw a man's thigh slice open, right across. Now if the rest of the events didn't follow as they had, that man was dead anyway. His femoral artery was severed and blood was spurting out of him as he collapsed to the floor.

Those around him, if they were in panic-mode before, then they went fucking ape-shit then.

An old woman, not ten seconds off that train, was trampled just about twenty feet in front of me. Her skin was like paper and a stiletto heel tore through the back of her hand and crushed her bones in an instant. She was screaming as others tripped on her legs and fell on top of her. Some of them stood on her legs and managed to keep their balance, and hopped off her, never bothering to try to assist her.

I saw her head smack off the floor and her... was it her left eye or right eye? One of her eyes anyway. It was completely ringed with blood where the orbit had shattered. It looked like the eyeball would just slip out onto the ground any second.

A young lad got shoved down so that his right leg got stuck between the platform and the train. People kept pushing and shoving and then someone fell on that poor bastard. I saw his leg snap just below the knee.

But the worst was yet to come, if you can believe it.

The thing that these two were fighting over, this thing they stole from the museum, Sitchin got his hands to it. Fischer slashed at him with the knife one more time and Sitchin just walked into it with his arm outstretched. The blade caught his forearm, and by God, it bit deep. If it wasn't down to the bone I'll be damned.

Sitchin just turned and sort of held the blade towards his body and turned a bit more so Fischer's arm was almost trapped. The knife was slipping back out of his arm, sawing through the gristle, right round the underside of Sitchin's forearm. He was screaming, Fischer was screaming, everyone was fucking screaming.

Sitchin took that knife out of his own arm by holding Fischer's hand and he ran at him, pushing him over onto that woman who was cradling her blinded son. They were too entangled and although I was getting closer, I still couldn't risk a shot.

Sitchin pulled away from Fischer and scrambled away to the side, among the crowd, shoving people back over towards me.

Fischer got to his feet, his arms outstretched, eyes wide, just fucking psycho-wide... and the chanting grew louder. He clenched his fists and I thought that detonator was going off.

I pulled the trigger.

Andrew Irwin (PPI salesman): Over all that noise down there on the platform, the screaming, the shouting, the cries for help, I heard this popping sound. Those two policemen, they were stood so that they sort of formed a triangle with Russell Fischer, with Fischer at its point, if that makes sense.

His head just sort of burst. He went down and they kept shooting. His ribs, his back, everything, it just seemed to erupt.

The other one, though, the one who had been fighting with him, he had made it onto the train. I knew he wasn't trying to escape. That train was going nowhere. I just assumed he was buying himself time to detonate his bomb.

But you were still there?

I was rooted to the spot. I don't know what it was, but I just couldn't move. Is that strange? I think I was in shock. My legs were like jelly. Do you remember that cartoon, Scooby Doo, when they get scared and their legs just wobble and they can't run away from the bad guys? It was like that. I felt nauseous and I swear to God, I just thought it was the end. No chance of escape.

His head. Jesus Christ, his head just wasn't there anymore.

Ross Davidson (occultist): The artefact believed to have been stolen from the museum is known as the Rod of Pathophas. Pathophas was a demon of the order of Fire. He was a demon renowned for his hot temper and hasty actions. This temperament often brought him into the poor favour of his commander, the demon King Jamaz.

Pathophas was a loyal soldier to Jamaz, however and grew to gain the ability to raise up to a thousand souls at his command at any one time. Not only this, but he was able to prevent or reverse decay and could kill with a single word.

What word?

Nobody knows. Pathophas was supposed to have been killed around two thousand years ago. His problem was that he was easy to summon. With the correct combination of incense and perfume, he could be enticed from Hell. The rituals were not complex and so he was drawn from his home for prolonged periods. It was a matter of time before someone discovered how to kill him. The rod is reportedly one of his femurs, dipped in gold and adorned with jewellery.

I've never seen the Rod of Pathophas before, but I have read about it. Apparently it is simply the thighbone of man and that is why so many believe it to be a fake relic. Others have reasoned that when summoned, he would have taken the form of a human sacrificed in his name and that the femur belongs to the last vessel to bear him before his death.

For years the rod was used in shamanistic practices for some of the Bantu peoples who migrated to South Africa. The rod apparently had some healing properties, but was more commonly used in delivering a sort of Last Rite, to the dying.

After the Second Boer War, a young officer named Marcus Hamilton was believed to have located the rod and brought it back to England with him, to Leeds, in fact. As far as I knew, though, this was considered to be a myth.

Sarah-Louise Nimmo (member of the House Grandier): What kind of organisation is it? Well, some people would call us a cult, I suppose. But I like to think of us as a family. We all take care of each other. We each put some money in, and those who are having a bad time, they get to draw some funds down, that sort of thing. We have plenty to eat and drink. Good company. Great company... I've met some great people through House Grandier, including Simonas and Russell. It was a shame about what happened to those two. I really liked them both. Especially Simonas. I mean, he and I sort of had a bit of a thing. I was pleased that he kept coming even when Russell quit.

Kept coming?

Yes. Russell left House Grandier, but Simonas kept coming. Simonas didn't have to agree with everything Russell said or did. High Priest Dover said Simonas was being groomed for duties in the higher order. That would mean a Priest, in case you don't know.

I was under the impression that Simonas and Russell had left together.

I'm not sure who you've spoken to, but he was definitely here on his own for a long time after Russell left.

High Priest Dover told me.

Perhaps I'm mistaken... I should check really, before I say these things. The High Priest will be correct. I must be mistaken. Just forget I said anything, strike it from the record.

It doesn't work like that, Sarah.

I won't let you print this. I want that recording destroyed.

I bet you do.

Listen, I could be in real trouble. There's obviously some issue here. You could get me killed.

I thought it was like a family. You take care of each other, right?

Well... it's more like the mafia. A family who could kill you if you say the wrong thing.

Sounds lovely.

Caroline Gebbie (department store assistant manager): That man who blinded my son, he wasn't saying Allah, by the way, like some of them have been saying over the years. Jay heard him, he liked copying things, especially if he heard words he considered funny or hadn't heard before. I'll never forget these words because they are the last words I heard my Jay say: "Cados, Adonai, Elohi, Zena."

It went on, but those were four words Jay copied. Any idea what they mean?

I'm afraid not.

I wish I had been allowed to keep the little pendant thing I found. The man dropped it and I don't know why, but I picked it up. It looked maybe Egyptian; it was like an eye or the sun or something like that. I have no idea why but I put picked it up and squeezed it until it cut into my palm, and I shoved it into my pocket.

The police took it from me later. I wasn't allowed to keep it. I could have shown you it; perhaps it has some meaning in all of this.

Wayne Cross (former West Yorkshire Police Constable): When those first shots went, I saw a small metallic object fall from Fischer's hand. Immediately, my mind went to grenade pin, you know? I jumped onto him, pressed my body down over him, my fingers were sliding through the ruins of his head: pieces of skull, brain matter, teeth and bits of his tongue. Usually that would make me feel sick just thinking about it, but there I was with my bare hands slipping through the mess, with nothing more on my mind than my body was going to take the blast and the shrapnel.

I was yelling my head off, trying to get people clear; Mullins did the same.

After a moment or two my eyes fell on the metal object and it was some sort of charm, resembling an eye. I know it now to be the "Evil Eye". I also know now that the Evil Eye is considered to be a protective talisman, warding off evil, despite its name.

Do you believe that?

What does that have to do with anything? The point is that Russell Fischer believed in it. Don't you see? I shot him in the utter belief that he was some sort of religious zealot who was going to detonate a bomb. He had the backpack, the sweats, he had a knife for Christ's sake, he jumped the gate, he was sprinting for a train... What the hell else was I to think?

Of course at the time, I didn't have time to think about what he did or didn't believe in. At the time, I had to act, because when I stood up, Mullins was shouting, telling me that Sitchin had boarded the train.

I instructed Mullins to hit the fire alarm and just get people out of there.

I broke through the crowd, all those poor bastards panicking, trying to get away from that train, trying not to look at the blinded boy, the trampled woman, the bul-let-riddled body of Fischer. It was like swimming uphill, and of course more and more people were tripping over and being trampled in the panic that broke out.

Anyway, I got onto the train and what I saw when I got on there... I don't know... Maybe it would have been better if Mullins had made it onboard and I had been on the platform.

Lisa Wood (marketing consultant): Standing out on New Station Street, a couple of vans full of police officers arrived and we were herded away towards City Square. People stopped in their tracks, though, and pointed up to the sky. I looked up and I swear I have never seen anything like it in my life.

Imagine the sky above the city being struck with blots of black ink, and that ink begins to spread, these blots reach-ing out for each other as other ink drops land, stretch-ing out, connecting. That is the only way I can describe it. Within about thirty seconds the city turned from late summer evening - still daylight, essentially, to pitch black.

People had been running away from the station, crying about terrorists and what have you, but when that sky changed so quickly, we had no idea what could cause it. But everyone had to know, as I knew, that this had nothing to do with terrorists and it couldn't be a coincidence, could it?

Saying that, though, when the lightning struck the train station, in that first second or two, I thought a bomb had gone off.

Andrew Irwin (PPI salesman): I had finally managed to pry myself away. I was trying to stay ahead of the crowd, running for the exits, when the lightning struck. I hit the ground, I think everyone did. You could feel the building shake. Again, I just thought, this is it. There was an explosive after all, I thought; it must have finally detonated.

Glass showered down onto the spot where all the madness had broken out earlier. There was already a sort of deafening roar of screaming and shouting as everyone fought to get out, but when the glass fell, and I saw it coming down, you could hear, from the other side of that train, individuals crying out, above the background roar, really screaming in agony.

I could only imagine what was going on.

Caroline Gebbie (department store assistant manager): A piece of the falling glass sliced me right from my shoulder down to my wrist. I've never really had full use of my arm since then. The worst part though, is that happening caused me to drop Jay's head and his shoulders hit my legs, but his head smacked the concrete. Even with all that noise around me, I heard that smack. I practically felt it.

There were still others running around, pushing and pulling one another, falling, trampling each other. It was terrible. Tilly was knocked to the ground, and I was trying to get one hand to her, and my injured arm under Jay's head, but he kept slipping and hitting the floor, I couldn't hold him.

Tilly's cries made me look back at her and she was sort of crawling towards me, trying to reach me. Her left forearm was snapped about halfway down... Her hand was hanging down. The sound... I could hear her bones rubbing against each other. It was... it was the worst sound I think I've ever heard.

I glanced at Jay. The back of his head was pouring blood. That was my fault. I did that to him. It was my stupid fault...

Wayne Cross (former West Yorkshire Police Constable): I've seen people do all sorts of things to themselves, you know. When I was on probation I had to cut down this suicide... He had hanged himself, but with razor wire. The way he had done it, he had snipped the razors off a good length of it, so the wire would slide and the slipknot worked fairly well. When those razors had bitten into the fucker, his head had nearly come off.

I've seen someone try to take their own eye out with a broken bottle. Another one bit through her own wrist right in front of me as I tried to arrest her. She made a good job of it, too. I never thought that was possible.

None of that, none of the things I have ever seen before, prepared me for what I saw on that train. I know I will never see anything like it again unless I am damned to Hell.

Are you ready? Do you want me to tell you what I saw?

I was hoping that you would.

Oh, I'll tell anyone. The trouble is, when I told my superiors they had me fucking sectioned. Never mind. Here it is. I was in the vestibule on the carriage Sitchin had jumped onto. I was only feet away from him and thirty or so people were in the carriage with him. I couldn't for the life of me understand why they hadn't run off. Surely, I thought, they saw the shooting, heard the screaming, why haven't they fucking run?

Sitchin was sat on the floor, sort of half in the lower luggage rack. He was only feet away from me as I say, with the vestibule door keeping us apart. He had something in his hand. At first I thought it was a piece of metal, but then I could see it was shaped like a human bone, painted gold, with gemstones stuck on it or mounted into it. He held it up in his left hand. Now I had witnessed the damage done to that arm out on the platform when Fischer had stabbed him, so how the hell he could hold this bone up, I don't know, but there he was, holding it out.

I hit the button to open the vestibule door, but it wouldn't respond. I tried to force it. Jamming my shoulder against the little handle part, but it wouldn't budge. Not even an inch.

The train's lights flickered and I noticed that the station was very dark. An explosion outside the train, above, at the roof of the building, which I'm told was the station actually being struck by lightning, sent massive glass shards falling onto the platform.

A man looked up on the platform and a huge wedge of glass just chopped his face in half. A woman ran around with her severed arm in her other hand. A teenager, or a girl in maybe her early twenties, she had a piece of glass embedded in her face, stretching from one cheek to the other. Her jaw hung loose beneath it and with every breath, a fountain of blood burst from the lower section of her mouth, beneath the glass, pouring down her chin.

Turning away from the carnage on the platform, I wrestled my attention back to Sitchin. I stuck another magazine into the pistol, but I didn't fire a shot. I couldn't. I froze. I can only assume Sitchin wanted me to see this and somehow he compelled me to look at him. He used the knife he had taken from Fischer, and sliced down his right trouser leg, about the length of his thigh. He put down the knife and the bone, using his hands to rip the material further up, towards his hip, and further down, past the knee.

The first cut, I could see, had scored his thigh, but that didn't matter because he picked that knife up and sliced right through his flesh, right through the muscle and down to the bone. His femoral artery was sliced open at this point and the blood came gushing out of him. I sort of thought then I had nothing to worry about. I thought he'll be dead in minutes with that injury.

I wasn't the only one on there watching him; those other passengers cried out, one of them vomited. Sitchin? He was out of his mind, screaming out and yelling. He felt it, I don't doubt it, but pain didn't stop him.

He sliced down into the meat at his knee, sawing across from left to right, then again in an upward diagonal at the top of his thigh. It was wet work, mind, and ugly. The blade kept slipping and by the end he was practically pulling the meat apart as he worked.

Sitchin, having created two great flaps of flesh and muscle, proceeded to tear these flaps open at either side, occasionally jamming the knife in again, to snap tendons and free the muscle from his femur.

Passengers rushed away from him, to the opposite end of the carriage, overcome by the sight of his grisly work, but they found the exit barred. The door at the far end of the carriage was evidently as jammed as my own.

Sitchin then placed his right leg up on the armrest of a seat opposite him; he picked up the golden thigh-bone and pointed it down the carriage. Immediately, a woman charged along the corridor towards him and she just jumped onto his right thigh. Her feet slipped and she fell over, half onto the chair where Sitchin's leg was propped. Her shoes ended up down on his groin, with this sodden mass of muscle and skin torn away.

He raised the bone again and another passenger sprinted down, landing his arse down on the woman's legs and Sitchin's. Even through the door I heard the bone snap. The man climbed off and wandered down the carriage, not to where the others stood, but he sat down, like he had calmly returned to his seat after buying a sandwich and a packet of crisps. The woman, she pulled her legs away from Sitchin and remained in the seat where she had toppled.

Sitchin's femur was snapped in two. He jammed the blade of that knife down under his knee-cap and just popped it out, slicing away at the cartilage in a deft move. His concentration was spell-binding. He wasn't screaming anymore, just really pre-occupied. It was like he knew that nobody could pose a threat to him, so why care?

He was deathly pale. There was definitely very little blood reaching his brain at that point. He wasn't about to collapse, though, although the sheer blood-loss and the broken leg should have placed him firmly into physiological shock. I noticed as well, that the blood wasn't spurting from his leg anymore. His blood pressure was very low. I just thought he had to be close to the end.

Like pulling a lever, he yanked up the top portion of his femur, bending it out of that massive wound of his. With both hands, he heaved on the bone, trying to pull it vertically from his body. He had his teeth clenched, eyes squeezed shut. The effort he was putting into the operation was enormous.

Sitchin stabbed away with his knife again, up inside his groin and he sort of reached right under, sawing under his buttocks.

He heaved again, but his bloody hands slipped off the bone. He wiped his hands on the seats, the floor, his t-shirt, all of which was already blood-soaked from his artery pumping out everywhere.

Somehow he managed to gain more purchase and the bone started to give. He braced his right shoulder against the luggage rack and pulled over to the left, dislocating his hip. And that was pretty much that, really, he just kept pulling and the top of his thigh came out.

With a little more cutting and pulling, he had the lower portion of bone clear, and then it was a simple matter of shoving the stolen, golden femur into his leg.

I glanced out at Mullins, and could see him ushering people away. Two of the station staff were with him and Mullins looked in at me, pointing up ahead. He did a gesture with his hands, showing the fists interlocked, then parted. He was getting these men to uncouple the train ahead of the carriage I was in. I nodded to him. A good move, I thought.

This was when Sitchin stood up. Now if you haven't already decided to write me off as a fucking nutter, then you just might, now.

He stood up, ok, on this leg that he had just voluntarily mangled and stuffed some sort of decorated bone into. His left forearm, sliced to buggery before, sealed back up right in front of me. It was like someone slowly fastening up a zip on a coat. I looked down to see that that mutilated leg was going the same way.

Sitchin turned and looked right at me. He pointed to the carriage behind me, which was the last one before the rear-facing locomotive. I turned around and saw the passengers there had been trying to escape, with no success. I had assumed them to be safely off the train and hadn't even looked at them or thought about them while watching Sitchin's improvised surgery.

I wondered what his fucking game was and when I turned back to Sitchin, he was walking down the carriage, further away from me. He touched that woman, the one who had jumped on his leg. She stood up and her face started to corrode, flesh dripping off her jaw. A rough hand-print shape was left on her face, where I could see right into her mouth; teeth exposed, jawbone right up to her eye socket.

He worked his way down the carriage and touched a few of them like that, on the hand, on the top of the head, on the shoulder, and wherever he touched them, the skin just putrefied and rotted away.

Whatever was in his touch not only had the effect of decaying their skin, but it made them take an interest in me, too.

PC Val Neeson: I didn't get to know PC Mullins, really. I had met him I think only on one occasion. He was assigned to North Leeds, you see, so we didn't cross paths frequently. That was before he went into Armed Response, and I didn't see him then.

What I know of him, he was a good copper. Some of the lads criticised him from his early days on the force. They said he always wanted to be second, but in my experience, that can be valuable. It wouldn't do to have a whole constabulary of Wayne Crosses would it?

Caroline Gebbie (department store assistant manager): One of the policemen had gone onto the train, but the other one, he stayed on the platform. I begged him to help me, but he was moving people on, getting anyone who could move to do so. I think it was he who hit the fire alarm.

He did come back to me though, only for a second. He could see that my children were badly injured and that I was hurt too. In all the panic, there was nothing he could really do, I just pleaded with him to get my kids out of there.

When he told us to keep our heads down for a few minutes more, I screamed at him, I called him all sorts of names. He just ignored me; he clearly had more to deal with than me. I hate it, but I can understand it now. How could he save as many people as possible, try to figure out what was going on, and give first aid to people? There were too many people needing his help.

I think I could have handled this more if Jay had just slipped away quietly then, or if Tillie had gone into shock and remained oblivious to everything that happened next, but... there's no point... I can't think like that now, because what happened... happened, it's just so hard to... make sense of it. Someone who knows about these things told me that they weren't themselves... that they wouldn't have known, but... I don't know... I hope to God that's the truth.

Wayne Cross (former West Yorkshire Police Constable): The... I don't know really what to call them. The decayed people in the same carriage as Sitchin, they started banging on the vestibule door, but the door didn't open and didn't budge, as before, when they tried to pull at it and get in with me.

The door behind me, though, that one opened and I was rushed. A woman scratched my face - she almost took my eyes out. I smacked her with the grip of my firearm, but another took her place. I punched him, I kicked the next woman. The first woman climbed to her feet again.

I glanced behind me and out on the platform to see people sprinting towards the train. Their eyes looked different. Wide, staring, with evil intent all over their faces. I've seen some bad people throughout my career, but this, like I said, this was evil. They looked insane, detached from reality, full of... hate. I couldn't just wait for them to join me, so I hit the button and closed the carriage door.

A man slammed against me with his full weight and I was pinned up against that door. I was thankful that I had thought to close it, or I would have been out on that platform right then, with my head cracked open.

Fingers stabbed into my mouth, someone actually had my tongue between their fingers. It was a woman; her long nails felt like they would come tear right through.

Someone was calling to me through the radio, but I couldn't respond. The man who pinned me kicked at my shins and I cried out, as much as I could anyway, with my tongue almost ripped clear of my head.

I... I lost it then.

Andrew Irwin (PPI salesman): You have never seen as many police as this. I mean, there was a ton of coppers pouring through the gate. They had the full MP5s and all that. The armed officers spread out, checking each of us who were still on the floor. We lifted our hands, you know, I wanted them to see that I was unarmed and everybody else seemed to be doing the same.

They stepped past, moving up the stairs. Some of them fanned out along the nearest platform, where they could see into the train over the rails.

A row of unarmed transport police and West Yorkshire officers followed, but one of them helped me to my feet. Around me, others were doing the same. We were led out onto New Station Street. To safety. Ambulances were all over the bottom of Park Row and they had set up sort of a makeshift hospital to tend to injuries.

They treated me for shock, kept me warm, kept me talking, that sort of thing. But, it didn't really register until later. I mean, I still can't get that image out of my mind. When that man's head just disintegrated. It was like a red cloud full of all these solid bits.

And that little boy... I mean, I only heard the worst of what happened later, but you don't know what's true and what isn't. All I know is we were all of us warned not to talk to the papers, not to talk to the news...

When you think of these terror attacks and police shootings and all that, there's always a hundred people on Sky News telling you what they saw, but with this thing in Leeds... nothing. It's like it didn't even happen. But something bloody massive happened in the station, and if what I heard is true, most of it happened after I got outside.

Caroline Gebbie (department store assistant manager): The policeman on the train was being attacked, I could see that. I shouted for his colleague to help him, but he was up ahead with two men who seemed to be, well, they were uncoupling the carriages. That's what they did, because when they finished, one of them blew a whistle and the front end of the train pulled away, leaving behind two carriages and the engine at the back.

But before they separated the train, lots of people who had been running to safety, they turned and came back. It was terrifying. They weren't the same anymore. I looked to my left because there was just this roaring noise and it was this mob of people streaming back down the stairs and across the platform.

I felt Jay move, and as I tried to stop him, he lashed out at me, breaking my nose. With the pain and tears I was blinded for a moment or two and when I cleared my vision, I saw that he had run off, and Tilly was gone, too.

The crowd spread alongside the train as the front section pulled away. Some of these people tried to cling to the sides, but they fell off and came back. Some of them dropped down onto the track and attacked the men who had uncoupled the carriages.

Tilly and Jay seemed to have been swallowed by the crowd and I stood up, hoping I would see them. I heard a gun firing on the train. Again and again and again it fired and I ducked down, not knowing where the hell the noise was coming from at first, and not knowing if they were firing at me... After a few seconds I had my head up again and kept looking for the kids.

I saw Jay first. I couldn't see what was happening to the men on the tracks, but I could hear them screaming. The policeman had left them, he was shouting into his radio, but seemed to be getting nowhere. One of those engineers or whatever they were, he tried to climb up onto the platform and that's when Jay ran over to him.

Despite Jay's eyes being... gone... he seemed to be able to move around fine. He stamped on the man's hands, like he wanted him not to get up from whatever was happening on the track. The man lashed out at his legs, trying to swipe him away, trying to stop him, but Jay kept kicking out.

He kicked the man in the face, not just once, but he got him again really quickly. The man's nose, well it just exploded. Jay then grasped this man's face and he... Christ, this was my little boy... I still can't understand it... He grabbed the man's head and smashed it on the edge of the platform. I mean, how was he strong enough to do that? How could he with the injuries? He couldn't even see the edge of the platform.

He kept slamming the man's head down again and again until his forehead just split open, right across. Jay kept going. I think he cracked the man's skull, but whoever was on the tracks pulled him back and that was him out of my view. Jay ran straight away, with no hesitation, right back into the crowd.

It was then that I saw Tilly. She was on the shoulders of one of these others. They were all banging their fists on the train windows, but Tilly was swinging her broken arm, just flailing it against the glass.

The next thing I knew, the policeman was at my side. He must have known I was ok... I mean, not like the others, because he started pushing me towards the stairs, behind the crowd. He told me to keep moving.

He had his gun out. I couldn't think. I didn't know what he was going to do. I was crying because if he was going to shoot at whoever was involved in the trouble, then he was going to get Jay and Tilly.

I begged him not to hurt my children. He kept telling me to move along and keep moving. I was begging him and begging him, though. I grabbed him and shook him. He slapped my face and pushed me away. When I got up, I ran at him. My God, I ran at him and I hit the pistol he carried. His arm swung back and he dropped the gun.

He dropped the gun and he's dead because of me.

Some of them in the crowd had turned on him. They grabbed him, it was like they got their hands down between his armour vest and his back, and they just pulled him back. A black briefcase came down over his head and he was knocked to his knees.

I just kept screaming, "I'm sorry. I'm sorry," and the look on his face… he wanted me to help him, but I couldn't do anything. I couldn't think of what would help him. I don't know anything about guns, and besides that, I couldn't see the gun he dropped, I think someone kicked it away.

A woman crouched over him; it looked like they were kissing. When she came away, one of his lips was gone.

They bent his fingers back and snapped them; they twisted his arms until they popped out of the sockets. When they stretched him out on his front and grabbed his head, I couldn't bear to watch any more. I wanted to get out of there, but I couldn't leave Jay and Tilly behind. The decision was taken away from me, though.

I collapsed into the arms of a police officer who had come down the stairs behind me, and I knew nothing else until the cold air outside hit me. I have a faint memory of that, I think I can remember seeing blue lights flashing in the darkness, but then that was it. When I woke up in LGI, it was three days later and my kids were both dead. And the police have threatened me with all sorts if I speak to anyone about it. Well, what can they possibly do to me, eh? What more can be taken away from me?

Wayne Cross (former West Yorkshire Police Constable): I knew I was ending my career as soon as I squeezed the trigger. They would never understand this, and I knew it at the time. I blew the top of a man's head off and he fell away from me and I slid down the door. I thought I would pass out with the pain because my tongue was still in the grip of that mad woman.

I fired a shot through her arm, shattered her humerus. Bone exploded out through her jacket. I had splinters of the man's skull in my mouth, in my eyes; the woman's blood had blinded me for a moment or two.

These bastards just kept coming through into the vestibule. I grabbed a handrail above me, next to the door, and hauled myself upright. The next person to attack was an overweight woman. I stuffed that firearm into her fat fucking gut and pulled the trigger. Her legs gave out; I had hoped to damage her spine and I think I got my wish. No good going for headshots, you know. It's not like the films. The head's just a little target, relatively. Aim lower, don't miss. I pressed one of the first attackers up against the wall and put a bullet into her heart.

I had only a second to try to see where Sitchin was at that point. He had gone right to the furthest end of the carriage, behind a meat-shield of these poor bastards with their faces and arms corroded by his touch. They stood there, waiting for me, like some sort of honour guard. It was like they were daring me to come in after Sitchin so that they could get at me.

Those out on the platform had become frenzied. Bloody hands banged on the windows, knuckles breaking, skin splitting, blood oozing out on the glass. They picked up a dead man from the concrete and used him as a battering ram, four of the bastards, one on each limb. The top of his skull compressed on the first impact and snapped in on the second. His neck broke, head hung limp and they just carried on. In a few seconds the old guy's spine was breaking through his flesh and snapping off in great big fragments.

Whatever Sitchin had done to these people, and I don't care what anyone says, he, or whatever he had become, courtesy of that fucking thighbone, is responsible for all of those people going on a rampage; whatever he had done, those people had absolutely no fear of my weapon, no apparent fear of death.

I saw a couple of folks on the train, holding back by the curving toilet cubicle of the next carriage. They weren't staying there out of fear. They glared at me, grinding their teeth like a bunch of pill-heads. They just waited for the right opportunity. They were coming for me, of that there was no doubt, but they had watched their cohorts being cut down and they wanted to be more effective than that. They wanted to be the ones to kill me.

That was when I caught a glimpse of something black out on the opposite platform, across the tracks. My colleagues, armed response officers, MP5 submachine guns at the ready. The relief. I have never known relief like it in my life.

One of my colleagues pointed at me and pointed a single finger to the ground. "Duck," he was telling me. I didn't argue.

Shots ripped through the vestibule and the carriage to my left. The air filled with glass, splinters and shredded upholstery. Those two who had been lying in wait for me, they made their move, only to be torn apart by gunfire. I was grateful.

I don't know... the strangest feeling came over me while I lay there, and I have to say, it comes over me almost every day. I mean, we're talking about people being possessed here. I thought about these people riddled with bullets, or their heads popped or their spines blown apart and I just... I wondered what would happen when Sitchin was stopped. Like, if I had just hit them with the taser, would they have woken up with the spell broken?

The truth of the matter was, I was frightened, and I did panic in there, and I shot to kill, or to cause the most damage that I could.

I didn't want to die.

And while my colleagues making themselves known had been a Godsend at first, the problem was when Sitchin saw them.

PC Val Neeson: The reports of an armed officer attacking other officers in that station... they're completely false. I mean, it's ridiculous to even suggest that. The detonation of that device ended the lives of 143 people, and that is all there is to it.

Wayne Cross and Justin Mullins took Russell Fischer's life, yes, that is true. There have been many statements given by senior officers and pathologists better informed than me, who have said their piece on the death of Russell Fischer. An inquest presented its findings and the IPCC presented its findings.

They hung Wayne Cross out to dry, don't you agree?

Look, as I've already said, Wayne's statements were unreliable. Ghosts and goblins have no place in an investigation. It's a miracle that Wayne survived; he was so close to that blast.

There is a time discrepancy. The blast was reported at around 6.00pm, but eye witnesses say the train was intact then.

This needs to be laid to rest, Stuart. Honestly, it does. You need to know something about these situations, these stressful situations. Time speeds up or slows down. A bomb went off. A man was riddled with bullets on a train station platform. People were in shock. Do you think they checked their watches, Stuart? Honestly, do you?

Well... I'm just saying that there are some very interesting accounts out there.

This tragedy was not interesting, Stuart. It was horrific; I shouldn't have to remind anyone of that. I lost so many friends and colleagues in that blast, Stuart. Some of them I'd worked with for ten years, some of the even more. We can't just keep retreading the old ground, it does nobody any good.

When we got to Hasib Nazir over in Harehills, a week after that explosion, then that was it. Mission accomplished.

When he was sentenced to life imprisonment, that was those victims avenged. He was the extremist who built the bomb. He was one who gave those two the order.

Simonas Sitchin and Russell Fischer were members of a cult. They weren't extremists of any mainstream faith.

Witnesses heard one of them shouting Allahu Akhbar, all the way through and right up until the explosion, so there you go. Now this interview is finished and I would advise you to leave all of this alone. If people like you, vultures like you, keep picking at this, it is never going to heal.

Wayne Cross (former West Yorkshire Police Constable): You know what I'm saying in my account. You know I'm talking about possession, right? Whatever was held in that bone, it caused Sitchin and all those civilians to be possessed and Sitchin, or his body anyway, seemed to be the centre of it all.

Then why didn't Sitchin just possess you? Why didn't he get you to turn the gun on yourself? Same with Mullins?

We're talking about demons, Stuart. Whatever demon was responsible for this whole thing... that bone... they call it the Rod of Pathophas, did you know that? Pathophas was a demon. Did you know that?

Let's say it's true and to be fair, it's the most fucking rational explanation for what I saw and experienced in that station. That demon couldn't touch us, Mullins and I, because we were evil. We had just killed someone. We shot a man only seconds before. Killed him right there on the spot.

So by that rationale, then, Caroline Gebbie, she's the lady who had the two children with her on the platform.

I know Caroline, yes. I know her well since all of this.

By your reasoning, she must be evil, then?

Not at all. She was carrying the protective talisman. She picked up the charm Fischer dropped. I'm right, you know. I'm right. If you don't believe me, listen to this next bit. When the armed officers on the far platform, closest to the gates, had finished firing into the remaining carriages, the other team moved onto the platform closest to the train.

Not one of them made a difference, because a bloke I had done my firearms training with, another new member of armed response, George Ferguson. We called him Geordie, because, well, he was a Geordie. Geordie was like Justin and I. When he went into the station he had never taken a life.

He shot every single one of those ten men and women in the base of their skulls at point blank range and he must have done it in seconds. At that range, no armour or helmet was going to help them.

Now, from inside the train, I saw the men on the far platform opening fire at somebody on the tracks. One by one, they were injured and dropped to the platform or dropped to the tracks.

At that point I had no idea it was Geordie, and there was nothing I could do anyway. The only thing I could think of, that could possibly bring an end to all of this madness, was to take out Sitchin himself.

But let's talk about what was going on all around me. The boys had emptied the carriage to my left, or at least rendered the enemy incapable of posing a threat.

Out on the platform, Sitchin's mob increased the intensity with which they attacked the door and when I say intensity, I mean it. A man was punching that glass so hard that his skin had ripped to bits and was hanging off his fingers like a bunch of fucking used condoms.

I heard a clicking noise among the thudding impact of his strikes as his bone connected with the glass. He couldn't see the futility of his actions; he hadn't even caused a crack to appear in that glass.

Again, four of them picked up another body and proceeded to use it as a battering ram but I noticed this time a spider's web of cracks starting to form in the bottom left corner of the window. That told me I had only minutes, maybe only seconds left to live.

I opened fire on the vestibule door, breaking the locking mechanism and the unseen hold Sitchin had applied to it. The woman with the partially rotted face, at the front of the queue of enemies beyond that door didn't wait a second; she yanked the door aside and took a bullet to her ravaged face, for her trouble.

That dropped her and the bullet tapped into the forehead of the bloodthirsty man stood behind her, putting him down, too.

It's not like I was ever trained to deal with that situation, so I had no idea if a headshot would even keep them down; as I've said the headshot's not great because you can easily miss and I had to conserve the little ammunition I carried on me.

The corridor down the carriage was blocked with these zombie-types, Sitchin had seemed to convert with just a touch. Sitchin, I could see right in the background. His leg, what I could see of it through the tattered jeans and the blood still fresh on his skin, looked as though it was sealing over, healing. But the skin, it wasn't the usual flesh-tone you'd expect to see, it was like a black, hard bark, it looked like a tough hide.

Sitchin was smiling at me as his pawns attacked.

I fired a shot into the chest of the first man to attack me. I went right for his heart. Now where that had finished those who had been turned by Sitchin at range, it did nothing on these fuckers. So I put one into his brain and that did the trick. It seemed I had to destroy the brain to stop them. My every thought was fixed on survival, so that took me only seconds to figure out.

To the right of me, a small army of these converts of Sitchin's hammered the glass with anything they could get their hands on, bins, dead bodies and each other. A little girl was on the shoulders of big, tall, rugby-player type man. This girl's forearm was snapped in half, bones protruding through her flesh. She swung her arm so that her little hand smacked the glass like a flail. I saw the last threads of soft tissue snap, and her hand flew off somewhere behind her. The girl didn't even flinch. You know what she started to do? She head-butted the glass instead. Her doing this gave the rest of them the idea.

Dozens of them, completely out of control, completely oblivious to pain, or the damage they were causing to themselves, pounded their fists and heads against the glass. Some of them, their flesh cracked on the first impact, so hard were they going at it; others took a few hits before the blood started to gush.

As I blasted a path through Sitchin's meat-shield on the train, the window to my right became awash with blood.

A decayed mouth bit into my hand, I screamed, terrified this was like a zombie-film, and I was going to become one of them. I almost dropped my gun and thank fuck I didn't. I punched this guy so hard, some of his teeth stuck in my arm when his jaw broke. I stuck the pistol muzzle under the roof of his gaping purple-black fucking mouth, and pulled the trigger, painting the ceiling with him.

While I slipped another magazine into the Glock, I had to kick and punch to keep another couple of these fuckers from biting me. Then, from the platform right over on my left, Geordie, it seems, had finished executing the rest of the team, and I hadn't noticed.

He looked in on me, took aim and fired.

I grabbed the old bloke in front of me and held him up to the left, letting him catch the bullets from Geordie's MP5. I kept pushing further into the carriage, running straight into a teenage boy whose left side of his face was just a blackened skull. The boy, as well as the old man I was carrying, both snapped their teeth at me.

You see this piece of my ear? See the scars there where they reattached it? The teenager almost had that completely off.

The collision caused me to fall, of course, so I had this old one practically on top of me, and this teenage one with the split face beneath me. Geordie didn't stop firing, though. His bullets smashed the windows on the platform side. Yeah, he took out a few of the converts who were there, trying to smash their way in, too, but there was a fucking legion of them out there. They had to get up a little way to get in, the carriage windows being well above the platform, but they had their entrance right there and ready made for them.

I head-butted the old bastard I held, smashing his nose in, hoping to rob him of his sight for a moment or two. I then knocked the side of my head down onto little 'Two-Face' on the floor, hoping to do the same to him.

I brought the gun round to the back of the old guy's head, praying to fucking Christ I wouldn't shoot myself. I fired, once again taking a wonderful shower in skull and brain matter. I scrambled over Two-Face and put one into his head as I passed.

Geordie had exhausted his magazine and was in the process of reloading it and I found myself face to face with Simonas Sitchin himself.

Rosie Ost (Russell Fischer's former partner): I don't know. I mean… I thought it would have been impossible for a demon to be killed by a man. I don't think you could outright kill a demon. They have to be like a demigod, or something, by comparison to us. Wouldn't they just slip out of the human form they had taken, and return to Hell? The bone that had Russell so excited… that had to be just a human bone, really, I would say. Even if it was a human who had been possessed by a demon, or a demon in human form... they would always have another form to escape to, don't you think?

I don't know what I think, Rosie, to be perfectly honest with you.

Ross Davidson (occultist): There isn't much to go on to really get the truth about what killed Pathophas all those years ago. He had taken on the body of a man and of course, one can reason that a body can die. A demon's healing abilities, if he has them, and if he has vitality left in his form to utilise them... would make it very difficult. A sustained attack by men with extraordinary stamina must have been required back then.

Those men were probably tribesmen who had been at war and had killed, tainting their souls so that Pathophas could not simply command them to carry out his wishes. It would have been one hell of a battle, I would suppose.

For a man... any man... or group of men, to have the stamina to render a demon incapable of healing himself, or forcing him to jettison his human shell... I mean, that would be a huge undertaking. Huge, but not impossible.

What do you think gives the Rod of Pathophas its power?

I'm not sure what you mean by gives it its power. I haven't experienced its power first-hand. Off the top of my head, though, this thing is supposed to be an unholy relic. A part of the body that Pathophas inhabited when he was killed. It is entirely possible that embedded within the material of that bone... imprinted on its DNA, perhaps, is some trace of the demon's power. Perhaps if allowed to grow, who knows? Pathophas might be resurrected by it, or perhaps it allows him to take control of your mind.

So in your opinion it would be a trace of Pathophas in there, not his whole... being?

I suppose that is my theory, yes. I think that trace of him might infiltrate a person who comes into contact with the rod. Maybe that could grow, who knows? This is very specific, Stuart. I think perhaps you know, or suspect more than you are telling me.

Wayne Cross (former West Yorkshire Police Constable): The engine started, with just a wave of his hand. A couple of seconds later and the train started to move off, back in the direction it had come from. Thank God we got moving before that lot out on the platform had the chance to climb in.

Sitchin leapt at me and all I could think about was that skin running off those other bastards he had touched. I dropped my pistol and grabbed his wrists, trying to keep those poisonous fingertips away from me. He was strong, though; he forced me back like a truck and all I could do was retreat. Of course, I got less than half a dozen steps before I toppled over one of the bodies that lay about the place like blood-soaked litter.

That made things somewhat more difficult, what with all of his weight crushing down on me.

I could hear his minions crying out from the platform as we passed, starting to gather speed. They sounded desperate to scramble aboard, like panicking children left by their mother. That impulse terrified me; what if Sitchin was going to keep it running slow so they could get on with us?

My arms began to buckle and I tried to brace myself against anything at all around me, but my elbows slipped on the gore streaked up the plastic on the side of the seats.

I heard gunfire behind Sitchin; glass shattered. I heard bullets thudding into metal and smashing plastic somewhere up past my head, back where I had first entered the carriage. Sitchin seemed to go limp for a moment and I used the precious seconds this had bought me to shove him upwards and back. I caught just a glimpse of Geordie entering the carriage through the vestibule door he had blasted open at what was now the back of the train.

My fingers slid through the blood and gore on the floor and I found a discarded pen. You will never know the feeling of finding that pen. It was like I had just been granted a second chance. I had that pen straight in Sitchin's right eye, and back out again and I just kept stabbing through that busted eyeball, right back through into his skull. I was able to get to my haunches as Sitchin staggered back.

Geordie had either realised he had shot his master in the back and injured him, or Sitchin was commanding him not to fire. Whatever the hell it was, I grabbed my pistol from the floor and put Geordie down with one to the head - I couldn't miss from that range and he was too dangerous for me to leave to chance.

The train was slowing again, and we hadn't even made it out of the station. The pen had stuck into Sitchin's brain and... possessed or not, he needs that brain to control his body and everything else, right? I grabbed the headrests of the chairs to my left and right, hopped up and stuck my boot right on the end of the pen and drove it deeper into his skull.

The noises he was making were like no man or animal I have ever heard before. Howling, crying, cursing... but it was all these noises at once. He was frantically trying to get that pen out of his head.

I helped him with that, when I blasted a hole right through his skull. He dropped to the ground, silent and still, but something told me that wasn't enough to keep him down.

The train ground to a halt and through the smashed door, I could see Sitchin's loyal cohorts racing toward me and that told me that Sitchin, or whatever the hell controlled him, still lived. I glanced about for the knife Sitchin had used earlier, but I couldn't see it in the chaos of limbs and shattered skulls.

I levelled my Glock at Sitchin's right leg and opened fire. It took a few shots, but the tough hide eventually tore open. I blew his kneecap out and blasted at his hip, shattering bones to free up that femur.

My ammunition was gone. My time ran out. Hands appeared at the door and the brainwashed puppets scrambled in. I grabbed a big dagger of the reinforced glass from one of the shattered windows, at first I thought about jabbing it right into my neck, but then I thought no. I have to fight. I hadn't survived all that just to lie down and die.

I dragged Sitchin back by the foot, hoping to buy a few seconds as I worked with the knife, sawing away at the holes in his leg created by my shots. In the dim carriage light I could just see the rivulets of blood sliding over the golden bone.

To my right as I moved backwards, other slaves rushed the train. They boarded. I was surrounded.

I reached into the leg, grabbed that golden femur, and yanked.

Hands clawed at my hair, dragging my head back. Someone clawed at my throat, tearing my skin away. Fingers scratched my eyelids. I lashed out, fought for my life, elbows flying this way and that; punching like a maniac.

Then Sitchin woke up and his fingers curled round my forearms.

My limbs went cold as the nerves died. I could actually feel the flesh dying. It was agonising... like plunging my arms into liquid nitrogen, or at least, what you'd imagine that to be like.

Sitchin's followers were all around me, attacking me. I felt my jaw break mid-scream. That was when my vision finally started to go. If I fell, I knew I would never get back up.

My left hand stopped responding and I let go of his right leg, twisting my arm around his, trying to break his grasp. As I rotated my arm, his fingers just slid through the soft tissue and his nails went down to the bones. He released my arms and pressed his palms around my face. I could feel liquid running down my cheeks and down, under my chin.

With my right hand, I grasped his femur again, but I planted my feet, one on his right shin and one on his left leg and I heaved with every ounce of strength I had. I collapsed somewhere during that last exertion.

When I woke up, Val Neeson was there. I had the femur in my hands. Sitchin was dead at my feet. I was surrounded, completely surrounded, by the corpses of those who had attacked me.

I looked at my arms. They were scarred up like hell, but the decay was gone. I asked Val something about my face... I think I asked her if I still had one.

PC Val Neeson: Before you go, I'll tell you one more thing, I'll tell you about when I found Wayne. Every available constable in the city had been summoned to the station. When I heard that Wayne was in there and that there was a chance he could be alive, I wasted no time at all. The idea that he could be saved got me past all of those other bodies, all those other colleagues, all those friends.

That carriage was an abattoir, I swear to God. An absolute nightmare. I didn't think for a minute he could be alive in the wreckage, but there he was, buried in a mound of the dead. They must have been between him and the bomb, taking the blast and the shrapnel and somehow leaving him alive with barely a scratch on him.

A visible scratch anyway. He was found to have suffered a severe brain injury. What he can't comprehend, he just makes up on the spot. Confabulation, they call it. I've been to see him up at the Yorath place a couple of times, but I don't know if it does him any good to see me. It just triggers him off and he goes on again, trying to convince me of the whole demonic possession story.

Rosie Ost (Russell Fischer's former partner): Russell's body was eventually released to us. That is, his family and I. We had a hell of a job getting it back. It was like they didn't want him to have a proper service or anything.

What is a proper service for a lifelong demon worshipper?

Well, we didn't go to the House Grandier for a service, although Professor Dover offered. I didn't think it was right, given how Russell felt about him. We just arranged a humanist ceremony, with burial at his family plot, which satisfied his parents' desire too.

I had a few drinks at The Green Goblin later and met another demon-worshipper, he was an American called Dane. I told him all about Russell and we had a fuck on his grave later. It's what he would have wanted.

I'm sure it is. What happened to Simonas' body, then? Do you know?

I heard a rumour that Professor Dover claimed the body eventually. I assume he held some sort of service. I wanted to go. It seemed the right thing to do, but the professor denied even having the body, so I don't know what happened, really.

Ross Davidson (occultist): It's hard to know what to make of that story. Like you, I picked up on little bits here and there. There were things on the internet one day and then they were gone, you know. Somebody had something to hide, that's all I can say.

A lot of people say that second explosion they heard was bigger than the first. Some of them say the first blast was a lightning strike and not a bomb at all; they say there wasn't a bomb in there until the police took one in.

Let me ask you something, you might know this... does Cados, Adonai, Elohi, Zena mean anything to you?

That's an easy one. Ask me another.

Seriously? You know where that comes from?

Absolutely. It's a little snippet of the Conjuration Of The Sword. Te Gladi, Vos Gladias, trea Nomine Sancto, Albrot, Abracadabra, Jehova elico... I conjure you, O Sword of Swords, by three Holy Names, Albrot, Abracadabra, Jehova. Be my fortress and defence against all enemies, visible and invisible, in every magical work. There's more to it, but those names you said are named in the spell, yes.

It sounds like a request for protection.

That's correct, that's what it is. A person chanting that spell would be trying to protect themselves or those around them, from evil. Depending upon how powerful the evil, you might have to shout it, or you might have to say it over and over again, barely taking a breath. So I suppose if you ever hear anyone chanting that, Stuart, definitely don't interrupt them.

I'll bear it in mind.

19

—·—

ABOUT 'THE BAPTIST'

In January 2016 I watched a documentary on Channel Four about a suspected serial killer stalking the canal towpaths of Manchester. They called this mysterious killer *The Pusher*, linking him or her to the deaths of some sixty individuals whose remains were fished out of Manchester's canals over six years. Many of the revellers pulled from the water are from Manchester's vibrant gay community, centred around Canal Street which, as the name suggests, runs close to the body of water in question. Does the Pusher haunt that area with some homophobic agenda, hoping to catch lonely victims on their walk home? Is it a killer who wants to take out anyone, attacking vulnerable drunken pedestrians indiscriminately, simply catching a higher proportion of gay victims because his hunting ground is close to Canal Street?

The police claim there is no Pusher, merely victims of excessive drinking, mis-stepping at the canal-side and, in their drunken states, being unable to save themselves. They may be right, but the idea stayed with me, and *The*

Baptist became the second of my Leeds-based horror stories, after *Anti-Terror*.

Leeds itself features the canal structure of the River Aire, as well as a vibrant gay social scene, and of course, a history with serial killers as it was part of The Yorkshire Ripper, Peter Sutcliffe's hunting grounds. The River Aire runs by an area known as The Calls (where a very good friend of mine used to have his office, in a building that used to be a brothel, which always amuses him no end!), from which you get to Call Lane, one of the most popular streets for socialising in Leeds, and is a focal point of the city's gay scene, much as Canal Street is to Manchester.

So there are the puzzle pieces, folks. I just find them, lay them out, put them together and hope you enjoy them. So here it is, previously unreleased, it's time to get wet with...

20

The Baptist

Ollie is perfect. His hair never seems to grow, it always looks like he just had it cut and styled. He's got this amazing social life, a demanding job and he always has time for the gym to keep that tanned body perfectly toned. I'm watching him now, even the way he sips on his mojito keeps my attention fixed on him. The tip of his tongue runs around his lips, catching the lingering taste of mint and rum, that same flavour I've tasted on his kisses since the start of summer, when we started having these secret little meet-ups. Now, the nights are darker, longer and the autumn chill makes me think about what it will be like to wander around the German Christmas Market later in the year, arm in arm with him. Even though I know that little scene won't happen, can't happen, I have to admit it, I'm totally head-over-heels with this man.

The problem is, he knows I'm with Tom, and I know he's with Richard and us getting together like this means we don't stand a chance long-term. We're showing each other that we're unfaithful and that would create problems later. We would each think the other was out on the prowl, looking for the next replacement, each about to make the other the next Tom or Richard. So I'm going to enjoy everything I can get from him now and accept it, and expect nothing more.

I know Ollie loves film – not movies – so I run the risk of conjuring up the spirit of my full-time relationship in order to have a conversation I know he'll get into. "I saw that new DiCaprio film the other night."

"The Revenant?" A warm grin spreads across his face. I know he isn't wondering who I went to the cinema with.

"Yeah."

"What did you think?"

"It's fantastic. I came out of there thinking I wanted to go and live in the wilderness for a year or something."

"A year, Nick? You wouldn't last an hour without your Tassimo, handsome."

We chuckle together because we both know it's true. If I was living within that film, I would have died somewhere in the trailers beforehand, I wouldn't even make it on-screen. We talk about the beautiful scenery of the movie, the lingering moments of nature's majesty, captured through the camera eye. We talk about the scene with the grizzly. We talk about Tom Hardy and I tell Ollie how I love Tom Hardy in *RockNRolla* and *Inception*, but I go off him when he's too big, like when he was in that Batman film.

"I don't know," he says, "I think he looks like he'd throw me around a bit. Might be kind of nice."

There is a pause, a silence, and in that space, my head swims a little, as though I have been punched on the forehead. Ollie thinks it would be nice to have a really big guy throw him around. I don't look anything like that. I'm toned and tanned and trim, like him. His fantasy is something else. I know that Richard isn't a hunk, either and I've been kidding myself, believing that I fulfil some sort of fantasy for him, but clearly I don't. I grab my mojito and drink it and the rum tastes good and Ollie looks good and the music in the bar is good and before long he's slid around to my side of the table and we're kissing.

I have the faintest hint of stubble, and so does he. We grate on each other ever so slightly as we connect. Another omen for the future, I wonder.

Justin Bieber's latest song plays and we talk about how great he looks now he's a little older, and how his new stuff is actually good. I fall short of telling Ollie that I masturbated to a picture of Justin on my phone only this morning. And then, as though the very thought of my phone brought it to life, I feel the vibrations of an incoming call in my jeans pocket.

I know it's Tom. Ollie knows it's Tom. His arm unwraps from around me and he clears his throat as he slides away, only a couple of inches, but still, it hurts me. I want him to be close.

"Sorry, I have to get this."

Ollie smiles and says, "It's okay, I understand."

I'm looking him right in the eye and I can see there's no jealousy there. He's simply giving me the space I need to be able to take the call safely, without being caught out. Why is there no jealousy there?

I feel sick as I pull the battered i-Phone 4 from my pocket. Tom's smiling face radiates out from the screen and I slide my finger across the display to accept the call. "Hi Tom," I say, in a voice absolutely devoid of all enthusiasm. "Yes, I'm just in Rev's down Call Lane. You're where?… No, I'm not coming all the way along there now. I thought you were going to meet me here."

Tom works in a call centre for the insurance company with the little nodding dog. He doesn't finish his late shifts until 10pm, so I always head out before him, usually to meet up with Ollie for a while, as Tom goes back to his flat to shower and change before coming out to join me.

"Tom, I've got a great seat, the music's good, I'm chilling out with a mojito waiting here for you. Why do you want to spoil things?"

I knew that Tom wouldn't meet me here. His anxiety prevents him from entering bars alone. Literally, he would turn around and go home rather than step through the door alone. When I have to leave and meet him, we always go somewhere else—somewhere Olly isn't. I don't know why, but tonight I feel like being mean, even though I know Tom can't help it and even though I'm the one cheating on him, I just feel like making him feel like shit a bit because Olly wants to fuck a Tom Hardy lookalike—BIG Tom Hardy, not normal, cute Tom Hardy, and he's not jealous that I have a boyfriend.

"Okay, I'll meet you there in half an hour."

Ollie sighs as I hang up and put my phone away.

"You need an upgrade, badly," he says.

"I love that phone," I tell him. "The battery life is about ten minutes after a full charge, so I have an excuse for being out of reach."

He raises an eyebrow. "And why would you need to be out of reach?"

"Come outside with me and find out."

Ollie takes his time with the mojito. He won't risk spilling watery rum down on his pristine white Hugo Boss shirt. He places the glass of ice and mint leaves on the table and flashes me a dirty grin, and I know exactly why his grin is so dirty—because this impeccably presented, BA in graphic design-holding marketing executive loves nothing better than a fast fuck in the shadows of Leeds City Centre.

It just goes to show that no matter how polished we appear on the outside, we're just a bunch of animals in the core. He holds the door open for me and I step outside, pulling my grey wool coat tight around me, and I warn him, "Don't come in me and don't come on me."

I fasten my brown leather belt and take a quick selfie with my phone. The flash blinds me for a few seconds, but when my vision clears I see that my hair still looks pretty good. That's the bonus of having my hair chopped and textured for rough spikes with a dry paste product—it always looks like you've made the effort to make it look like you've made no effort.

"Where are you meeting him?" Ollie asks me, tucking his white shirt back into his grey trousers.

"Down by the Oracle," I tell him.

We walk out of the grubby alleyway together, knowing exactly how it looks to those who see us emerge from the darkness, and not giving a shit either way. "Be careful down there, okay?" Ollie says, grabbing my shoulder.

"I haven't had that much to drink. I won't fall into the river if that's what you mean."

"Never mind falling. Haven't you heard about The Baptist?"

I roll my eyes. "What, the Yorkshire fag Ripper?"

"Don't kid about it, Nick. I'm bloody telling you, start meeting Tom somewhere else. You've lived here, what? Five years now, is it? You must know what they say about him."

I rolled my eyes. "I know. I just don't believe it."

"Well, a guy from my work has been missing for two days now. Not even his flatmate has seen him. I'm telling you, someone's out there doing this. Every time we get a heavy downpour, like the other night, when the Aire burst its banks, people go missing."

"Yeah, probably pissed up, walking close to edge of the path and they slip into the river. I never get that rat-arsed."

"There are people who went missing just out walking their dog, Nick. Not even a beer in them. And, by the way, it's not only us who The Baptist gets. He takes them straight, men, women, he doesn't care. If you're along the river and the water level's up, he's on the hunt, and you're fair game."

I widen my eyes and waggle my fingers like some Scooby-Doo monster, "Fair game, and he comes for you and wets your head and off to God you go. It's a fucking crap name for a fake serial killer, by the way. But there have been no bodies, Ollie. Nothing to say those people ended up in the water. I mean, even when the river burst its banks, it was hardly like a bloody typhoon hits and swept families and cars away. The buses ran late along Kirkstall Road. And even then, probable not that much later than they always run."

"Well, I wouldn't be down there this late, that's all I know."

A memory pops into my head, as we cross from Call Lane to The Calls. "I remember my great aunt telling me about that warehouses over there. She said it used to be a brothel. She told me that two barges crashed a couple of miles downriver on the day she got married. Loads of her friends' husbands were there, helping out at the scene and she had to delay her service for four hours because of it. Anyway, they say when they used another barge to pull the wreckage away, all these tiny bones floated up from the river bed, from all the concealed births thrown into the river from the brothel, she reckoned."

"That's grim." Ollie hugs me and gives me a brief kiss on each cheek. It's like he's saying goodbye to a friend, not someone he's just fucked stupid. I have a funny feeling we won't be doing that again. And with that kiss, he's gone. Strutting back along The Calls to go and find out where Richard is, probably.

He didn't say. "Same time next week?" or "See you on Monday?" or try to find any other opportunity to hook up again. Maybe I was just a summer thing for him. Maybe autumn and winter are for him to snuggle in with Richard. The stinging pain of this apparent ending is surprisingly dull. That superstitious Dad-talk¬ about The Baptist made me cringe, and I wonder if he's anything near as cool as he appeared.

Call Lane is quiet. Saturday nights haven't been the same since the credit crunch. Lots of people just get pissed at home then head to a club later. It's the only way anyone can afford to drink until morning. I watch a guy with long, dark hair, in some t-shirt he probably picked up at some grotty heavy metal festival, as he throws up against the stone arch of the railway bridge. Steam rises from his vomit in the cold night.

My phone vibrates again. I'm late, and I can't be bothered listening to Tom whining at me, so I just ignore it. I'm two minutes away from him, so fuck it, he can wait. A shorter buzz indicates the arrival of a text message, no doubt some paranoid rant, or maybe just Where are you?

I cross the stylish white metal bridge linking High Court Lane to the cool cylindrical structure of the Oracle bar, and I can't see Tom anywhere. Usually he would be sat with his back to the Oracle, watching me cross the bridge, but he's not there.

The first thing that enters my head is The Baptist. I quicken my pace and get down to where Tom usually meets me. There is absolutely no sign of him along the waterfront. I see a cigarette butt and pick it up, using the flame from my lighter to inspect the brand. The pale gold lettering at the edge of the squashed filter says Regal, and Tom's would say Marlborough. I don't know if this is a good sign, or a bad one. I don't know what I'm doing.

I whip out the phone from my pocket to discover that I am officially out of reach. My battery is dead and now I can't call Tom to find out where he's gone. I doubt that he's walked up into the city without me—he wouldn't go into a bar and even if he would, he would have headed for Rev's and I would have met him along the way. I walk past the little Sainsbury up onto Dock Street, and buzz his apartment at number 1. There's no answer. He's either not in, and his housemate isn't in, or they're ignoring me.

My apartment is in the Velocity Complex, only a five-minute walk away. I decide to jog back home and plug my phone in. All I can think of is a tall man in a long, black coat passing Tom by as he sits smoking, waiting for me to arrive. I imagine the tall man asking him for a light and Tom producing his lighter, extending his hand, only to be grabbed and stabbed and thrown into the river to bleed and freeze to death and drown. I fight against the worst of my imagination. There was no blood, I tell myself. But that doesn't mean he wasn't thrown into the water.

I arrive at home and the first thing I do is dash into the kitchenette area, where my phone charger lies on the breakfast bar, plugged into the corner socket next to the chrome microwave. I click the connector in place and after a second or so, the phone pulses once and the screen shows a little battery and lightning flash symbol. I use the en-suite in my room and as I evacuate the long piss that had felt like a block of ice in my bladder as I ran home, I can't shake the feeling that Tom didn't just go home.

I wash my hands and dry them, but it all feels like someone else is in control. I return to the lounge and snatch up my phone. I have sufficient charge to access my voicemails and so I press the icon to do that. I have one new message.

It's from Tom: "Hi Nick, where the fuck are you? I'm freezing my arse off here." Then there's a shuffling noise and I realise he's put the phone back in his pocket and not disconnected the call. I hear rustling and the sound of his lighter sparking. "Shit," he mutters, and I know his lighter must have been running low. I hear a long draw on a cigarette and a slow, exasperated exhalation. And the next sound I hear chills the blood in my veins.

Tom screams. He doesn't just sound scared, he sounds absolutely terrified. The pitch, the volume, the duration of the scream... his panicked breaths. It all amounts to absolute terror at whatever is happening to him.

Tears streak my cold cheeks as I hear the rustling of clothing – it sounds like he's being dragged. He's still screaming and then comes the splash.

I cut off the call and, my fingers trembling, I call 999 and my voice cracks as I try to squeeze out the words to describe what I think has happened to my boyfriend.

"I don't want to see you," I cry, shoving Ollie's hand away. "You have to stay away from me. I can't see you anymore."

"Please, Nick. I'm here for you… let me try to help you. Let me be your friend, if nothing else."

I clamp my hands on the railings and the River Aire rushes by beneath my feet. My shouts have echoed through the tunnel and attracted the attention of the dozen or so folks walking to and from Granary Wharf. They stare at me, assume I'm being a drunk, dramatic queen, but they don't know the first fucking thing about me.

"Just go back to Richard, you arsehole. Leave me alone."

Ollie strokes my back and I feel the urge to throw myself over the railings and into the swollen, brown, cloudy water below. I don't want to join Tom. I didn't love Tom. I just can't stand the guilt. I was being fucked while someone dragged him to the edge of the path and threw him into the water. In two weeks, not one trace of him has been found.

I killed him. Not physically. It wasn't me who put him in the water, but I know that if I had been there to meet him, he would not have been there at that time for The Baptist to get him.

"Come home with me, Nick. You need a couple of days leaving the drink alone. You need to process this."

"Process? You were inside me while he was being murdered, Ollie. How the hell do you think you can help me process that?"

"Is this guy bothering you, Nick?"

I look up and it's Curly. He's left The Hop to come and find me. Curly is one of the nicest blokes I have ever met, and he worked with Tom. They were good pals and I really like him. He's got this great mop of curly brown hair and a fantastic physique. A rugby player, but his face isn't all smashed up. He's gorgeous. And so is his girlfriend. Lucky bitch.

"He's just leaving, Curly."

"Nick, please."

"Ollie, just leave me alone."

Ollie backs away and I watch him as he turns and walks off along the tunnel known as the Dark Arches, away from Granary Wharf, towards the city centre proper.

Curly eases me away from the red metal railings and I release my grip willingly. I allow him to hug me.

"Come on, let's go back in," he whispers. "Don't stay out here on your own, pal."

I'm shaking and sobbing, I press my hands against his chest and push him so I don't mark his light blue polo shirt with my tears. "I'm not coming back in. I'm going down by the Oracle."

"Don't Nick. Don't go down there. It won't help you. Come in with me. We'll all have a drink and a cry and we'll feel a little bit better in the morning. Come on, pal."

I shake my head. "No, I can't. I have to go down there. It's the only place I feel... close to him. It's stupid, I know."

"Listen, I'll walk down with you, then. You're not going down there on your own."

I know by the look on his face that he's not going to take no for an answer. And I know he thinks I'm going to hurt myself. It's less hassle just to let him come with me, so I nod to him.

"I'll just send Linzi a text and let her know."

As Curly taps out the message on his phone a half-dozen guys in matching printed t-shirts enter the tunnel. I assume they're here for a stag party and staying at the hotel on the wharf. One of them puts on a camp, sibilant tone and bends his wrist. "Evening, ladiethhhh," he lisps, to the delight of his friends who whoop and howl with laughter, slapping him on the back.

I say nothing to the bunch of pricks and let them pass, not wanting any trouble from them. Curly's eyes burn holes into the backs of their heads, but I am relieved when he does nothing. He hits send and we walk on together.

Curly fills the silence as we walk, talking about Linzi training for a fun-run for Cancer Research, talking about her mum who swears like a trooper and makes dirty jokes, talking about his job and how the jumped-up prick of a line manager he works for went to school with him and how Curly regrets making fun of the guy's inability to throw a javelin, now that he gives him all the shit jobs.

I'm only half-listening, though. I'm bracing myself as we walk over the bridge and I retrace my steps from that night, I'm replaying the scene in my mind, the vision of the empty bank sliding over the soggy, brown, wilted bunches of flowers tied to the railings where the bridge meets the pavement. Tom's shrine. Those dead, washed-out bouquets, dozens of them, show just how loved he was. And the one person he loved wasn't there for him at the time that mattered the most.

As I crest the bow-shaped bridge, I notice two police constables, one male, one female, slowly walking along the pavement at the riverside. It seems the West Yorkshire Police have increased their presence on the Aire, hoping to catch the killer, no doubt, or at least to keep people moving along as dusk sets in and another night of drinking and partying gets underway.

A sad thought crosses my mind—that Tom had to die for the police to take tales of The Baptist seriously. I turn to the left and walk down the short slope to the river's edge and peer into the murky, churning, dirty floodwater. He could be lying under there, I'm thinking, he could be just under the surface, hidden in the filth, waiting for a barge crash to bring his bones to the surface. And yet, I know it's impossible. I know the police divers would have done a thorough job and with the pace of the river, bolstered with all the heavy rain we've had this month, he'd never have stayed in one place anyway. No, he's long gone, flushed away, and I know it.

I look up across the river, to the Victorian warehouses, some of which are now smart office blocks and some are cool bars. The one that has my attention, though, directly opposite me, is derelict. A murderer, who had stoved in the heads of an old couple out by Scarborough, hid out in there a few years ago, not long after I moved to Leeds. I remember hearing some guys found him in there and instead of reporting it to the police, they found some chains lying about in the old warehouse. They wrapped him in the chains, weighing him down, and they just threw him in the river. One version of the rumour was that it was actually a bunch of off-duty coppers who did it to him.

Everyone has a different story of what happened to that bloke, just like they all have their opinion about what happened to Tom. I catch people whispering, then they see me, just a second too late, when the words have already caught my ears. Did he fall? Did he jump? Was he pushed? He was a druggie. It was a deal gone bad.

I step back to the centre of the pavement, turning my back on Curly and that terrible, thick water. I stare at the spot where I found the cigarette butt, until I hear footsteps pounding along the pavement towards me. I look up to see the police racing in my direction.

"Grab him," the policeman shouts.

Confused, I turn around to see that Curly is clinging to the bridge railings, his arms stretched to their full extent, his face contorted in agony, his whole body forming a straight diagonal line with his arms outstretched above his head, and his legs pointing down to the river, like he's being stretched on some sort of rack.

"Nick," he screams.

And then I see what's got him in this position. Dark brown, rusted chains, strung with dark moss hanging in triangular clumps are wrapped around Nick's ankles, twisting over his trainers and up to his calf muscles.

The two police officers burst past me, one on either side, grabbing Curly's arms, his belt and waistband, anything to keep hold of him.

"Try and take the chain off," the policewoman yells over Curly's terrified screams.

"I can't hold on. My legs are going to break."

"Don't stand there gawping, lad. Help," the policeman shouts at me.

"You'll be okay, just hold on."

I'm frozen to the spot, though. It's terrifying to witness, so God only knows how Curly feels right now. I know one thing though, those screams he's letting out, they're just the same as Tom's were on the voicemail. The screams of someone who realises they are seconds away from death.

The water breaks and another rusted chain appears, lashing around Curly's waist, trapping the policewoman's arm. She cries out and I hear a solid snap moment later. A third chain thrashes up out of the water, finding the policewoman's legs, whipping them tight together, throwing her off balance. She falls right in front of me and her weight pulls on Curly and in a second the chains whip them both flailing and splashing down into the murk.

The policeman leaps in after them and he disappears beneath the surface for so long that I think whatever this is, throwing chains out of the water, it's got him, but he appears after a while, clearing his eyes, spitting out muddy water, taking a deep gasp of air and then he's under again.

I'm so out of my mind with fear and confusion that it takes me a while to register that he hasn't resurfaced for a couple of minutes. I step to the edge of the footpath, hoping I can catch a glimpse of his hi-viz jacket, or reflection from his equipment or the metal details of his uniform. Something shifts between billowing mocha clouds beneath the surface. He's coming back up for air.

The water breaks and a dripping, rusted chain cracks across my face, splitting my cheek and the back of my head. Can't breathe. Fingers grasp at throat. Chains too tight. Can't budge them. I fall, I go under, dragged across the river bottom.

Through the brown, a lumpy grey, fleshy mass stretches out of a trench in the riverbed, close to the old brothel-warehouse. My left arm drifts lifeless, numb, broken. The chains are so tight, but I can't scream.

The lumps in the flesh take shape. I see noses, I see foreheads. Hundreds of milky eyes peer at me and dozens of arms protrude between the closely-packed, bloated faces, pitted and blistered. Rotting hands claw at me, some yank the chains, reeling me in like a fish.

The faces mouth words at me, others appear to shout, or weep, or scream, but the only sound is the rush of the river. The faces are clearer as I am drawn to the fingertips of the grasping hands. I see I see babies, I see men, I see women, I see Tom, I see Curly, I see all the terrible secrets of the river. I see its sorrow. I see its horror.

I see nothing.

The Humble Author's Plea

Dear Reader,

So you made it this far. I hope that means you enjoyed my book. I'd like to thank you for giving me your valuable reading time, and the opportunity to to entertain you. Telling stories is much more than a job to me, it's been a love of my life since I was a little boy, drawing comics to read to my little brother. All the same, I only have this job because of people like you - people kind enough to choose my books and to give me a chance to be read, by spending your hard-earned money on my work. For that, I can't thank you enough.

If you enjoyed this book and you would like to help, then please leave a review on Amazon, Goodreads, and anywhere else you share feedback on stories with other readers. Positive reviews have a HUGE impact on how well a book sells, so in leaving one for me, you are directly contributing to my journey as a writer.

If you would like to find out more about my other books, then please visit my website for full details. You can find it at https://www.jackrollinsfiction.com

FREE STORY

If you've enjoyed these Jack Rollins horror tales, jump into the nightmarish world of The Victorian Vampire Chronicles, with 'Tender Morsels' - **free** when you join the Jack Rollins Readers' Club. Join the club to get this **exclusive** story **unavailable anywhere else**, and you'll get chances to become a named character in a Jack Rollins book, exclusive behind-the-scenes info, members-only alerts for 99c/99p launch days, be the first to know about limited edition books and more!

Head to **jackrollinsfiction.com** now.

to accept the existence of a realm beyond the world around him?

Dead Shore

They're coming for you and your child. How fast can you run? When a group of teenagers mess around with a washed-up dolphin carcass, Karen and her toddler Charlie are caught in a wave of chaos and violence as one by one the residents of Ashmouth fall prey to a deadly virus, transforming them into relentless, violent zombies. Allying herself with Dean, one of the teenage boys, Karen must stay strong and alert as the world she knows crumbles around her and there appears to be no way out. Is the village doomed, and will this zombie outbreak remain contained?

Tread Gently Amidst The Barrows

Jack Rollins returns to the Victorian era for a chilling, thrilling tale as the progress of mankind and technology trespass into the world of the mythical in Sweden. A series of night-time disappearances among the workforce of railway engineer Oliver Stroud threaten to bring the construction of a new railway bridge to a standstill as local superstitions give rise to unrest and desertion. Stroud is left with no choice but to investigate an ancient burial site to bring closure to the matter once and for all but there is no peace to be found among the barrows of Old Uppsala, for neither the dead, nor the creatures of myth who live among them.

ACKNOWLEDGMENTS

A big thank you to David Basnett for helping to gather the ashes back up for this volume. Thanks also to Miranda Kate for sending kind words and for guiding me through a lot of the behind-the-scenes work that goes to getting books out into the world. Endless thanks to Alice J Black without whose friendship some dark times would have been even darker.

ABOUT JACK ROLLINS

Jack Rollins was born and raised among the twisting cobbled streets and lanes, ruined forts and rolling moors of rural Northumberland, England in 1980. He is the author of The Victorian Vampire Chronicles, the novella *The Seance* and a range of short, dark fiction and horror tales, many of which are collected in this volume.

Jack lives in Newcastle, England.